Long O

By Patrick Forsyth

Best wishes

Patrick Forsyth

This Edition Published by Stanhope Books, Essex, UK 2014

www.stanhopebooks.com

Cover design and format by Tracy Saunders © 2014

ISBN-13: 978-1-909893-24-5

Dedication

In memory of Sue:

so much loving support, so many good memories.

Note: The cover design is by artist and graphic designer Tracy Saunders (perhaps best known for her marine paintings) who is, appropriately, resident close to the initial setting of this book.

PROLOGUE
Not what you expect on the way to work

April 2014: Maldon, Essex, UK

The ambulance seemed to be taking a long time to arrive.

He had set off to walk to work on what seemed like a perfectly ordinary Tuesday. It was a bright spring morning and everything seemed right with the world. But that quickly changed. He had never seen a dead body before, though as far as he could see Abigail was dead: there was nothing to be done for her, nothing that would make a difference, but phoning the emergency services seemed to be what was called for. He had dialled 999.

"Which service do you require?" A man with an efficient sounding voice answered him promptly.

"Ambulance. And police too, I think. Yes. She's dead, well I think she is. Maybe ... I'm not sure, just send help."

It was not the most articulate sentence of his life, but he had been taken systematically through the details and had explained the situation to the operator. He wanted to shout at them, their cool professionalism seemed almost like indifference, but he supposed it was what was called for in the circumstances. It was a necessary routine.

He had given his name and the addresses – hers and his - and been asked, well told was more like it, to wait. It was a beautiful bright spring morning and he stood in the small front garden in front of the terraced house nervously shuffling his mobile phone from one hand to the other and looking up and down the road. Abigail sat in the directors'-style chair just outside the front door her head a little slumped back on a cushion wedged between the back of the chair and the wall of the neat terraced house, and did nothing. The mug of tea on the small table next to her was half empty and cold and a book was spread open and face down next to it. He recognised the cover and couldn't help thinking what a shame it was that Abigail had evidently not finished reading it. Her walking stick was propped against the wall alongside the chair.

The sound of a vehicle approaching made him turn, but it was a car not an ambulance; it went on by. He waited; he found that he had one foot on a flower bed and was crushing a primrose. He moved his foot, and muttered a mild curse at his inattention; after all most of the small garden was paved. He was going to be late for work. He had thought about moving on – leaving the scene it would be called, after all there was surely nothing he could do and officialdom would be there soon enough - but he had given his name and address and doing so might cause complications. Besides, it was not something he would seriously consider.

6

Miss Frobisher wasn't going to like it. With Margaret off sick the library was already short staffed and he was due to set up the sale already announced for next week that would, it was hoped, clear out a backlog of old and somewhat damaged books. He liked the idea of making room for new titles and editions, though the money raised by such sales was always minimal. He contemplated phoning her, but the library, twenty minutes' walk away through the town centre, would just be opening, Froby, as they all called her behind her back, would be ensconced in the manager's office with her first cup of coffee of the morning, and interrupting the first moments of her ordered day would be even worse than being late. He'd phone in a few minutes when he had a better idea of how long he'd be held up. He imagined her peering at him through her narrow framed, ultra-modern spectacles, which he was sure she thought made her appear hyper-efficient, and telling him that it was "not good enough".

He glanced at Abigail again; then he quickly turned away, and his eyes went back to scanning the road, his mind full of confused thoughts: this was not at all how his walk to work normally went. He was just contemplating sitting down on the thick wooden rim of the raised bed that filled one corner of the small front garden, when a police car pulled up outside the gate. Policeman do not look like the friendly figures of yesterday, he thought, the one who came forward from the car was in shirtsleeves and had a profusion of technical kit belted around his middle. Despite his seeming youth, for a moment he thought the man looked quite intimidating.

He could not remember when he had last had any contact with the police. He had once called them to get a drunk evicted from the library, and impressively they had managed to do so without disturbing anyone, but before that it might well have been when he dialled the emergency number just to see what happened. He had banged the phone down quickly once it was answered, but they had tracked him down and before long a policeman came knocking on the door. He was six at the time. He didn't do it again.

"Are you Mr Marchington?" A business-like tone introduced the constable.

"Yes, Philip Marchington. I dialled 999." He waved his mobile in front of him absently.

"And this is the body?"

"Well, yes, I think so, it's Abigail Croft and she's ..."

Their conversation was then almost immediately interrupted as an ambulance pulled up at the kerb behind the police car. Two people, a man and a woman in reflective yellow jackets, came briskly through the gate, the man with a bulky green canvas bag over his shoulder. They clearly knew the policeman, just nodding to him and stepping quickly across the garden to bend over the figure in the chair. Philip and the constable both stood back.

"Well, I am afraid she is dead," said the man, adding an "I'm so sorry" directed politely towards Philip, though of course he knew nothing of his role in the matter.

Philip had irrationally held out some small hope that it might be a false alarm. Perhaps Abigail was just unconscious, perhaps she would be okay, and maybe ... well anything was preferable to her having died. Now he found that he was shocked to find that there was nothing more to be done; at least not by him. He turned to the policeman.

"Oh, dear, that's so sad." Then, feeling awkward and wondering what to do, he added "Can I go now?" he said "I'm running late for work".

Work would wait of course, but he had no role here and felt he would absorb the news better alone as he continued his walk. He withdrew from his thoughts as the policeman spoke again:

"Just a second, sir, I need to get some details from you first."

He produced a notebook and Philip gave his name and address again then, conscious that he really knew comparatively little about Abigail, explained that the lady was really just an acquaintance – "We sometimes spoke as I went by, I live just up the road and pass her house every day on the way to the high street." He had called out this morning, got no reply from her and had gone through the gate into the small garden to see if everything was all right. Clearly it wasn't. Everything was very far from all right. He had shaken her shoulder gently in an attempt to rouse her and her arm had dropped from her lap and hung limp; he did not tell the policeman this, he had found it to be rather unnerving. The policeman explained that he might need to get in touch with him again, then allowed Philip to go on his way. As he headed on up the road he heard the ambulance man speaking on his radio, presumably arranging whatever must happen next. The words were soon unintelligible then faded to nothing behind him.

As he had predicted he was late arriving at the library and despite the call he had made from the high street, also as predicted, Froby was not pleased. She insisted on making him describe what had happened again and tut-tutted throughout his explanation. It seemed to Philip that stumbling unexpectedly upon a dead body and the attendant actions in which he had become involved provided a more than adequate excuse for his late arrival. It was surely not a sign that his attendance record was likely to cause any great problem in the future; not unless his neighbours started dropping like flies, and that seemed a somewhat unlikely event. Though, when he thought about it, and judging by the marital rows he had overheard on occasion, he would not be a bit surprised if Mr McCann who lived a few doors down actually murdered his wife one day; or vice versa.

He left Froby still muttering, hung his cord jacket on a chair and tried to concentrate on work. Philip had worked at the library for almost twenty years, since the blessed Miss Frobisher was practically in kindergarten, as he liked to tell

9

himself. In the past whoever held the post of Head Librarian had been an ambassador and a bridge between the library and the local community and, above all else, a book lover. Now, and certainly this was true of Froby, such people seemed only to be there to see to costs, accounting and Health and Safety issues – he doubted if Froby opened a book from one end of the year to the next. Certainly he had never known her check one out. It was obvious to him that she was planning something, some change or other; she had hinted at it often and from what he knew of her Philip was convinced it could only bode ill. Her whole attitude to the place was at odds with his. She had previously worked in some central administrative office, somewhere heavily allied to finance. He still resented her being in charge and wondered why someone with her obsession for administration had been appointed.

There was a well-known phenomenon amongst library members: known amongst the staff as the 'one-minute-to-closing brigade'. These people whisked in just before closing time and if challenged always said something like "I know what I want, I'll only be a second" before taking long moments to return to the counter with a book or, even more annoyingly, disappearing in due course with nothing, saying "I'll come back", meaning the wait had been fruitless. It was awkward, but this was a library and Philip believed the situation demanded courtesy to the member and that a short wait was therefore to be tolerated. It characterised her that Froby was fierce about such things, demanding that such members were immediately challenged and ejected. He had seen Froby do this herself on one occasion and the member concerned had beat a hasty retreat; she could be seriously scary.

At the end of his working day he left for home a little later than usual and as he walked back down the high street he considered the morning's events. It was sad, but Abigail was old and she had presumably expired from natural causes. It wasn't as if there was a knife in her chest or anything. Yes, all very sad. She was such a dear and lively in her conversation, even if she could not get about so much of late. Her walking stick was always there alongside her chair and, provided the weather was reasonable she always sat outside watching the world go by, her white hair neat and tidy and her eyes sparkling behind her large metal framed glasses. Indeed it was her desire to interact with the world that had led to their meeting. Now he would miss their little chats. It seemed like the end of a chapter, though as yet he had no inkling of how her death would turn his own world upside down.

As Philip walked past her house all was quiet. He saw that Abigail's front door was shut, the chair no longer visible outside. He presumed the police had secured the house and was grateful for that. Abigail was very house proud. Arriving at his own house a further few minutes' walk down the road the first thing he saw was a police car parked at the kerb. As he approached his gate, a policeman was coming out, he imagined after knocking at the door and getting no reply. It was not this morning's policeman, but another, similarly clad, this evening's policeman, thought Philip.

"Good afternoon, I'm PC Barnet, are you Philip Marchington?" Philip admitted that he was.

"I need to talk to you about Abigail Cross."

"Come in, though I'm not sure how I can help."

"You reported her death." It was said as a statement, but somehow a question mark sounded at the end of the sentence. They were sitting in Philip's small living room, a neat, comfortable space, though punctuated by piles of books and papers. He lived alone and never seemed to quite attain the level of tidiness that was his goal. He liked to think he kept things tidy, but as one thing was tidied away something else seemed to demand to take its place. He could do with a cup of tea, but the constable had declined his offer of a drink.

"You know I did," said Philip, resisting adding that otherwise the policeman would not be there.

"Yes, of course." The PC produced a black notebook and asked further, "Why were you there?"

"I go by her house most every morning and evening. I work at the town library and always walk past on my way to and from work. Sorry, I just said that. We often exchange a few words when the weather's good and Abigail is sitting outside. Well, we did, I mean ..." His voice tailed off. Then he added "I hadn't known her all that long" as he wondered why even such an innocuous encounter with the police should make him in any way nervous.

"How did you know her?"

"Well, it was because of the whistle. Sometimes as I walked along past her house, I heard a whistle; you know the sort of piercing whistle that's made by putting two fingers in your mouth. Not something I could ever do ... anyway I heard it a number of times and never knew where it came from. Kids, I thought. Then, I must have turned more quickly on one occasion and I spotted Abigail taking her fingers out of her mouth. She grinned and I waved. Then, on my way home we had a chat. She used to love to whistle like that. 'You're the first person who's spotted me' she said 'Most people look round and wonder where the whistle came from, but they always ignore me as a possible source – a little granny-like figure sitting in the sun. No, surely not.' Sorry, I'm sure all this isn't of much relevance to the police. Anyway after that we talked regularly. We had tea together sometimes when I delivered and collected her library books."

"Do you know who her next of kin would be?" the policeman asked, pencil poised above his notebook.

"No, I don't. She never spoke of relatives and I rarely saw anyone else with her. We were just acquaintances really, though she was a lovely lady."

"Right ... I see."

The policeman seemed somewhat nonplussed by all this. He had obviously hoped to get a name from Philip and now presumably other action would be necessary. He had written almost nothing down in his notebook.

"I'm sorry I can't help more."

The constable seemed disappointed with the outcome of his visit, but he took his leave with a polite "thank you" saying that "it might be necessary to talk to you again".

But as the next few days saw no constabulary return and as Philip walked regularly past Abigail's house and saw no sign of activity there, he began to wonder what, if anything, would now happen. He had once asked Abigail if she had any family and he remembered her telling him that her husband had died many years back, then her saying "So no, not now, not really." With hindsight it seemed an odd way to reply, what had "Not really" meant? Then a further thought struck him. There was someone she had spoken of regularly: Mac. "Mac would hate me saying so" – "Mac would never agree, but I think ..." He tended to be mentioned as a prefix to comments in her conversation rather than as a topic of it and she had never explained who it was or anything about them. She might have been referring to a friend or relative, though for all he knew it might have been the name of a pet cat; not that he thought Abigail owned a cat.

If the police made a return visit he resolved to mention it to them, though he was sure whatever procedure was underway would cope with matters perfectly well. Surely there must be a relative somewhere? He hated to dwell on her death, but he did know that he would miss her, though he was yet to discover that she was not done with him yet.

Six months previously things had been rather different.

CHAPTER ONE
A nice cup of tea and a good book

I've not kept a journal for years, though I always did so as a child. Then I did again that year things were all so difficult; for a while at least. Now I have decided to start again, well I'll give it a go – just some occasional thoughts, not a daily entry. My old notebooks are long gone I think, though I'll have another look, but I do have the last one. I'll fill

these last pages here till I see how it goes –
a new friend - a new chapter.

He's a nice young man, well I say
young, he's probably forty or so, but
then I'm well past seventy so anyone
seems young to me. He heard me whistle.
It's a new game of mine and until then
no one I startled had spotted it was me.
He did. He turned and wagged a finger
at me. He called me a rogue, but grinned
as he said it. We got talking later, he
stopped on his way home, and I suppose I
interrogated him a bit. His name is
Philip Marchington, he lives a little way
down my street and works at the library
in the high street, has done for years
though I don't think I ever noticed him in
the days when I could walk there.
Probably just my memory. I love the
library. I love books. But it's a problem
getting them these days. I can order
from Amazon and they drop through the
letter box, but mostly I don't need to keep

books once I've read them and besides I am a bit slow with the computer, I've never used it much and now my fingers are getting stiff.

Philip seems nice. He has a kind face and I asked him if he could get a book for me if I gave him my library card. He readily agreed but I couldn't find the card in my bag. He said he would check something out for me, so I scribbled a note of several titles on a sheet of paper. It took a minute and when I looked up he was glancing at his watch. He saw that I'd seen and immediately apologised explaining that he must get on to be on time for work. Even so he took a moment longer to introduce me to Miss Frobisher, a right old dragon by all accounts – the library staff call her Froby - and a stickler for punctuality. Then, with a cheery wave, he was on his way. Perhaps it was a bit of a cheek to ask, but this could be a lifeline for me and he had seemed happy enough to help.

At ten to six there was a knock on the door and Philip, now homeward bound, was on the doorstep with, as good as his word, not one but several books; I offered grateful thanks, which indeed I felt. I hobbled back to the living room and offered him tea: well I instructed him as to where things were kept and sent him off to the kitchen to make us both a cup. They say to be careful inviting a stranger into your house but if you can't trust a librarian then who can you trust? Besides, I don't think mad axe men make such excellent tea.

October 2013

Philip read slowly and clearly, holding the book just a little away from him so that he could see beyond it to his audience.

"Madrigal was a bit of a witch in her spare time, but she didn't look like one. She wore black mini-skirts, jangly bangles and a silver stud in her nose.

She longed to look taller by wearing a witch's hat at the school where she had a part-time job."

A few sentences in and the twenty or so children in front of him were mesmerised. The tale was by a local author, Elizabeth Webb, who had had several books of short stories published, and he always found children loved them. Today they were obviously hooked. Madrigal was a great character; she had studied witchcraft through a correspondence course and was just beginning to get her spells pretty much right, well mostly. She was assisted by a toy puppet and a cat: naturally the cat spoke and the puppet came to life. Both helped her use her magic to help the children in the school where she worked as a dinner lady. In this first story the puppet, Raz, came to life for the first time: "All of a sudden, Raz unfolded his long legs and leapt onto the table. He landed in a bowl of porridge." And it set the scene for further stories to come, this one ending with the words "'Witchcraft (lesson two)', she read, and settled down to choose her next spell."

Elizabeth had done several readings at the library and Philip felt the stories, which the author described as "an ideal length to read at bedtime" worked just as well during the day. At a session like this at a local primary school he could read two or three stories and they allowed a small break in between so that the youngest children could enjoy a new start. He loved this aspect of his work and was never slow in volunteering to speak or read at any of the schools round and about; anything he could do to enhance the way children learnt to read he regarded as good. Philip felt he embraced modern ways, he accepted that the library offered CDs and DVDs on loan as well as books, but he was also passionate about the library's traditional role, and this was surely an important aspect of it.

As Philip finished a story he held up a puppet - Elizabeth had had some made to help her publicity - and spoke to it directly.

"Right, Raz, I think we must stop now. Do you think the children enjoyed hearing about you?"

Amidst a murmur of agreement a hand was raised by a little girl, clearly one of the youngest present. She cleared her throat and spoke up.

"You do know he's not real, don't you?"

She spoke with unarguable logic, Philip laughed out loud and the teacher took over.

"Okay, children you can take your break now, but first we must thank Mr Marchington for being here to help us today and for the lovely stories." The teacher began to clap her hands as she finished speaking and the class all joined in, then the children scrambled up and headed for the door. Their shrill chatter receded down the corridor and took a moment to disperse.

Philip picked up the mug of tea he had brought to the table, realising that he had forgotten all about it and that what remained had become cold. Barbara Ross was the teacher concerned; she turned to Philip, asking "More tea? Yours always goes cold." He smiled at her but shook his head.

"The children love these sessions," she told him "I just wish we could give more time to reading aloud, but the curriculum is so busy these days and anyway it is not so often we get volunteers like you. You read so well."

"It's just part of my job really," said Philip, "but I do enjoy it and I'm pleased if it helps."

He did love it too, especially when the children took turns to read, and he had loved it all the more in recent months. Since Miss Frobisher had been appointed to head the library he was only too happy to spend time outside it. She was, he had decided, a cross between the worst sort of "jobsworth", a stickler for every obscure rule and regulation, the less necessary the better, and an uncaring literary vandal. She seemed to care only about the processes involved, always quoting –It's how it must be done, Philip – like a mantra, rather than thinking about the outcome, about what the library actually did for people. She wanted the library to be orderly and incident free rather than meeting the needs of the local community.

She was so hard on the younger staff too. Poor Margaret, who was the youngest and newest member of the little team, seemed perpetually to be addressed as "you silly girl", yet in Philip's view she was doing very well. Philip told her not to worry and that "it would all be fine", but he did wonder for how long she would put up with it. Last time he had picked up the pieces after she had been taken to task, Margaret had been reprimanded for being late with some task or other after taking time and moving heaven and earth to find something for a member, who had been delighted to be so well looked after. Okay, the admin had been delayed, but no harm was done and the member had been well satisfied. Philip had told her so, adding that he reckoned that a perfect day for Froby would be one when the library did not have a single visitor, no books moved in or out and she, indeed the whole staff, could concentrate entirely on administration for the sake of administration. Margaret had smiled at that, but he could see she hated being made to feel she was inadequate.

Philip had rather hoped to get the top job himself, but the powers that be had decreed otherwise, administration winning out over more literary considerations. With hindsight he knew he should have emphasised his administrative abilities much more in his application, they were perfectly good after all, but he found it impossible not to wax lyrical about books, reading and just the sort of thing he had been doing today: visiting schools. He knew that he needed to think more about Froby and her new broom. In fact he was beginning to form something of a plan; indeed he felt it was just possible that she was not in fact unstoppable.

"Can you do the same day next month?" Barbara asked.

"I think so, yes, let me give you a ring though, I need to check the date with the library system. Unfortunately under the new regime this sort of thing is more difficult to fit in." Philip's voice slowed, wishing it was not so, then brightened again "but I'm sure I can work something out."

He said goodbye, and with Barbara's thanks ringing in his ears, went out to the car and drove away with the books he had brought to read tucked away in his bag. He knew at least some of the kids he had met today would likely appear in the library in due course asking for "a Madrigal story". And he would be well pleased to find that they did.

He was not going back to the library until the next morning. Once into the town and driving down his road he slowed down a little before reaching Abigail's house, there were numbers of parked cars nearby but he was able to pull up almost opposite the house. She was hobbling about in the front garden. He got out and gave her a call: "Got time for a cuppa? I've a new book for you." She smiled broadly and waved him in. He had met her perhaps six months back and immediately they had fallen into a routine, at least a couple of times a week Philip would call in, books would be delivered and collected, inquests about their relative merits held, tea drunk and biscuits eaten as they chattered on about this and that. She was interested in his work at the library; in fact she had begun to collect a bit of a catalogue about his life over the months and she had also begun to find him small chores to do for her around the house on his visits.

"Before you make a drink, be a dear and pop up to the bathroom would you. There's a spider in the bath the size of a soup plate and I just hate them. Do you mind?"

Philip went into the kitchen first to put the kettle on saying "I'll do it while this boils."

In the bathroom he found a largish spider had indeed set up residence in the bath and having captured it under a mug he deposited it out of the window. Back downstairs, with

Abigail thankful for his having helped her avoid an unpleasant arachnophobic encounter, he made the tea. She always let him do that for them and it saved her a walk into the kitchen. He put the mugs on a tray with a jug of milk, she always insisted on a jug, saying "must do it properly". Neither of them took sugar so no more was necessary; he waited for the kettle to boil.

"Had a good day?" her voice sang out cheerfully from the living room, where he knew she would be sitting in her usual chair, a smile on her face, her spectacles hanging round her neck on a pink cord, and a pile of books on the table alongside her.

"Yes, I did actually. Hang on, I'm nearly there." He poured the tea, added milk, and carried the tray into the other room; he had brought a packet of biscuits with him and put some of these on a plate adding a couple of Abigail's paper napkins from a kitchen drawer. "No napkins, no biscuits" she always said.

"I was at one of the local schools this afternoon, came straight here from there, in fact. Not only a Froby-free afternoon but I had a great session at the school too. Not a class I knew this time, I bet I see some of them in the library now." He continued, turning to books "What have we got to swap?"

Abigail pulled a copy of The Eyre Affair, the first of Jasper Fforde's books about his heroine literary detective Thursday Next, from the bottom of a pile of half a dozen books on the table alongside her and held it up.

"The school things must be fun" she said, then waving the book and continuing: "You recommended this one. I did wonder about it at first, but I just loved it. I would never have picked this one out myself, but it was wonderful - funny, exciting and full of clever links to the world of books. It's weird to start with, all this flitting in and out of fiction –

surreal – but once you accept the premise then it's magic, I got lost in it ... and better still there's a sequel."

Her eyes sparkled with the thought of something else to look forward to reading.

"There are several more in fact, I'll put the next one on the list for you. Now I have something else here I think you'll like just as much ..."

He fell silent as he got a book out of his bag, then he gave her a quick synopsis of it, aiming to enthuse her about it while not giving any of the plot details away. She nodded at his description, indicating that she felt it sounded good.

"This one's a bit special," said Philip. An idea had occurred to him, he hadn't picked the title at random. "It's not just your cup of tea, it's the next one chosen for discussion at a reading group that meets regularly in the library. I think you should join, read this and then come and attend the next meeting when the group will talk about it. I'm sure you would enjoy it."

"Oh, I don't know, I'm not one for going out much these days."

"That's rather the point," continued Philip, he had been thinking about this and had resolved to be assertive, "It will get you out and about; and don't say that you can't get to the library, all you have to do is get in my car at the curb here and get out at the door. Your trusty stick will do the rest. The group meets on the first Thursday of every month."

"Well, I suppose I could try, if it's not too much trouble for you. Let me read the book first and then we'll see."

"Oh no you don't! Read the book first of course, but promise me now that you will go to the meeting."

Abigail smiled and gave in. "Alright, I can't say no when you are so kind about getting me all these books. It's a deal. Here, have one of these."

She produced a bag of sweets and offered him one. On her infrequent trips into town, she sometimes got a lift to the top of the high street so that she could walk slowly down and then on home, she liked to visit the old fashioned sweetshop half way along. The shop was lined with traditional shaped jars and sold old favourites like pineapple chunks, pear drops and summer creams. He took one, thanked her and they chatted and drank tea for a while longer, until Philip cleared the things away, washing up and returning the mugs to the cupboard, and made to set off for home. Just as he was at the door Abigail stopped him.

"Philip, thanks again for the books, you're very kind. I wonder if you could ..." she hesitated, continuing, "No never mind, another time."

She had come with him into the hall, now she pulled the front door open for him and Philip did not pursue what she had said, there was clearly something and, if it was important, then she would surely raise it again. He was well pleased with his day: two useful things accomplished - one at the school and one here. Abigail had even written the group's meeting date down and he'd put her note of it on the pin board above the kettle in the kitchen, writing underneath – Don't forget! Such things were not rocket science and they wouldn't change the world but he found these little successes very satisfying.

The first few months after his wife died - her heart problem had taken her within what seemed like moments - had been utterly miserable. Mostly people had been very kind and gradually he had got through it and in some ways it now seemed like a far distant memory, but his life had changed. There was so much that he and Penny had done together. Now while he enjoyed his job and was more than happy to be helping Abigail, who despite the difference in their ages had quickly become a friend, there was still something of a void. Making regular visits to Abigail was probably the only new thing he had done for a while. People, including his sister, told him to "get out more", but it was difficult somehow. He acknowledged that he was in a bit of a rut, and now the situation at the library promised to change his view of his job.

Maybe, he thought, he needed a complete change.

Perhaps he should join a group of some sort himself, just as he had encouraged Abigail to do, but what would suit? He needed a change, he vowed he would make one, but nevertheless he remained unsure how to go about it. Maybe, he thought, as was so often said, something would turn up.

Inside her house, sitting in her comfortable armchair, Abigail opened her new book, but before she began to read she resolved to put the question left unasked to Philip soon. She had hesitated, but was now sure that it was a good idea and besides, she was sure that Mac would approve.

CHAPTER TWO
Some information and introductions

We chatted again yesterday, mostly about books – I had arranged the three he had brought in the order in which I planned to read them while he made the tea: first the new Alistair McCall Smith that would transport me to Botswana for a while and make me smile too.

This morning he lent over the gate as he walked by and gave me a cheery good morning as I sat outside with a first cuppa. Receiving his greeting was indeed cheering and I wondered if I would see him this evening on his way home, after all we had made no arrangement for returning the books once I'd read them and he now knew of my difficulty in visiting the library. Already I feel he's a friend. It is just what I need. And I'm sure Mac would like him.

October 2013

Miss Frobisher was clearly building up to announcing some changes. She wanted to make her mark and seemed to think that the way to do that was not just to embrace technology, but to wrap it in bureaucracy and let it predominate. She seemed to be considering what to do and how to do it. Meantime she had had every staff member attend a meeting one evening after the library had closed so that they were all in no doubt that change was certainly coming.

Philip found it all excruciating. Afterwards he had recounted the gist of the meeting to Abigail during one of his early evening visits, putting on Froby's precise little voice and found he couldn't help exaggerating more and more as he went so that he made it absolutely clear just how dreadful her manner was. "I suppose it was a bit like this" he began.

"Well, good evening everyone, I've called this meeting to instigate some changes so let's get down to business straight away shall we?

First, let me say that I'm sorry the meeting had to be called at such short notice. But it is urgent, and it is important. I am sorry too that there was confusion about where it was to be held. The meeting room was unavailable because of the painting. So thanks for all squeezing into my small office, I hope you are okay on that stool Margaret. The result of all this is that the meeting is starting nearly half an hour late. I know Harry's not here yet, but he will just have to catch up when he arrives; something about a school visit he said - some people have no sense of priorities and that seems to apply to Harry more than most; that man's always ducking and diving - there are two things I dislike about him - his face. Let's move on: coffee will be here soon

The team convened here is very important: Margaret is a relative newcomer but obviously no new plans can be made without involving her as she's handling petty cash at present - more's the pity.

Philip is here because he will, in his usual fumbling way, attempt to project manage the new scheme. You will all remember the fiasco of firing that idiot assistant he recruited. He disobeyed orders: he was shoddy, constantly late and wasted precious funds. He burnt down the cookery book section for goodness sake - you can still smell smoke all around the building - but it still took four months to fire him by the time I had issued all the necessary warnings, initiated the labyrinthine disciplinary procedures and dotted all the i's and crossed all the t's. It was a complete disaster and all too typical of how things seem to work nowadays.

Anyway, the rest of you know your roles apart from George, I'm not sure what you can contribute, but I expect I'll think of something. And, no George - don't speak yet - when I want your opinion I'll give it to you.

Right let's get on. This is potentially an important project. Well it seems to me to be the only way forward and I cannot commend it highly enough. There may be other ways of proceeding, and my setting out a plan that we do this is, of course, only a suggestion; though that said I hope you will bear in mind who's making it. I very much want your inputs, I want any decision I make to be based on a consensus and I want to hear what you have to say and to suggest. No, not yet, George, when I want your opinion I'll give it to you.

They both giggled at this point and Abigail opened her mouth to comment, but Phillip immediately shushed her and continued in character.

The trouble is that so much that goes on here is downright unproductive. For instance, all of you seem to spend hours chatting to library users when you could be doing something useful. I want everyone to pull their socks up, gird up their loins and get down to some real work. The future's uncertain: I know it's difficult to see the writing on the wall when your back's to it, but we have to re-double our efforts and get things really buzzing. There's no excuse for procrastination. You do all know what that means don't you? Shush George, don't speak, I'm sure you do, especially as you're so very good at it.

Oh do come in Harry, here you are at last. No don't apologise, we knew you were going to be late and had more important things to do than join us on time.

Right, we must wrap it up now. I for one have more important things to get on with; these changes won't implement themselves. We've covered a lot of ground this session, I think it has been very useful, but clearly no decision can be made today. Think about it and we will meet again soon. Trust me: we will get this right if we all pull together. Thank you all for your contributions today. No George, say no more now for goodness sake, save it for the next meeting ... besides, and I'm sure I said this already, when I want your opinion I'll give it to you.

And one more final thing – next time we meet let's have a bit more order shall we? I don't want you all talking while I'm interrupting."

Abigail chuckled as he finished, asking "Was it really like that?" and Philip had to confess to a degree of exaggeration, though he insisted "Not too much. She made absolutely nothing clear and no one else was able to get a word in."

April 2014

As the days went past Philip heard no more from the police, too busy chasing parking offenders he thought. Though he was not a major car user himself he saw this as a ubiquitous fault. His daily walks to work did not seem quite the same any more without his regular exchanges with Abigail. The whole business of her death had shaken him somewhat. It would have been bad enough to find that she had died, but it was worse that he had discovered her body. Since his wife, Penny, had died a couple of years ago he had found himself disproportionately affected by anything to do with death. They had been, he supposed, childhood sweethearts. They had both been brought up in the town and had attended the same school. Having gone their separate ways after that they met again when Philip returned having finished university, and though his shyness meant it took some time it had seemed natural to get together; they already knew one another and liking turned to love. They had been happy together and content in their life. He had good memories and time would heal the sadness eventually, though he certainly felt that somehow he should be into a new chapter soon.

While he tried not to dwell on Abigail's death, as the days went by he was regularly reminded of it. He saw her house standing quietly uninhabited and unattended as he walked by and remembering, realised that their meetings had become really rather important to him. Pondering the future, a thought struck him: there was the question of her library

30

books. It might be a minor matter in the circumstances, but those she had at the time of her death would soon be overdue and the library system would show not only that they had not been collected personally, but that he had taken them out. It was a fact that Miss Frobisher, still busy pondering her changes, would certainly pick up on; she loved nothing more than tidying up loose ends.

In his lunch break Philip walked round to the police station.

"Is PC Barnet here?" He had elected to ask for the 'evening policeman' as he got to the desk, reckoning that it was best to start with someone with a connection to the matter. The relevant PC was duly summoned and Philip asked what was happening about Abigail's possessions and house and whether there was a relative he could contact.

"Not that we know of here," replied the PC "I know the ambulance crew summoned a doctor and she was officially pronounced dead. I heard it was later recorded as death from natural causes; I think she had a stroke. Still, she was a good age. I hope I go as peacefully."

"Would it be possible to get into her house?" said Philip and apologetically explained about the "minor matter" of the library books. PC Barnet told him that he didn't know, but he promised to find out "in whose remit" it now was. He wrote down Philip's home telephone number and promised to give him a call.

⚐

The phone rang before he left for work the next morning; it was a woman's voice. "Is that Philip Marchington?"

"Yes, hello."

"Good morning. It's Sergeant Jayne. I'm calling from the police station - about Abigail Croft."

"About the house?"

"Yes, but I think it might be best if we had a word. Might we do that before you go home from the library today? I could call in there to speak to you."

The police station was not far round the corner from the library.

"Well, yes if that's convenient for you," he said "I'll finish work today about six. Is that okay?"

It was agreed she would ask for him at the counter. He did not know what he would be doing at the end of the afternoon but he resolved to look out for her. His meeting a policeman in the library, even if it was as he finished work, was bound to raise eyebrows, especially Froby's. Her eyebrows rose at no end of things; having christened her Froby he thought that her middle name had to be nit-picker.

In the event he was at the counter for the last minutes of his day. In Philip's experience this was when librarians were regularly asked bizarre questions. This evening his first such encounter had been with a man of about his age who asked, "Do you have a poetry book that might contain something suitable to read at a funeral?" Philip said he would look and escorted him to the relevant section, offering condolences as he did so. "Oh, no need for that," said the man, "it's my little girl's pet rabbit." Really!

At ten to six an attractive woman who looked to be in her late thirties came in. She put a large floppy handbag on the counter, the sort that always made Philip wonder what on earth women carried round with them that needed such copious space. She smiled at him as she took a book out of the bag.

"I'm afraid this is a bit overdue," she said "I must confess I completely forgot about it; I'm sorry." Philip realised he knew her, well, knew her as a regular user of the library anyway ... and admired her too, if he was honest. She always smiled and had a word with him, even if he was away from

32

the counter she would say something if they crossed paths. It would be truer to say that she attracted him. Since his wife died he had not been out with anyone, but if he did, he told himself, he would like it to be someone like this.

"Right," he said briskly, conscious of the time and his imminent meeting with Police Sergeant Jayne. "There's a fine to pay I'm afraid, not too much though." He passed her a slip.

She handed over the money. "Worth it anyway, it was a good book." He slipped the money into the drawer below the counter thinking that the transaction was over. But she didn't move away.

"Well," she said, looking at him directly "Where can we talk?"

"Talk?" He looked nonplussed.

"I'm Sergeant Jayne. Sorry, I thought I'd been in here in uniform before and that you would recognise me."

"Oh, yes, sorry."

Philip was flustered. In truth he did recognise her, but had completely forgotten her occasional rare appearances in uniform. He muttered something about only belatedly recognising her and suggested that they sat at a table in the corner, currently empty but mostly habitually inhabited by those with time on their hands and who were too mean, or too poor, to buy a magazine. All libraries had, in his experience, numbers of members who used them as much to keep in out of the cold or out of the way of a spouse as anything else. He wondered whether he should offer her some tea, but the staff room kettle took an age to boil and somehow he was embarrassed to suggest it.

"Mrs Croft's house: I thought I would just have a word about this informally. I shouldn't really do this," she said. "But we can't have the public deprived of her library books, now can we?" She smiled, seeming to display a hint of conspiracy, and continued, "The keys are still with us at the station and I guess I could let you in for a moment ... as we sort of know each other. It won't cause a problem and it will be a few more days before the keys are handed on. It seems that the lady may have no relatives; certainly no one's come forward immediately. If that proves to be the case it will all start going through official channels soon."

"She certainly told me she had no family," said Philip, adding his thanks and then asking when and how book collection might be affected.

"I could drive you there now," she said glancing at her watch "If you don't mind being seen in a police car." Again she smiled. "I have to go that way. Are you finished here?"

"Well, yes. Just let me get my case."

He grabbed his trusty satchel and they walked along to the back of the police station. She left him standing by a police car while she went inside to collect Abigail's house keys. They drove in silence to the house. For a few moments Philip couldn't think what to say. He rejected "perhaps we could put on the siren", despite the almost irresistible appeal that riding below the flashing blue lights would undoubtedly have had, and settled for a "this is very kind of you" and then, when they became stuck behind a parked delivery lorry in the narrow high street, repeated his story about his contact with Abigail. He paused and chuckled when the driver came out of the shop alongside his lorry, caught Jayne's eye, mouthed an apology and quickly climbed into his cab and drove on.

"They don't all do that," she said, returning his smile. Such deliveries were a perennial problem in the narrow street.

He continued his tale about Abigail: the whistle, the meeting, the routine they had fallen into. He presumed that kind of detail was not recorded at the police station; certainly the sergeant seemed to listen with interest. She drove down the high street and turned off at the bottom into an area that lay behind Hythe Quay where the small stream of the river Blackwater entered the estuary. It was a feature of the town and well known to the boating world. They got out of the car and she unlocked the front door while Philip stood in the little garden, disconcerting memories of the morning Abigail had died flooding back to him.

Once inside, they found the hall was dimly lit by only one small window above the door, but as Jayne clicked on the light a pile of books was immediately apparent on the small hall table.

Philip pointed: "That's them." He gathered them up and popped them into a book bag he had got out of his satchel in the car. The house seemed unnaturally cool and silent; somehow it already had the distinct feel of somewhere currently unlived in. He remembered the last time he and Abigail had sat and had tea together. Her death seemed such a waste: a nice house and maybe with no one for it to be passed on to. He said as much to Sargent Jayne.

"Yes, it is – but it's not so uncommon, you know; you might be surprised by how many people die without a will and even with no family at all."

"What happens in such circumstances?" he asked.

"Well it's a while since I last came across such a situation, but don't worry, usually there's someone. It may well be okay. But I can check and let you know if you like."

"That's kind; I would be interested to know." He quite liked the idea of another opportunity to talk to Jayne. He didn't know her first name but calling her that, in his mind at least, seemed rather nice; it was almost familiar.

She turned back to the door, they went out and she locked it behind them. "Where to now?" she said more cheerfully "Maybe I can drop you somewhere."

"There's no need, I live just down the road, number 28, that's how I knew her – remember."

"Okay, yes, of course, well I must push on ... but I know where to find you now, don't I?"

She smiled, raised her hand in a small wave and went round to get into the driver's seat. In a moment the car pulled away in one direction and he walked slowly on along the road in the other.

Philip wondered if he was reading things correctly: surely there had been a friendly element to the encounter; her farewell had not seemed to be solely business like. But he had been married for the best part of twenty years until his wife had been taken in what he regarded as the prime of her life – his too, they were the same age - and he realised all too readily that he was totally out of practice at reading women. Sargent Jayne was either just refreshingly pleasant in her dealings with the public or had intentionally ... well, intentionally what? He walked slowly home and put the books on his hall table ready to take to the library in the morning.

He went through to the kitchen and made himself a mug of tea.

As he returned he noticed that the book spines were visible where the books poked out of the bag. There was something odd about them. Three of the titles were books he had delivered to her. She had told him how much she had enjoyed one of his early recommendations, The Time Traveler's Wife.

"I love something a bit different," she had explained "If it is difficult to say 'It's rather like so and so' about a book, then that always seems to me to be a very good sign."

So that had become his recent brief. The three books were: The curious incident of the dog in the night time, Winter in

Madrid, both in that sort of category and another of her beloved Alistair McCall Smith titles. Though undemanding reads these too had a unique and amusing character and were assuredly cleverly written. "I love him," Abigail had told him "Opening a new one of his is like getting into a warm bath – it's classic comfort reading."

But it was now clear that the last book was not a book at all. It had caught his eye that there was no white sticker from the library on the spine. It was book-sized but was in fact a note book of some sort. He opened it at the first page and saw a recipe: strawberry cheesecake, and a list of ingredients starting "6ozs of sweet meal biscuits". He started to flick on through it but immediately a dozen or so photographs tumbled out and fell to the floor. He stooped to collect them up and gave them a superficial glance. Most of them seemed to be of a visit to Scotland; the name "Dunoon" was written on the back of one of them in pencil. There were mountains and lochs and a shot of Abigail apparently taken on the pier at Dunoon, which he knew to be a small seaside town west of Glasgow that had grown up way back as a place Glaswegians liked to visit to get away from the city; he knew too that quite a few of its houses were built to be second homes for those made rich by the industrial revolution.

Philip got an envelope from his desk and tucked the photos inside, then put them back in the book and put it aside from the library books which he left in the hall ready to return to the library the next morning. Neither the recipe nor the photographs appeared to be of any great significance, but he resolved to have another look at them later.

Soon after 8 o'clock the following morning, just as he was starting breakfast, his telephone rang. It was Sargent Jayne. She told Philip that such matters – that is a death with no relatives apparent to take care of the funeral and estate - were referred to the Treasury Solicitor, a grand sounding name for a department of the civil service.

Philip made a note, as she concluded, "There's a bit of work to be done by someone by the look of it. It's so sad when there's no family to carry things on when someone dies. But that's life, I suppose." She seemed to realise what she had said and Philip heard her stifle a chuckle.

"Sorry, death is never a laughing matter, I just meant that sometimes such things happen, however regrettable. Besides it may still not apply in this case. My job's not all doom and gloom; a lot of what we do is helpful and positive, but it can have its dark side."

She excused herself saying that "business called". Philip thanked her, wondered what the business was – the small town had vanishingly few bank robberies – and again found himself thinking that she was a tad chatty for a police officer dealing with a member of the public. He was surely imagining it, though it might be nice if there was a more social element to their contacts. He would look out for her in the library.

He went through to the kitchen to finish his breakfast toast, spread out the Daily Telegraph on the kitchen table and clicked the kettle on again. He reckoned that he could just get in a second cup of tea before he left for work.

ᚦ

The next day was Saturday. He was not too busy and he was not working; although the library opened on Saturdays and staff had a rota to man the place. He had quite often worked on Saturdays in recent times: since his wife had died there was no one to co-ordinate time off with. So still with Abigail in mind he started the morning spending an hour or so doing some research. The police had asked about relatives and as far as he knew there were none. But if not, what exactly happened then he wondered? You can find anything on the internet these days and, although by no means an extreme computer buff, he had no trouble looking up the Treasury Solicitor's Office. The relevant department had an odd name:

Bona Vacantia, which he discovered was Latin. Roughly translated the words meant ownerless goods, and as Jayne – he was still adopting a familiar tone with her in his mind – had said, when there were no relatives it was their job to investigate and then wind up an estate. Any money there might be in such an estate went to the Government. It seemed a rather soulless process and he was pleased he had a will and would not be in that position, and yet, of course, sometimes it had to be done. Someone had to make arrangements.

He found that the Treasury Solicitor, whoever that might be, did not actually arrange funerals. A few more clicks and the ubiquitous Google had explained this too. If no relative appeared Abigail would have a "Public Health" or "Welfare" funeral; this was, he discovered, an element of the Public Health (Control of Diseases) Act of 1984. Philip wondered what happened before that date, there must have been something or unclaimed bodies would have rather piled up. A macabre thought. This kind of funeral was arranged by the local authority and ultimately paid for out of any monies left by the deceased or, if there was none, by the tax payer.

On a whim he looked up Abigail herself. One thing, or rather one click, quickly led to another. He found her birth certificate and quickly discovered how much basic, and personal, information is readily available on line. She was born in 1938 and was thus 76 years old when she died. He discovered that she had been married – to a James Croft – though her husband had died a while ago in the Nineties. The internet is somewhat addictive, Philip didn't notice the time going by, and then, with a few more clicks, another discovery brought him up short.

"Heavens, she does have a relative," he said out loud.

A son, Michael, had been born in 1970; he would be – he counted on his fingers – 40 years old. But where was he and why had she never spoken of him? He went further back and checked for there being any siblings, thinking perhaps that the Mac she had mentioned might be Abigail's brother. But, no, it appeared she was an only child. Suddenly hungry he switched off the computer and decided to leave it for a while and go out for a walk and some lunch. He was no great cook; Penny had always joked that if he threw the scraps out for the birds after he had cooked they would throw them back. And he had found that since his wife had died a pub lunch at a weekend had become something of a habit.

He had always enjoyed walking. It helped him think when he was alone and before Penny had died one of the things they loved doing together was exploring the district on foot, not just in the immediate vicinity but also to the north of the town and up into Suffolk. Now he decided not to get the car out; there were no garages in the terraced street in which he lived and Philip kept his small Honda Jazz in a boat yard down by the quay close to where the old-style sailing barges for which Maldon was known tied up. He checked the time and after walking to the top of the high street got a bus to take him the three or so miles to Heybridge, He walked along the canal for some twenty minutes to where it met the River Blackwater at a lock, back from which a line of boats were moored along both sides of the canal. Heybridge Basin was a mooring place accommodating boats of all sorts and was a temporary stopping place too for boats from as far afield as France and Holland. Here there were two pubs and a café, the latter run by a local company, Wilkins, famous for their quality jams.

"Posh, expensive and well worth it," Penny had always said about their distinctive jars; she had particularly liked their marmalade.

He saw the tide was coming in, water moving almost visibly across the shining mud that stretched out beyond the lock. The weather was fine and he immediately saw a friend sitting on the stone wall bordering the river opposite The Old Ship pub and drinking a pint. At his feet was his golden Labrador, Topper. Richard worked for the town council and they occasionally had contact over work and also saw each other around the town and had a coffee or beer together. Richard and his wife had known Penny and they had sometimes met up as a foursome.

"Topper," he called as he got closer, and the dog jerked its head towards him and Richard turned, too. "Hi, there."

Richard smiled: apparently out for a lone walk with the dog he seemed pleased to see a friendly face. "Hi, are you going to eat?" he asked.

"That's the idea."

"Get me something too would you, so that I don't have to take Topper inside."

They agreed on sausage sandwiches and Richard passed a ten pound note over to him. Once Philip had gone into the pub and given his order, and got a pint of beer for himself, they sat and chatted for a while at a table near the lock, where a few boats were lining up to go through to the river once high tide was reached and the lock gates could open safely. The Basin was a popular and busy sailing area; indeed in the summer months the whole estuary was alive with boats. The sound of water spurting through small gaps in the imperfect lock gates made a background to their conversation.

"Have you found yourself any female company yet?"

Used to such banter Philip just raised an eyebrow.

Richard had known Philip long enough to comment in this way. "I'm sure Penny wouldn't mind. Sorry, that was a bit blunt, but you know what I mean – you need to get out more."

Philip nearly told him he had some thoughts about that, but his liking for Jayne was embryonic to say the very least and, in all likelihood it was totally one sided too.

Embarrassed, he mumbled, conscious of others sitting around them in what was now a busy seating area, "I don't know about that, though I was thinking, well, it's been more than two years now and I do seem to have been living in something of a daze. I know something needs to change, I ..." He faltered, then a sudden thought enabled him to change track. "Actually I did meet a lady recently, but then only a few days ago I found her dead."

"You ...what on earth do you mean?" Richard gasped and Philip, realising that pitching into that just to get out of mentioning something Richard had no inkling of, needed some explanation. He told his story: how he and Abigail had met, the whistle, their chats, the library errands and how he had found her sitting dead in her garden.

"I suppose I'm part of an official investigation now. I had the police calling round at home and at the library and now, if no relations can be found, your lot must arrange a funeral for her. I suppose the authorities may talk to neighbours too. Their first job must surely be to see if they can trace a next of kin."

"Seems to me you're probably not sufficiently close by to be counted as a neighbour, but if the council talk to the police then you may get a call. You reported her death after all," said Richard.

"It's sad, at first I thought there were no relations but I now know there is a son, Michael, or there was. I checked it on Google. But she never mentioned him to me. He might be a few streets away or dead too for all I know."

"They'll track him down I'm sure. Are you walking back to the town?" Their sandwiches eaten, Richard put his empty glass down as he spoke. Topper sensed that it was time to leave, standing and tugging at his lead.

Having agreed to move on they chatted some more as they made their way back alongside the canal, though the path was narrow and squeezing past the occasional fisherman they had to walk in single file. They parted company as they came to the road and Philip walked on into town, climbing the steep twisting slope of Market Hill that rose into the high street after the road crossed the bridge over the river.

He was puffing a little when he got to where the hill joined the high street; he passed the pedestrian crossing and then ran straight into Jayne, now dressed imposingly in uniform, coming the other way and apparently aiming to cross the road.

They both stopped and then, in unison, said, "Hello again".

"I've found out a bit more about Abigail Croft," said Philip.

A look of interest flashed in Jayne's eyes, but remained there only for a second. She just said, "Good, but I've got to move along, I'm due to be somewhere. Another time, perhaps?"

"Right, fine."

Philip couldn't help but feel some small disappointment in her reaction, but he immediately wondered why he should. "Okay," he said, "goodbye then" and walked on. He had only gone a few paces when he heard a call from behind him. "Hang on, Philip."

He turned, instantly registering, and slightly thrown by, the fact that she had addressed him by his first name for the first time.

"Yes, what is it?"

Just as he spoke a woman approached the sergeant and appeared to ask for directions. She signalled to Philip that he should wait and he watched while she directed the enquirer, pointing this way and that as she did so; a common occurrence Philip imagined remembering his childhood and his mother impressing on him that if ever he was lost he should ask a policeman. The police were mostly men in those days and, many would say, much more evident on the streets than they are now. In this case the enquirer went on her way apparently well satisfied and Sergeant Jayne turned back to Philip again.

"Sorry about that, occupational hazard. I wonder ... can you do me a favour, well a big favour actually?"

What do you say to a police sergeant asking you that? Especially an attractive one.

"Yes, I guess ..." he said and waited.

Jayne stepped forward so that they were face to face again. A couple of people passed close on the narrow pavement and the two of them flattened themselves against the church wall that faced the road.

"Well, it's just ..." She hesitated, looking uncertain. "I wondered whether ..."

She paused again, prompting Philip to butt in with, "Wondered what?"

"Okay, right, I'll come straight out with it. Can we have dinner together on Monday night? It's my fortieth birthday – terrible, please don't laugh – and I can't face a fuss being made and some of my colleagues at the station are hinting that we should do something, something well 'partyish'. That's the last thing I want. I'd hate it. I really need a good excuse. Will you? Please? We could go somewhere in the town after work – I shouldn't be late getting off that evening. And ... well, then you can update me about your old lady."

Finally it had all come out in a rush as she found herself responding to the coincidence of events and her feelings with some impulsiveness.

Philip was at first surprised and then elated at the thought, the latter feeling rapidly diminished by her apparent need for an excuse. Did she want to spend time with him? Was there a hint of embarrassment about her request? Was that because she was asking him for a date? Or was it because it was just a ploy to enable her to avoid something unpleasant? He wasn't sure, but he didn't hesitate.

"Sure, that would be nice," he said, even as these thoughts flashed through his mind "Would you like to try the Thai restaurant at the top of the town or is it too near the police station?"

"No, fine, sounds nice – can we meet there at about seven o'clock?"

"Yes, I'll call them and book a table. Do you have a mobile number in case there is any problem?" They solemnly swapped numbers.

"That's good. Now, sorry – really must get on. See you then." She was gone.

Philip walked slowly back down the high street towards his home. Puzzled, he wondered why he had picked a restaurant he had never been to and which served food he had eaten only very occasionally. There was, he felt, some feeling between him and Sergeant Jayne. But what exactly? She surely would not have asked just anyone to help her escape a birthday catastrophe. At the very least Monday evening promised to be interesting.

CHAPTER THREE
A written request

Not only has Philip called in regularly and continued to supply books to me, he has recommended some too. I am just loving reading the Shardlake stories – historical thrillers I can't put down – I can't remember the author's name. The historical background is excellent, they are real page turners and so well written too. They just fit my category of being difficult to compare with anything else. I hope I'm not presuming on his time too much. I get the impression that since his wife died he has time on his hands – all the things he and Penny used to do together have gone or don't have the same charm any more. I remember the feeling. When James died I ... No, I'm not going there again.

I'm sure Philip quite enjoys our chats, even when I badger him. I'm working hard to get him to stand up to that awful Froby woman; making some progress too I think. Maybe he can help me. I wonder if I could raise it with him. I won't press him, but he might be just the one. How to raise it? I can't think how I might ... perhaps I could write to him. It's old fashioned these days, I know, with all these texts and chatters flying about, but maybe I could. No, really, I will.

April 2014

Monday morning. He put the library books back in the canvas book bag; he always kept this folded flat in the battered brown leather satchel he habitually carried. Later, in the library he went to return them to the shelves. He could have just put them on the books-returned trolley but somehow wanted to complete the process himself. He had taken the books out and delivered them to Abigail, indeed he had recommended most of them, and he would now put them back too. He had cancelled the electronic record inside the books as he arrived for work. Now, as he reached high to the appropriate fiction shelf, to set an Alistair McCall Smith title back in place, he noticed a sheet of paper slide out a little from inside the book. Perhaps it had been used as a book mark. Not likely, he thought, Abigail had had a collection of bookmarks and given a new book she always went to a drawer and selected one carefully; the first time he had seen her do this she had explained "I feel it has to match the book somehow, but don't ask me quite how." She'd laughed at the nonsense of it.

He pulled the sheet out. It was a single sheet of cream coloured writing paper folded in half. He opened it up and saw that it was a letter addressed to him, or certainly to someone named Philip.

"Can you spare me a moment Philip?" Miss Frobisher's voice intruded on his thoughts. She had wanted to discuss something with him "as soon as we can fit in a moment" and the moment had clearly arrived. He said he could, and refolded the letter and slipped it into his jacket pocket as he followed her towards her office and spent a boring hour discussing the need to update Health & Safety regulations and make sure all the staff – there were only five others – knew how to react to something like having to use steps to get to a top shelf. Vital stuff. Not so, he thought, but at least the meeting was not about cost cutting or pushing the library towards her particular vision of extreme modernity. They did not, it had to be said, see eye to eye on that and much else besides. Nevertheless he took a moment once the Health and Safety matter was ended to float a few ideas of his own with her about her embryo grand plans for modernisation.

It was only later back at his desk that he was able to pull out what proved to be Abigail's intended note to him and read what it said. It was hand written using blue ink in a clear, crisp hand. This did not surprise him. When Abigail was at school Philip imagined that learning to write in such a way was mandatory. She would have had to write carefully, positioning letters between the lines of an exercise book just so, though the resultant style seemed to display character too.

What he read, however, surprised him a good deal. Below her address it said:

Dear Philip

I suppose we don't know each other very well, hardly at all really and certainly we have not done so for long. But I have so enjoyed our little chats and your errands on my behalf, especially to the library, have been a godsend. I have caught up on my list of "want to read" books and you have introduced me to some great reads that I would never otherwise have found. I am halfway through "The Time Traveler's Wife" and am enjoying it immensely; even if traveller is spelt the American way. Fancy this being a first novel, it's such a clever idea and despite being totally implausible it just works and works so well. A woman author, of course!

So first a big thank you on the library front, and then ... but there is something else. I don't like to raise this with you but you have been so kind and, well really there is no one else.

It's about Mac. I have not seen him for many years. There was a falling out, quite soon after my husband died, we lost contact and I have never heard from him again. It broke my heart, but time goes by – years – and I kind of got used to the fact; I had to. Well, I never stopped thinking about him, but I rather stopped constantly expecting contact or thinking that he might get in touch. To have thought that would have made life unbearable.

But as I get older I wonder. Is he okay? If so where is he? What is he doing? Might we be in touch again? It will soon be too late, I have a heart condition; oh, don't worry it's manageable, if I am careful and remember my pills then, who knows, I may go on for years, but maybe not.

I wonder if there is anything I can do, even after all these years, I wonder if you know ... if you could help I would be so grateful. I know it is a lot to ask and I hesitate to even attempt to involve you in my problems but

The writing ended half way down the second page leaving the letter unfinished. Philip sat at his desk holding the sheet and feeling rather stunned. Suddenly he was involved in her life, or he was about to be before she ... he sighed, how sad he thought, just as she had resolved to try to renew an old contact her life had ended. A single moment had changed everything. He would never know the details he realised, maybe she would not have actually sent the letter, after all it wasn't finished, but he knew what it said and, as a result, he felt he must do something. Abigail's estate might well be about to be wound up, her possessions sold off and her money taken away by the state. He hated that thought, it didn't seem right somehow however much it was the law. Maybe this Mac was a relative. If so, and if her son could not be found, then maybe this Mac person could be. Besides, presumably if she had thought her son could be found she would have asked about that.

He put the letter away and went back to library work. Almost at once he was approached by a mother with a child of perhaps six or seven in tow.

"Can you help please?" she asked. "She just loves all the Beatrix Potter books, but her latest passion is dinosaurs. Did Beatrix Potter write anything about them?" Philip raised an eyebrow but politely prepared a counter suggestion.

At lunchtime he paused only briefly and just had a sandwich, after all he was eating out in the evening. He wondered what the evening would bring. It might well prove to be nothing, just an opportunistic way for Jayne to avoid an unwanted party, but it might actually be a date, indeed he rather hoped it was. If so, then for a start he must find out what her first name was; for the moment it was a date with Sergeant Jayne - if it was a date. He chuckled to himself about the name even as he became aware that Margaret, who was sitting with him in the staff room, had asked a question.

"What do you think?"

"Sorry, I was miles away, about what?"

"Well this guy, the one I was out with last night. Tony. He seems nice and his friend is too. It was a foursome with Mary and Wayne. She likes Wayne, says he's a tiger, know what I mean. He looks smart and dresses well and "so quickly too" as she said last night." She giggled. "Maybe he's married. He's older than we are, he's ..."

"Sorry Margaret, I wasn't listening properly – things on my mind. I'm sure he's fine, but take care, eh? I must get on now."

He felt bad for not giving her any time, but also felt old; certainly he felt that he had little in common with someone of Margaret's age these days.

As he headed back to his desk he made a mental note not to ask Margaret for romantic advice, that is if he ever needed it.

There he found a new note from Froby about reorganisation and "extending and updating our tech cred profile"; which he imagined meant technical credibility. Remembering the memos that she had sent since her appointment, he wondered again how a librarian could write such gobbledegook. He sighed. She wanted him to reduce the number of books in stock again and was intent on putting in another row of computers. Computers were in danger of taking over, there was already a whole line of them. Undoubtedly they were useful, they were well used and people with no computer at home relied on them, there was so much that had to be done on line these days. Philip felt that was more than enough though, especially if adding more would take more money and space away from books.

It was anything for an easy life with Froby, he thought, and certainly computers were far easier to look after than books. Library users simply sat down and logged in to use a computer using their library card number as a code. Computers did not need to be checked in or out, sorted, arranged or catalogued and if one of them needed attention one of the staff stuck an out of order sign on it and sent in a request for the area IT guy to come and fix it. Of course he knew that computers were virtually essential to modern life now but, in a library at least, Philip thought books should predominate.

In fact, he thought, he would try to make sure that the traditional library roles were not overpowered by Froby's unthinking rush for everything modern, trendy and, not least he suspected, designed to make her look like she was an innovator leading the way to a bright new future. He had simply resented what was going on for a while now; too long. Now he had a plan of his own: he would, he had decided, continue to feed her some ideas; maybe he could influence things for the better in the long term.

In the middle of the afternoon, he had a phone call. The library environment made personal calls somewhat awkward and Froby, who had no such problem herself as she had her own office, frowned on them. Since she arrived she had had a profusion of new notices posted: "Silence!", "No Mobile phones!", "No eating!" and more. The number of such signs had doubled and one or two earlier ones that Philip rather liked, one was in the form of a tombstone on which was engraved "Here rests the last person to eat in here: don't do it!" had been unceremoniously removed as "unsuitable". Philip had certainly liked the tombstone one, it made people smile and he could not remember when he had last seen anyone eating. Maybe he could add one somewhere saying "Froby-free zone" Philip thought mischievously. He had at least persuaded her not to post six copies of a notice saying "We do NOT sell lottery tickets" around the library even though they were occasionally asked if they did.

He made few telephone calls as a rule; indeed he discouraged people from calling him at work even though there was not actually a rule forbidding staff from receiving calls; well, not yet that is. This one was from Richard.

"Sorry to call during the day," he said as Philip stood to one side of the library counter. "I won't keep you long. I can't give you the details, I should not even know about it really, but I heard something in the corridor about your old lady and I thought, well, I thought you'd like to know."

"Right, that's kind of you. What's going on?"

"It seems she had a son, Michael, but he disappeared nearly twenty years ago. As far as can be discovered there has been no contact between them since; and so there is little realistic prospect of him being traced now. I guess it's even possible he's dead. Anyway, the likelihood is that the Council will fix a basic funeral."

"I see. That's sad." He did not mention his own research, but made a mental note about the funeral.

"Yeah, it is, I won't keep you now, but if I hear anything more then I'll let you know. Might you be having a snack at the Basin on Saturday?"

Philip thanked him and acknowledged that, if the weather was still good, then they might well cross paths at the pub.

At the end of what had been a busy day he had time to go home before his dinner meeting. He wondered what to wear. He should be smart he decided, but not too smart. Not a suit, he did not even wear a suit for work these days; that sort of formality had long gone. Was a jacket and tie too formal? He settled on a sports jacket and no tie, and then suddenly thought about why this dinner was taking place. It was Jayne's birthday. Should he take a birthday card, he wondered? Or even a present? It was too late to buy a card, but he looked in the small store of cards he kept in his desk. There was nothing with age 40 on it, but he hated cards with numbers on anyway, a dislike fuelled by those he received on his own fortieth birthday just a year or two back. He found one that was okay, wrote a brief message on it and secreted it in his jacket pocket. He only intended to get it out if events showed it to be appropriate.

Just before seven o'clock he turned the corner at the top of the high street and went towards the restaurant where he had booked a table earlier. He paused at the door and a car passed within inches on the narrow corner: if it was a date then he was nervous, if it wasn't then he would be disappointed; either seemed to indicate that a deep breath before entering was in order, so he took one and exhaled slowly. Then he opened the door. Jayne was already there, wearing a blue dress and sitting at a table towards the back of the restaurant. Her hair was loose, she looked very nice and she smiled as she saw him come in. It was, he decided, a charming smile.

He breathed deeply again and went forward to join her.

CHAPTER FOUR
The dinner that wasn't an excuse

I've decided. I'll ask him. I've written a
letter, well I've started it and I will send
it, really I will. I can give it to him when
he next calls. I'll put it in an envelope
and ask him to look at it later - then he
can think about it before he responds. I
have no idea what can be done, he may
not even want to get involved. Or he may
have no idea what to do or just think it is

too time-consuming. Or impossible.
We'll see.

Meantime I must finish this book before
he does come calling again. It's a nice
day and I can sit outside. I'm half way
through "The curious incident of the dog
in the night time", again a book I would
never have found without Philip's
direction. It presents its story through
the eyes of a teenage boy with Asperger's
syndrome; the way he sets out to solve a
mystery is riveting. I don't think I'll
ever forget the description of him
tackling the London Underground,
which he manages to do even though he
hardly ever goes out on his own. I can't
wait to see what happens.

She had got to the restaurant early. In the months she had been in Maldon she had got to know the little town well, even though the scale of operation of the small town police station meant that she spent as much time in Chelmsford and around the area as she did in the town itself. So she had often passed the restaurant, which was not far from the police station.

The restaurant was long and narrow, attractively decorated and looked to promise a pleasant meal to come. She was

57

shown to a table. She declined a drink, saying she had a friend coming and sat back to look at the unfamiliar menu. She recalled that the last time she had been in a restaurant was on a call out. A diner had complained to the restaurant manager that his jacket had been ruined by wet paint. The manager had explained that the wet paint was clearly signed and that this had been pointed out as he entered. They argued: voices and the eyebrows of other diners were raised. The man wanted not just the cost of cleaning the jacket, but of a replacement; the argument had become increasingly acrimonious and another diner, fearing violence, called the police. She had successfully calmed things down and no further action needed to be taken; she had left thinking that the man's jacket had seemed suspiciously tight and that it had all the appearances of a ploy to finance a new, better fitting one. If she was honest such incidents were in the majority; the area was a low crime one, though of course what there was upset people. Nevertheless she felt that her work acted to smooth the life of many people caught up in untoward accidents or incidents.

In the restaurant only a couple of tables were yet occupied. She scanned the menu thinking of how she had contrived the coming meal with Philip. It was not really like her to take such an initiative, especially in such a disguised way. Certainly she had wanted to avoid any forced birthday celebrations at the station, but she also wanted to meet Philip properly. Her romantic record was hardly good; married for some years in her twenties she was divorced when her husband had had an affair. It was unexpected. She thought everything was fine, but realised that her attention had been almost exclusively on her job. It was not the kind of job you could do half-heartedly and anyway she enjoyed it. In retrospect the marriage had been somewhat lack lustre she supposed and she had always hoped for something better.

But only a few ill-fated encounters with men had occurred since her divorce – she cringed at the thought of her last dinner date: the man concerned had turned out to have a phobia about the police and from the "so what do you do?" moment it was all downhill. She faced a gambit of questions from "When did you last help beat someone up?" to "Do you make a lot of money from the bribes?" Perhaps she was just not lucky with men.

Nevertheless it would be nice to have someone to spend time with and she had good feelings about Philip, though it was clearly early days. Brief encounters in the library and a chance meeting because of the old lady's death hardly qualified as the start of a romance and he probably didn't even regard their meeting as a date. Whatever it was it would be a chance to find out more about him. Having taken the initiative she resolved to run with it for a bit. She concentrated on the menu, quite an exotic one from her perspective, and reckoned that would be fun to investigate too.

She remembered what had brought her to Maldon and her resolution to make some changes in her life. Suddenly she saw that Philip had arrived and was walking through the restaurant towards her a smile on his face. She smiled back.

"Hello again." He'd said that in the street on the day this dinner had been arranged. "I hope you've not been here too long."

He sat down opposite her and she smiled at him.

"No, no, I've only just sat down – looks very nice here. Thanks so much for coming."

"So, you ducked out of the station do okay, did you?"

"Oh, yes, I said I had a date."

"And did ..." He was interrupted by a waitress, who was clearly English, not Thai, delivering a menu and taking their order for drinks: a beer for him, his standard tipple, and a lager for her.

"What were you saying?" she enquired as soon as the waitress departed.

"Oh, I said – do you?"

"Do I what?"

"Do you have a date?"

"I suppose I do. No. I see what you mean. Really it's just a coincidence. I did need a pressing engagement for tonight, but also this just seemed, well a good idea and so yes I do have a date, I guess - one I'm pleased to be having. How about you?"

"Yes, yes I'm very pleased, and pleased not just to be the get-out-clause too. I honestly don't know how long it might have taken me to pluck up the courage to say more than hello to you otherwise, especially seeing you in uniform half the time – you look great this evening by the way – and I ... but I don't even know your first name."

"It's Miriam."

"Hello again Miriam."

They both laughed and the awkwardness began to evaporate. For a second Philip contemplated commenting that Miriam was a nice name, but he rejected doing so. He might be out of practice at this but he did know to avoid such blatant clichés. A question was a better start.

"I don't know much else about you either apart from the sergeant bit, though I guess I could always look you up in the library records to see what you read, though that would probably run foul of data protection these days. Anyway, how long have you been in Maldon?"

"Fair enough. I ...." Again the waitress was back, an expectant look on her face and asking if they were ready to order.

"Give us five minutes," said Philip, "Sorry, we've been talking." He turned to Miriam, who was picking up the menu that had been moved in front of her with the drinks.

"What would you like?" he said, realising that he had no real idea how to order Thai food.

"No idea," she replied "And I've never been here before."

"Me neither."

In the slight hiatus that followed, Philip had an idea and he suggested that they order one of the set selections of dishes and share. Miriam agreed and, pleased with himself for thinking of it, he signalled to the waitress who duly returned and took their order. She chased off quickly; the restaurant was filling up.

"That's sorted that then," Miriam said, continuing, "I only arrived in Maldon not quite a year ago, I have one of the new flats in Wenlock Place, you must know it, off the High Street, and I transferred here from the suburbs in north London. I like it here, it's really very different to what I was used to over the last few years."

He knew Wenlock Place: a small passage off the high street with shops below and flats above, a small well planned little development he thought, just the sort of thing a small town high street needed. There was a pleasant deli and café there that had been a favourite of Penny's. Miriam must walk from home to the police station he thought and wondered how they had never crossed paths in the street; probably they had different working hours.

She continued: "And you're the town's Librarian."

"Regrettably not, I'm the number two. The chief number cruncher is Miss Frobisher – a greater advocate of computers than books, I'm afraid. Not my favourite person. Can you imagine she was put out by my being late in on that morning when Abigail Croft died? I would have thought discovering a dead body was a pretty good excuse for delay; if that's not exceptional circumstances, I'm sure I don't know what is. If that woman is ever found dead in a ditch let me tell you I'll be your main suspect."

"Hmm, I'd better remember that."

He resisted launching into a lengthy tirade against the attitudes of modern librarians. Froby would have hated a saying his mother had always used: "God made libraries so that we would have no excuse to be ignorant," and anyway he found that the mention of Abigail had Miriam asking about the current state of play.

"There are a number of things," he said.

He wondered how much to say about it all, but the thought that Abigail seemed likely to have a 'welfare' funeral set up by the council distressed him. Moreover she had sort of embroiled him in her affairs or it seemed that she had intended to. The letter might never have been sent, but he was increasingly convinced she would have asked him about Mac; it was him the letter had mentioned.

He went through the situation with Miriam as they tucked into the array of dishes that had now been served; it was all very tasty, though he found one dish was spicy enough to numb his mouth. He took a swig of cold beer conscious that such was not the best antidote to spicy food; he had been told that milk was better, but he could hardly order that in the middle of a meal. The effect was a little like a dental injection though it did not last too long.

Miriam listened closely to his update, then asked: "So where does that leave things now?"

"It seems she had a son but he has been missing for some twenty years. I have a mate in the Council who reckons that they have decided he is long gone and will go ahead with fixing a funeral soon. But then there is this Mac person.

Mention of him cropped up occasionally in my conversations with Abigail; I never knew anything about him, but I suppose it's possible he's a relation or a friend, maybe someone she thought could help her find her son. It's just a name though – how could they be traced do you think?"

"It depends what happened to them. For instance if the son ran away, well, moved away or wanted to disappear for some reason – from what you say he wasn't a child, after all – then he could have changed his name to confuse the trail and all these years on ... he could be difficult, if not impossible, to trace, especially if he still doesn't want to be found or has never been back. Certainly these things take time. I do think perhaps you should mention this Mac person to the Treasury Solicitor; it may be that the name ties in with some record in Abigail's effects. If so and if they have a surname that might well make a difference."

Philip agreed. He would be pleased to do something – anything – to help, but it seemed so little: just a short letter. He wondered if Abigail's letter to him had implied that she felt there were specific things to be done.

Despite the odd way the dinner had been arranged, they chatted amicably for a long time, adding another drink, a dessert and coffee and tea to their order. Philip told her how, earlier that day, he had had a library member asking if they had security cameras in the library. "We do, of course, and I said something about it being sad that this was necessary, then a little while later I saw them glancing round then taking a book out from under their jacket and returning it to a shelf."

Miriam laughed at the image it conjured up and said with mock seriousness "Maybe next time you should call me."

Philip was delighted to find that the meal concluded very amicably. Perhaps having the topic of Abigail to discuss had largely banished any what-does-this-person-think-of-me awkwardness of such a meeting. They ended with an agreement to meet again firmly in place. After a short tussle, with both insisting on paying, Miriam because she had invited him and Philip because as he said vaguely "well, I should", they agreed to split the bill and, as Philip dealt with it, the Thai lady who apparently owned or managed the place asked if they had enjoyed the meal.

"Yes, indeed" Philip replied. "Though one of those dishes was really hot."

"No problem," she told him. "Next time when you order just say mai pet, it means 'not too spicy'- okay?"

Philip thanked her and then walked with Miriam down the high street. As she turned off towards her flat half way along Philip suddenly realised that he had not given her the birthday card; indeed her birthday had hardly been mentioned during the evening.

"Hang on." He called back to her reaching into his pocket. "I got you a card - it doesn't say forty on it."

"I should hope not! I had practically forgotten it was my birthday. Thanks for keeping me company, it was very nice. See you soon."

She turned off towards her flat carrying the card and Philip continued on down the road towards the Quay and his home, content in the knowledge that she had not only agreed to their meeting again, but had charged him with telephoning her at the weekend to arrange something.

"And you can update me about Abigail too," she had said.

Indeed. By the weekend he would find there would be a good deal more for him to report.

CHAPTER FIVE
A little light investigation

I've written the letter three times – all
torn up and in the bin. I'm having
another go now. I will finish it, I will. I've
just a last chapter to read first, Philip's
coming this evening and I bet he's got
something else for me to read lined up.
The next reading group book is due too, I
don't know what it will be but I look
forward to it anyway. Philip was right, I
did enjoy the group meeting, there are

some nice people there, and though most of them are a bit younger than me they welcomed me in very easily. The discussion was interesting, though some comments were a bit ... bizarre. That Virginia seemed to see the whole plot as a representation of some failure in her own life and I don't think it's likely that the author even knew of that or would have given one jot if he had. All good fun though.

Midweek: and Philip had plans that did not involve the library. He had a whole day away from the dreaded Froby. He had always thought that a job that involved an element of shift work provided a bit of a perk in that he sometimes had a day off during the week. He liked to linger over breakfast on, say, a Wednesday, knowing that those living round about him were rushing off to get to their places of work as he sat idly. He usually read the paper with extra thoroughness on such a morning, but today he found he could not settle to it.

He made a cup of tea, though he had already had several, and sat down in his study and switched the computer on. He checked the address of the office of the Treasury Solicitor and typed them a short note.

```
Dear Sir

I write regarding the death of Abigail Croft.
```

He paused to check her full postal address, from her library card which still sat on his desk – she had affixed a small self-adhesive address label to it – and then returned to his typing, added her address and continued.

```
Just in case this helps you let me say:

She was only an acquaintance really, I met her only
a few months ago and used to help her get books
from the library, but I did ask her once if she had
any relations. I remember her reply specifically as
it was a bit odd, she said "No, not now, not
really"; well words to that effect. The "not
really" seemed a curious choice of words.

Sorry, I'm rambling, what I really felt you should
know was that she did mention someone. Just the
name Mac; I have no idea if this was a relation and
can cast no further light on their identity, but it
cropped up regularly and seemed important to her.

In case this information is in any way useful to
you I felt I should write.

Yours sincerely
```

He printed out the letter, signed it and addressed and stamped an envelope. He switched off the computer, wondering as he did so about the curious fact that this necessitated going to the button marked "Start"; he had always joked about this with Penny.

Next he made a phone call to the offices of the local paper, The Maldon Standard. He did not buy this himself, but they always had it set out in the library on the periodicals table.

He'd checked their number noting that curiously they had no offices in the town but were located in nearby Braintree. The fact that the paper was part of a small group publishing several newspapers around the area probably explained this.

When the phone was picked up Philip asked, "I wonder if you have an archive, is it possible that I can see past copies of the Maldon newspaper at your offices?"

"Yes, we do, but it does not go back very far and there are gaps. It's because the paper has been under several different ownerships over the years. When were you interested in?"

Michael had disappeared nearly twenty years ago and, when Philip mentioned a year, it rapidly became clear that this was too far back for copies to be available.

"Sorry we can't help, but try the Essex Records office in Chelmsford; they should have them."

Philip expressed his thanks and promptly made another call.

He drove the back way into Chelmsford, avoiding the A12, having decided that he could save himself a separate trip to the library there that he would otherwise have to make later in the week. He went first to the library to speak to someone about an author visit, then on to the Records Office to check out their archive of newspapers. Things there proved to be very straightforward. A helpful assistant led him straight to what he wanted. He started with copies of the Maldon paper that he felt were maybe a little earlier than any likely date for when Abigail's son disappeared. Richard had only given him an estimate, and so he flicked through each weekly copy getting nearer and nearer to the present day as he did so.

After about twenty minutes he found himself having covered a few months and was rewarded by spotting a news item; he read it through.

BOAT BOY MISSING

A local sailing enthusiast, Michael Croft, is reported to be missing. Michael had been living on the boat "Starcounter", an eighteen foot sailing cruiser owned by his late father James Croft and moored in Heybridge Basin, following a family row.

His mother Abigail Croft had been coping with the recent death of her husband and friction arose with her son who then moved out of the house a couple of months ago.

Mrs Croft declined to say what the row was about, but had been trying to set matters straight. "I have been trying to meet up with him and sort things out, but then I went to the boat and found it empty. All his things have gone. He's clearly not living there any longer."

For two weeks now no word has been received from Michael and the boat, used in the past by James Croft, remains empty. A family friend told the Standard that a difficult situation had arisen because Michael, who had won a place at Lancaster University, failed to take up the place as his parents hoped he would and preferred simply to work with boats. Sailing was his passion. He had been working on an ad hoc basis at a number of boat yards in Maldon and Tollesbury while planning a long voyage of some sort in "Starcounter".

There is no indication that anything untoward has happened to Michael, but the family are desperate to find him and ask that if anyone knows where he may be they should please say so. The Standard will pass on information. "We just want to know he is safe" said Mrs Croft.

So it seemed that he had simply walked out. It was perhaps understandable: he was only young and after the trauma of his father dying and a major disagreement he may well have acted impetuously. Philip could remember some moments at a similar age when he ... no matter, he concentrated on Michael. Perhaps the move had been spurred on by the fact that it had been easy to leave home: Michael had had a boat he could move into and it was not even located far away. But then he had evidently moved on again, surely following a more considered decision, to where or what though there was no clue. And he had apparently never looked back.

Philip's curiosity was quenched to a degree but his new knowledge was tinged with disappointment; he had hoped whatever had happened would point to where Michael might be found now.

However it seemed it did not.

He could find no further reference to the matter so he went to the desk and made a photocopy of the article, which had a picture alongside it. It was a shot of Michael taken as he stood on the deck of the boat holding onto the mast. The boat was amongst others at a mooring point; Michael looked young and fit, suntanned and happy. He smiled into the camera below a shock of dark, wind-blown brown hair. Philip was sure he knew the boat. But how could that be? One of his regular walks took him along the canal to Heybridge Basin and, thinking about it, he was sure he had seen a boat there named "Starcounter"; he remembered it because it had a couple of stars painted jauntily alongside the name on the stern. If he was right then the boat at least was still around, even if Michael himself was long gone.

He tucked the photocopy into his satchel, left the Records Office and drove home, out of Chelmsford and along the A12, a usually busy road today unaccountably quiet. He wondered what more he could find out, if anything.

He had had no lunch as yet so he turned off the A12 at Hatfield Peverel and came into Maldon at Heybridge; there he parked at the small clutch of shops at the corner and walked along the narrow canal towpath towards Heybridge Basin, the air filled with the sound of stays banging on masts as he got to where boats were moored. A little short of the Basin there was a car park, one he was always pleased to see still allowed free parking, and just before the car park he saw "Starcounter" moored on the far side of the canal. Though clearly of some age, the boat looked smart, it had been painted not so long ago by the look of it; the polished stainless steel rails round the deck shone in the sun. The two stars, or a recent version of them, still decorated the name on the stern. Boats lined both sides of the canal at this point. "Starcounter" was not covered by a tarpaulin as some craft were, and Philip could see that the door into the cabin was closed; no one seemed to be aboard. A woman was sitting drinking a mug of something on the boat just ahead of him, a motor launch called "Lazybones".

On a whim he spoke to her.

"Afternoon," he said. "I wonder if you know who owns "Starcounter" over there?" He pointed across the canal.

"Well, yes, I do, it's always moored just opposite us: it's Kevin Foster's boat. I know he's in The Old Ship at the moment if you want a word; he went off to get a sandwich."

"Thanks, yes. How would I know him?"

The woman laughed. "That's easy," she said "He's about a mile high and has a dachshund with him – the long, the short and the tall, you might say."

She chuckled again and Philip thanked her and walked on. Approaching the pub, Kevin Foster seemed obvious; otherwise there were two extremely tall men with long low slung dogs at the Basin. He was sitting alone at one of the picnic-style tables just outside the pub door and looked a bit like the image of the sailor on the old style Players cigarette packets, a bushy beard, flecked with grey, and a peaked navel-style hat above his jeans, open necked shirt and navy blue deck shoes. A retiree who loved boats Philip assumed as he approached him.

"Excuse me," he said. "Are you Kevin Foster?" The man nodded.

"You own "Starcounter", I'm told. If you have a moment, I wonder if you can tell me anything of her history before you had her?"

"It's my son's boat now," he said. "I'm getting a bit old for it. All that climbing in and out, you know. But yes, I bought it from people I knew slightly, though it was a good while ago."

"That would be the Crofts?"

"That's right, how can I ..."

Philip interrupted. "Sorry, I'm in danger of being rude. Look, I wonder if I can ask you a few questions about it – I'm just getting a drink. Would you like another?"

He indicated the virtually empty pint glass on the table. They introduced themselves properly and then when Philip returned with their drinks he told Kevin about Abigail, their meeting, her death and the mystery of her missing son.

"Since I found her body I can't get it out of my mind. As far as I can gather Michael has not been heard of for nearly twenty years. It seems such a shame if he can't be found. I just found out that he lived on the boat for a while before he disappeared and I remembered seeing it moored here on my walks along the canal. I remembered the name with the stars. Do you have any idea what happened to Michael? I would love to think he could still be tracked down."

"Not a clue, I'm afraid. I'm sorry to hear about Abigail's death. I bought the boat from her after her husband James's death. He and I knew each other slightly, we both worked in the city and saw each other occasionally as we commuted – bemoaning another late train at Witham, you know. With Michael gone she did not want the worry of looking after the boat – upkeep, mooring fees and so on. James was the sailor, not her ... and Michael too later on, of course. I've never regretted buying her - she's a great little boat."

The conversation did not seem promising in terms of adding any useful information about Michael's whereabouts. Philip took a bite out of the sandwich he had ordered at the bar and which had just been delivered.

Kevin turned away and shouted, "Graham! Spare a minute." The shout seemed to be directed at a group of men, women and children sitting over near the canal. A man about Philip's age detached himself from the group and started towards them.

"My son may know. He and Michael knew each other, at school I think."

Graham sat down with them and Kevin made a rapid introduction and explained that Philip was interested in the whereabouts of Michael Croft.

"I vaguely remember him disappearing," said Graham, "but that has to be years ago when we must both have been in our twenties. I only saw him occasionally then and I've never heard anything from him or about him since. Sorry."

He glanced across towards where he had been sitting where what might have been his wife was apparently reprimanding one of the children for throwing stones in the canal. Notices specifically warned against doing so as it could damage the boats.

"I must get back, sorry I can't help," he said. "Tell you who might know though. He was great mates with Roger Morris. They both did casual work at the boatyard just along the path, you know by the houseboat that the youth club uses. To the best of my knowledge he still does, I think I saw him the other day as I walked by."

Philip thanked them both, and Graham excused himself to return to his family, telling his father: "See you along at the boat before we go."

Philip downed the remains of his pint, thanked Kevin and walked the hundred yards or so to the yard, a small establishment where boats could be stored on land during the winter and repairs carried out. In front of the main shed two men were hosing down a boat in preparation for a paint job of some sort – pots and brushes were laid out on a bench.

"Excuse me, anyone know Roger Morris?" Philip called down the steps to the yard which was set below the path where the land sloped away from the river.

"That's me," one of the men replied. He appeared to be in his early forties and his hands gave evidence of regular manual labour. He was dressed in paint spattered blue overalls with a length of fraying rope tied round them acting as a belt.

"Can I ask you a quick question?" said Philip, moving down the steps alongside the crane set to swing over the wall by the river and bring out boats on a canvas sling.

"Give us a moment," he replied, putting down the hose "I was just going to take a break – can you come to the café for a few minutes? I need to get a cuppa."

Philip had the time and wanted to check this out thoroughly so he said, "Okay. Sure."

Roger stripped off his mucky overalls and came up the steps to the path. The café, which was only a few yards away, was busy: the terrace was a popular spot and afforded a great view along the river. They ordered a pot of tea and found a seat outside. Well... Roger grabbed the seats and left Philip to order – and to pay.

"Okay, what's this about?" Roger took a sip of his tea, which was delivered promptly despite the café being busy.

"I know it's a while back, but I think you knew Michael Croft and I wondered if you have any idea what became of him?"

"Knew him, oh, some twenty years back before he disappeared. Why do you ask?"

"Well, he's apparently never been heard from again, and now his mother's just died – I knew her and I sort of promised to try to track him down. Matters following a death with no relatives to be found can become complicated."

"Heck, well it's really going back isn't it? ... But I do remember Michael was planning a voyage, round the U.K. I think. He was a sailing nut, wanted to do nothing else and when he wasn't sailing he got enough work around about to earn his keep. I seem to remember that he was a brilliant carpenter, so he was in great demand for the fiddly work that's often necessary to keep a boat in good nick. As I remember it he'd saved enough money to make a long trip, but there was some trouble at home and he told me he was moving away instead. I seem to remember that he got a job, helping to move a yacht, I think. That's right – and, yes, it was out east, Singapore or somewhere, I'm not sure. He did send me a postcard, but I never heard from him again. I had really forgotten all about it."

"Did you think to tell anyone where he was?"

"Nope, don't think so, but then no one asked - and anyway his mother knew. I do remember that his card said something about his putting things right at home so I imagined he'd been in touch with her."

Philip pursued the point a little: "Do you know if anyone heard any more from him?" he asked.

"Not that I know of. His name came up a few times over the next few months, mainly in context of his carpentry – I seem to remember someone wanting him to construct a mast

– but when it was clear he was no longer around this slowly stopped. He knew lots of people in the local boating world, but I don't think he socialised much with them outside of a boating context. Look, I ought to get back if you don't mind. Thanks for the tea."

"Well, thanks very much for your help."

Roger got up and left, lifting his hand in a small wave.

Philip remained, sitting thinking for a few minutes and poured himself another cup of tea. Finally it looked as if he had got some useful information. It seemed reliable too. Roger had no reason to deceive him or claim to remember something he did not. It looked like Michael had gone abroad, possibly to the East, apparently intent on doing some serious sailing and then, for whatever reason, he seemed never to have returned, or had any more contact with home either for that matter.

The East was a big place; he could be anywhere.

Philip finished his tea and retraced his steps the way he had come; it was, he supposed, progress of a sort.

ﺏ

"Do you want a walk first before we eat?"

Philip had phoned Miriam and arranged to meet and go for Sunday lunch at a pub in Goldhanger, a small village set northwards along the river from Maldon. He had promised her an update about Abigail; indeed he found he was looking forward to sharing his findings with Miriam, not least because having something they planned to talk about would make it easier to combat his natural shyness. He had collected her at the back of Wenlock Way, where it ran through from the High Street to a car park. Now parked outside the village church in Goldhanger he suggested a walk before lunch.

"Sure, that would be nice." Miriam had been looking forward to their meeting as a real antidote to a busy shift at work.

"There's a particularly nice walk here: if we go through the churchyard we can go across the fields to the river, then along the riverbank and back into the village at the other end. It's about forty-five minutes. That sound okay?" He pointed to where the narrow road from the river came back towards the pub, saying, "Brings us back that way."

"Sounds good for the appetite."

They negotiated the metal one-person-at-a-time gate into the churchyard, walked through and climbed the odd v-shaped stile into the fields beyond. As Philip went over the stile he paused, his mind focusing on a flash of memory: this was a favourite walk for him and Penny, and was one they had taken many times before she died. Miriam noticed his momentary hesitation.

"Having second thoughts about having lunch with the long arm of the law?" She turned and smiled.

"No, no, not at all." Philip was quick to respond but then paused. "It's just ..."

"Just what?"

"Sorry, it's just that this was a favourite walk for my wife and I; she died a couple of years ago: heart, genetic thing."

"I'm so sorry, would you rather ...?"

"No, sorry, it's silly and it's all a long while ago now. Come on, we go this way."

He stepped out cutting off the conversation and led the way down the path, fields on either side of them and a view of the estuary showing across the field to the right.

They walked in silence for a while. Philip cursed himself, he liked Miriam, but he was so not used to this – getting to know someone new – and he now felt awkward. For the life of him he couldn't think what to say next and so fell back on Abigail as a topic.

"I promised to update you about Abigail. I had a free day during the week and did some digging about her or rather about her son. I went to the Records Office in Chelmsford and found something in an old issue of the local paper about his disappearance. I have a copy of the article in my pocket. I'll show you in the pub. She and Michael had a falling out, just after his father's death. He moved out and lived on his father's boat at Heybridge Basin for a while. The boat's still there – it's still called "Starcounter", well it would be, it's unlucky to change a boat's name – anyway, I thought I recognised the name, it's moored in full view as you walk along the canal. I found the current owner at the pub and asked him about it, he bought it from Abigail a little while after her husband's death and still has it – his son and family uses it nowadays."

"Did he know anything about Michael?"

"No, nor did the son, but the son introduced me to a friend of Michael's - they worked on boats together, I think, he only remembers Michael dropping plans to sail round the U.K coast in "Starcounter" and taking a job out east – he mentioned Singapore and thought Michael was to help as crew moving a yacht. He had a postcard from him, though he wasn't sure where from, and then he heard no more."

"Didn't he say anything? He must have known a search was on."

"I did ask him about that, but he said no one asked. Also he was sure Abigail knew. He said the card he got mentioned something about making up at home. I think he assumed Michael had been in touch with her too."

"But Abigail clearly didn't know where he'd gone, did she?" She didn't wait for an answer and went on: "You are becoming quite the detective, aren't you?"

"Not really, I'm not any nearer to knowing exactly where he might have gone, much less where he might be now. I feel there should be more that I can do, I feel I kind of owe it to Abigail somehow."

After strolling through fields for a while they reached the estuary. They climbed the steps up to the path atop the sea defences, a stout concrete construction built after the 1953 East coast floods, and turned right along the river path back towards the village. To their left across the wide expanse of the estuary they could see the old power station at Bradwell. To the right was Osea Island accessible by the causeway, or wet-road, only at low tide, an arrangement going back to Roman times. Philip paused at a seat facing the water.

"Let's sit for a moment" he said. "That's Osea Island." He pointed to it. "Sorry, you must know a fair bit about the area by now. How long have you been here?"

"A little less than a year."

"What brought you here?"

"Oh, I just wanted a change, and there was some trouble on my last posting."

She seemed to think better of saying more but Philip immediately asked for details.

"I was nearly stabbed." She saw a look of horror on his face. "Don't worry, I said nearly, threatened is more accurate. The problem was really after that."

"How?"

"Well, we got a call that shop lifting was in progress at a mini-supermarket. I went with a colleague, another sergeant, and because he was driving I got out first and went to the shop just as two youths came bursting out. The saw the car, and us, and threw the bags they were carrying at me, though they fell short. They dashed in different directions, the one who I followed turning into what proved to be a narrow alley and a cul-de-sac. He drew a knife on me. He lunged towards me and I jumped back just as my colleague drew level with me. We were off balance and just missed him as he barged his way out of the alley; I don't think he actually intended to hurt me, he was just a kid. Anyway... both lads were picked up later - and prosecuted successfully for once too."

Philip continued to look appalled. He opened his mouth but got no further than "That sounds ..." before Miriam continued,

"It sounds more dramatic than it was, but my colleague insisted on taking the credit, telling everyone that he had saved my life. Not true, but he never let it go, always going on about it and then in due course wanting his 'reward'; even if he had saved my life that does not mean I would have slept with him. The innuendoes turned unpleasant, bullying really, and, well... as I said, rather than make a thing of it, I put in for a transfer. Best thing I ever did anyway, I have really liked it here."

"Well, I for one, am glad you came. Not a nice thing to happen though."

"All in the past now." It had been a watershed and she had left intent on changing her life a bit and not being so bound up in police work. "Shall we move on?" She stood up, waiting for Philip to show the way and they walked on alongside the creek used by Goldhanger Sailing Club, which ran inland back towards the village. Gulls shrieked overhead and the usual retinue of wading birds searched for scraps at the water's edge. Philip took the opportunity to change the subject.

"You see the Shelducks?" He indicated the brightly covered pair just below the wall. "Back when wild ducks were regarded as food, they were rarely shot – there's an old recipe for them: prepare the duck, put it in the oven with a brick, when it's done take them out of the oven, throw the duck away and eat the brick. Seems they are not the tastiest thing around."

Miriam smiled as they walked on.

When they reached the end of the creek they looked back towards the estuary, there were a good number of boats about, lines of dinghy sails at one point indicating that a race might be taking place.

"This is lovely here; I've really seen so little of the district so far," said Miriam.

"Here is a favourite spot of mine. Nice walks and a good pub. The Chequers is a traditional village pub. With so many country pubs in decline or closing it is one that by offering good food now attracts people from a wider range round about than just the immediate village. It dates back too; it was a player long ago in the days of smuggling along the coast. And the building is supposed to be haunted. I've heard stories of poltergeists, but a free pint of bitter has never mysteriously moved onto my table, more's the pity, and until it does I shall remain sceptical!"

Miriam shared his scepticism. So far so good, Philip thought: we share an interest in a small mystery and neither of us believes in ghosts. It was still a bit of a way off a relationship, but they were getting on well.

They had a good meal, chatting easily together about many things. They discovered that they shared a love of travel, but reckoned they had never done enough, had some common tastes in music and books and would never do a bungee jump in a million years.

It was getting on for three o'clock when Philip dropped Miriam off in the high street. They ended with a quip: "Can I stop here for a moment without being arrested?" from Philip as he pulled up on a yellow line in the narrow road and a challenge from Miriam: "Don't give up on the Abigail situation, we'll keep thinking about it and something may pop up." She had read the newspaper article about Michael's disappearance in the pub and Philip felt she was becoming somewhat involved in the mystery too. He felt an increasing urge to take things further. If Abigail had asked he would certainly have done everything he could to help and he saw no reason not to do so now.

They said goodbye, with an arrangement for another meeting again in place, this time prompted by Philip, though, if he could have known, he was only a whisker ahead of Miriam in suggesting it.

Philip returned home thinking how she had said "we'll keep thinking about it" in a way that seemed to imply not just an interest in the mystery, but in on-going contact between them; he wondered what more he could do meantime. Was what he had discovered likely to prove a useful clue? Was the matter impossible or was Michael traceable?

Time would tell and he would go on trying.

CHAPTER SIX
A decision to make

I should never have spoken out like that, I suppose, but I'm sure he should be considering a career, a "proper job". James loved sailing but he was adamant that messing about in boats can't be real work. I only want what's best for him, wouldn't any mother?

But now he's gone, camping out on that wretched boat - as if there's room to swing a cat in there; it's all very well loving his sailing too, but for M it's an obsession. I shouted. I shouldn't have. But he walked out. We've the funeral coming and it's all just ... Bother and blast – Come back!

I'll have to go to the boat and talk to him. Please let it be alright.

1997: Maldon

"Starcounter" sat on a pontoon at the marina at Bradwell a few miles downriver from Maldon. While the old, now defunct, nuclear power station set along from the marina was still a brooding presence, and plans were regularly mooted in the newspapers about a new one being built on the site, behind the marina there was just a small village set out on a geographical limb and a longer drive from Maldon than one would first think. The road had to go right round the estuary, though by boat it was just a pleasant few miles sail.

Michael had left Heybridge Basin at high tide, guiding the boat out of the lock with the outboard motor and then setting sail down the river towards Northey Island and with its shore on his starboard side. Osea Island then lay ahead. Both islands were connected to the mainland by causeways: these dated from Roman times, and the islands could only be accessed on foot or by car when the water was at low tide, though both were private property.

The National Trust owned Northey Island and farmed the land; once or twice a year they ran walking tours and people were able to both see and learn about the place, he remembered his mother once doing this with a group from her Women's Institute.

Today he had tacked his way down the channel and sailed around the far side of Osea through the channel that remained navigable even at low tide and on along the estuary as it broadened out as it got nearer to the sea. The day was fine, the wind more than adequate and the sail had been a pleasure. Michael sat comfortably, tiller in one hand, the other resting on the sheet ready to pull the sail tighter. The sound of the water was pretty much all he could hear as the boat moved forward and the water swirled back along the hull. In due course Mersea Island was ahead and to port, but after several hours' sailing Michael had opted to put in at Bradwell. Here he could moor for the cost of a few pounds and, being a regular, he had a key to the facilities on shore where he could shower and shave. Being on a jetty he could just climb out of the boat and walk into the village.

The afternoon seemed to have quickly disappeared. Like so many people who enjoy sailing alone, he had been lost in the pleasure of controlling the boat and of the scenery around him. It was a pleasant day; other boats were about but as he got further down the river, and the area of water opened up, few came near. He had stopped, tying the boat to a buoy, at around two o'clock, and eaten a sandwich he had brought with him while watching the profusion of water birds that frequented the estuary: oyster catchers, egrets and a variety of ducks amongst others. Some fussed in groups, others squabbled rambunctiously amongst themselves and a few seagulls screeched above him diving occasionally to the water. No day was the same, the birds appearing in varying numbers and in different places as they sought out food.

He kept his eyes skinned and at one point got out the binoculars. A couple of times in recent weeks he had seen a solitary seal, he had gone about quickly to turn the boat and reverse course and tacked back to watch, then trying to keep station with it for a while. It seemed unconcerned by his presence, but finally moved off and was lost in the distance. Seals were regular visitors to the estuary and always a pleasure to see. Today there were no seals apparent, but the river was both tranquil yet alive with life. A fish broke the surface just beside him as he ate.

He had time to think.

Now, the sail over and with the boat tied securely to the jetty he walked briskly up the path to the nearby pub. He stopped on the way at the Marina office to pay the modest mooring fee and was greeted cheerfully by the man on duty.

"Going far this trip?" he asked.

"No, just a day out really, back to Heybridge in the morning," Michael replied. He handed over the money and went on to the pub carrying a notebook in his hand.

"A pint of your Best Bitter and a steak and ale pie, please," he asked.

The barman poured his drink and noted his food order on a slip of paper ready to pass to unseen colleagues in the hidden kitchen, asking "New potatoes or chips?" as he did so. Michael opted for chips. He could cook up quite a meal on 'Starcounter's' small stove but today did not want the distraction. He had some thinking to do.

"Stick the number on the table, they'll find you," the barman said automatically, though he well knew that Michael knew the form. "Be maybe ten minutes." He took the money proffered to him and handed Michael some change and a wooden spoon with the number 18 painted on the back of the spoon end.

Michael saw no one he knew in the sparsely populated bar, found a table in a corner, sipped his beer and opened his notebook. Then, almost immediately, he was interrupted.

"You're looking very serious. Can I join you?"

He looked up and saw a familiar figure. George was a little older than Michael and sailed a boat similar in size to "Starcounter"; he lived on Mersea Island and kept the boat on a mooring there. They didn't know each other well, but they crossed paths regularly during the sailing season.

"Sure," he said. "Are you moored here overnight?" George nodded. His boat, which Michael knew was called "C-side" – he hated names like that though he knew it was said to be unlucky to change the name of a boat and he knew too that George had inherited it - was evidently also moored outside on one of the piers.

"Yes. A meal's on the way. What are you busy with?" George asked, nodding towards the notebook Michael had closed as he had joined him. Michael considered. Though he did not know George too well he felt that another opinion could be useful, after all he had a lot to think through.

"Well ..." he hesitated and George cocked an eyebrow expectantly as he put his numbered spoon down on the table.

"Okay - have a look at this." Michael slipped a sheet of printed paper out of the notebook, unfolded it and passed it over. It was a print out from a page on an Internet site, the modern equivalent of a small ads page and one directed at the boating world. It was a notice from a skipper seeking crew to help move a boat from one place to another.

"Certainly sounds fun," said Michael "... says it would take a week or so, maybe more depending on the number of stops – he doesn't seem to be in a great hurry, wants to enjoy the trip and have some company and a helping hand."

George took the sheet, read silently for a moment, then looking up, amazement on his face, said, "But it says the trip starts in Singapore!" He sounded incredulous. For him, commuting to London from Colchester every day, sailing was just a hobby and a local one too. For all his keenness he had never taken his boat any further than where the Blackwater estuary merged into the sea.

"Yes, well, that's the attraction!" Michael said, raising his voice. "I can combine it with some holiday and earn a little money on the way to finance a stay in Phuket when the voyage ends there in Thailand."

"I guess so." George still looked incredulous, "You've got to apply first though and I bet a fair number of people would be after it."

"I thought so too, I nearly didn't bother. Then I thought 'what the heck' and sent off a reply. I thought no more about it, but a week or so later I got a reply. Turns out the guy's originally from Brightlingsea, just up the road so to speak. What sort of coincidence is that? He's probably moored up outside here in the past and eaten in this very pub. Anyway, he was rather taken with the idea of recruiting someone from around here. And ...well, he's offered me the job."

"So, will you take it?"

Michael paused for a moment, then spoke. "When I saw the ad I thought yes, that's it, but I never thought it would go anywhere. Now it has, I've got a firm offer and the job's mine if I want it, and ... well, I'm suddenly not so sure. I did exaggerate my sailing experience a bit when I wrote. Going across the Channel isn't quite the same as the South China Sea or wherever it is, is it? What do you think?"

Ever practical George asked about the boat.

"It's a fair size, 40 foot plus, certainly she'd be up to the journey. I can't see any problem there."

"Then surely you have to go for it. I wish I had done something like that after uni and before I settled into a job. You're the right age; it's not for ever after all and it would certainly be fun by the sound of it - and if you can link it to a great holiday. Well, go on, you have to go for it. Right?"

Michael was non-committal. He was not quite ready to make a decision and they fell to talking of other things. They had a couple more pints, bade each other goodnight and made their way back to their respective boats, moored on different sides of the marina.

"You'll let me know what you decide, won't you?" A parting shot from George received a promise to do just that. "Don't leave it too long or the decision may be made for you," he added as he walked away. Michael knew it was a good point: the question was how to decide.

CHAPTER SEVEN
Invitation to a funeral

I've sent him an email every day; I think they went successfully, though it's not something I'm very used to. I know he has his computer with him. But not a word back. Nor from the innumerable messages I've left on his mobile phone and he's surgically attached to that. He's not been at the boat yard since he left home either – I asked Sam, she didn't know and told me that they'd stopped seeing each other a month or two back, though he never said anything about that - shame, I rather liked her.

Three days running I've driven to Heybridge Basin and been to the boat. It's on the far side of the canal so I have to walk along to the end, cross over at the lock and go back along the other side - definitely a flat shoe job. He is clearly living there, there was washing hanging out last time I went, but of him there was no sign.

What's he doing? Is he just sulking or is there some other problem? I don't know how much to worry. It's the funeral in a while, there are things do be done, things he must do. I left an envelope for him tucked into the cabin door.

Philip was having a quick lunchtime sandwich in the staff room. As he ate his sandwich, he thumbed through the current local paper and then stopped with a start on seeing Abigail's name. The Council must be getting things organised and they had placed an announcement in the paper about her funeral: it was 11.30am in just three days' time. On

Thursday. He exclaimed out loud saying "Bugger" just as one of his colleagues walked into the staff room.

"What's up?" they asked.

"Nothing to do with work," he replied, "I've just seen a funeral announcement for that lady I found dead; you remember?"

"Oh yes, I do remember, not the way I'd like to start the day."

"No, it's not. Anyway I presume there is still no relative been found, the Council seem to have organised the funeral; it's all very sad."

His colleague grabbed a file from the top of a cupboard and excused himself with a quick "Must get on, I've someone at the counter. You're due to do a spell there soon aren't you?" Philip nodded. He finished his sandwich - his colleague disappeared back to his customer - and surreptitiously tore the funeral notice out of the paper, conscious that it was something they reprimanded library members for doing, and then went and slipped the paper back on the magazine area. He could have photocopied it, but Froby was more likely to spot that and ask what he was doing. He could imagine it all too easily – "The copier is not for private use, Philip."

He must go to the funeral. He realised it was silly to do so in some ways, but he was not only unwittingly somehow involved but increasingly felt a responsibility in the aftermath of Abigail's death. Besides he would like to attend, somehow it would feel right. He was still trying to think about how her son might be traced; if he was alive and well. It seemed extraordinary that he had simply dropped out of sight. Okay Michael and his mother had had a row, but that was some twenty years ago! Surely that was out of all proportion to the difficulties. A sudden thought struck him. He phoned Miriam's mobile. As expected it went to voicemail, he knew that she would never have a personal phone on while she was on duty. He left a message.

"Hi – it's Philip. How are you? Look, I've just heard that Abigail's funeral is on Thursday. This Thursday. It's at eleven thirty in the morning at Chelmsford Crematorium. I've no idea who might be there, rather few I fear, but I feel I must go. It seems the right thing to do and ... anyway, look...would you come too? Please. I'm sure you're busy, but ... do let me know if it's possible. See you soon. Bye."

He had switched off his mobile and gone to do a stint of counter duty and immediately found himself dwelling on death again as he tried to trace a book on handling probate for an elderly woman clearly having to sort things out after the death of a close relative, perhaps her husband. He preferred the silly questions like being asked for fictional novels or trying to trace a book for someone who said they knew neither title nor author but were sure that the cover was blue. Maybe Abigail had checked out about probate after her husband died ... as he had for Penny. Any death had repercussions for someone. Next a middle aged man tried to check back in a book that looked as if had had spent a week under water.

"I'm afraid I'll have to charge you for this," said Philip. "It's damaged beyond repair and will need to be replaced."

The man protested, admitting that the book had fallen in the bath, but suggesting that "it will dry out", that it was "too old to bother with" and that "surely you have a budget for this sort of thing". Philip was pleased ultimately to be able to deflect all arguments and take the requisite amount of money from him without tempers being lost; but it took twenty minutes to accomplish.

Next, an encounter with Froby.

Miss Frobisher was not happy.

"I thought we agreed you would find space for the computers we discussed. Something has to go to make room."

"Well, I have begun making a list, but a good deal of thinning out will be necessary to create the space you need." He purposely said "you" rather than "we". It was her idea and he hated the thought of getting rid of more books – what were libraries for, for goodness sake?

"I don't think we need a list, more a series of shelves or sections. If you identify things that way then it will make clearing the space much easier, no 'thinning out' as you put it, just batches going into boxes and away. I realise that you don't like the thought, but this is the 21st century you know. E-book loans will be the next thing. Now let's set a deadline for this current clearing shall we?" He reluctantly agreed a date.

Philip had to suppress an audible groan about what she had said about e-books and clearing in batches. He liked to think he was not a Luddite: yes, loaning e-books was doubtless a good idea, more and more people had electronic readers these days, and to be fair music and film sat comfortably on shelves alongside books and had done so for a while. It was just that every new move Froby took seemed to seriously dilute the more traditional roles of the library. The budget for events had been slashed, so opportunities for local authors were currently reduced and Philip even felt that various activities designed to help youngsters to read were threatened. He and Penny had had no children, but surely there was little of more importance for a library to do than to support reading initiatives for youngsters. He liaised with several schools nearby and well knew that many teachers shared his view. Hadn't the school reading he had done just the other day gone well?

He had grudgingly accepted Froby's deadline, then added, almost as an aside, "I do want this to be successful, you know, and rather than just extend the existing line of computers I thought perhaps we could set up a whole area dedicated to technology, I bet there are all sorts of things we could add, it would send a real message of modernity, don't you think?"

"Well, yes, I suppose, but it would need some thought." Froby replied non-committedly. She was not about to welcome any ideas from elsewhere, though she found it did give her food for thought.

Philip did not pursue the point, but he had been drip feeding tit bits about things for a little while; he just excused himself and went back to the counter. Margaret was in sole charge there and a queue was forming. Even so he took a moment first to note on the staffing wall chart his proposed absence on the morning of Abigail's funeral. He thought taking a couple of hours away from work was the least he could do in the circumstances. Then he was into a search for "something she can read now she's finished the last Harry Potter" in response to a request from an anxious small girl's mother who had added "... and with no blood, gore and vampires, thank you very much."

In the middle of the afternoon he checked his mobile phone to find a voicemail message waiting.

"Hi, it's Miriam. Yes, I can join you at the funeral. I'll make my own way there though, I'm in court in Chelmsford first thing, so don't worry if I should be late – I'll see you there, sorry - must rush. Bye"

As the message concluded Philip clicked the phone with a flourish, delighted not to be attending the funeral on his own and also, if he was honest, to have the opportunity of seeing Miriam again.

CHAPTER EIGHT
Decision time

1997: Maldon

Michael sat in the cockpit for a while reading a book, but his heart was not in it and his mind kept drifting off. Should he go? There were so many reasons not to, yet it was an opportunity that might set him on an entirely new course. At the least it would give him a break and a holiday. He had a little time to organise matters before he would have to fly out there, but he knew he must reply soon or his indecision would lose him the berth. George was no doubt correct: other potential crew members were bound to be waiting in the wings; indeed there could be additional replies still arriving.

He got into the book again, reading until it got too dark to see, at least in the cockpit - he had a gas lamp in the cabin so could continue there if he wanted. He looked up. There was a cloudless sky above and the stars were awesome. He gathered his washing kit, checked that the key to the washroom was in his pocket and climbed out of the cockpit. He walked away from the quay until even the few lights around were screened from view.

The light of the night sky grew in intensity as his eyes gradually became accustomed to the dark. One of his earliest memories of his father was of lying on the lawn as a small boy looking up at the night sky. His father said it was one of the great things about sailing, mooring up for the night somewhere isolated– the estuary was full of hidden creeks – and seeing the sky with minimum light pollution: each star a sun in its own right and shining from distances that boggled the mind. The number seemed countless, though he knew, again from his father, that it was actually only possible to see three or four thousand stars with the naked eye. The boat was testament to his father's love of open skies – it was the reason he had named her 'Starcounter'.

"I bet the skies on the Singapore trip would be amazing," he muttered to himself.

He would miss his father. He did miss him, though he, like his mother, had been against his working with boats and doing something that thus allowed his passion to be more than just a hobby and something he could spend real time on.

He walked back towards the boat via the wash room and prepared himself for the night ahead. Back on board, he crawled into his sleeping bag and settled down to sleep. But sleep would not come. He tossed and turned, brooding about the offer that had been made to him. It was attractive, but also it was a big step, maybe more than he could cope with; even if he replied realistically there was no guarantee that he would get picked.

He slept fitfully, turning the matter over in his mind and finally resolving to decide one way or another in the morning. One step at a time.

He woke the next morning with the light streaming in through the cabin window and the roof close above his head. He extracted his legs from the sleeping bag and swung them to the floor, sitting up and pushing his hands through his tangled hair. Then, almost before he was properly awake... finally, he was sure.

"I'll do it, it will give me a breathing space," he thought to himself. "I'll reply once I'm ashore."

He did not want the row with his mother to continue but he could not see it settled soon and felt some time apart would allow them both to calm down and help sort matters out. If all went well, perhaps later when he returned and told her about the trip, showed her photos perhaps, she would begin to appreciate things from his point of view.

There was a fair breeze blowing as Michael set off back towards his home berth. He guided the boat out of the mooring area and along the narrow channel to the river on the outboard. The wind was behind him at first as he set sail up river towards Osea Island; he made good progress and for a while thought he would be too early for the tide and have to wait around until the water level raised sufficiently to allow the lock gates to open. But, once past Osea Island, the second part of the voyage was slower though he still sailed at a good pace. It was enough to send spray up from the bows and into the cockpit - he tasted salt on his lips - but he had to tack to and fro across the channel and this took time. He arrived off the lock with only ten minutes to wait until the lock gates were opened; he joined the other waiting boats and entered the lock in his turn.

The lock keeper called out to him as he entered, "Not too far this trip."

"Just to Bradwell," he replied, then muttering to himself, "but next time it will be different."

He was soon back at base. Having tied the boat securely at "Starcounter's" allotted place on the canal bank, he changed his clothes and, after putting his precious laptop computer in a shoulder bag, he got a lift into Maldon with a fellow sailor also packing up after the tide started to drop. The last area they had sailed across would soon be exposed to the estuary mud. He hopped off at the roundabout below Market Hill and walked up the steep curving road. He had found a small print shop in the town that allowed him to use its connection for his computer. Some cafes were starting to have a wireless facility but Maldon had none such yet. He logged on and called up his email. There was another message from his mother demanding that they talk. Funny, she complained that she hated computers but seemed to manage sending emails to him every five minutes when circumstances dictated. He deleted it, together with a spam message offering discounts on duvets and a couple of newsletters he had requested but in the circumstances could not be bothered with.

Further down the list in his In-box he clicked on the invitation from Singapore. He drafted a reply accepting the offer and promising to be in Singapore on the due date; he included his mobile phone number, but then realising that would be no good overseas he also said he would get a local one as soon as he arrived in Singapore. He would get a flight that gave him a day or two to get accustomed to the time change ahead of his deadline to meet the boat's skipper. He began to write a to-do list in his notebook, starting by noting the point about checking that his phone would work overseas.

A little while later he had a list. Satisfied that he could be ready in time, he returned to the email he had drafted and clicked "send". It was done. He was committed. He imagined his message arriving on the other side of the world, then realised that it was probably the middle of the night there. Nevertheless, this meant he was on his way. As promised he called George, leaving him a message telling him what he had done.

So much of his mind had been tied up in considering and making the decision that, for the moment, he had completely forgotten about the likely date of his father's coming funeral.

CHAPTER NINE
An interrupted funeral

Philip does like his books, but he didn't know about the elephants. When he brought the tea in today I said "Give me a minute I'm just coming to an elephant". I had to explain. It was years ago when I was reading a book by William Dalrymple about his travels in the east, instead of asterisks to mark break points the book was set with little elephants, we adopted it – from then on a pause was always described as an elephant. A big elephant meant a chapter end and a little elephant meant a less major break point. Philip liked it and vowed to adopt it himself.

It was the day of Abigail's funeral and Philip had booked the morning off from the library. He pulled up and parked at the crematorium and walked alongside elaborate floral tributes, presumably laid out following an earlier funeral that made the small bunch of flowers he had belatedly thought to buy and bring seem rather inadequate. The sky was overcast, but it was warm enough, nothing to put people off coming he thought; if anyone else did attend the service. As yet there was no sign of Miriam.

He was early. A large, black hearse waited, parked alongside the building. Old and traditional in style its sober presence was somehow a sign of the atmosphere of the whole establishment, even though the building itself was modern. These places were like production lines he thought: one in, one out. Well, destruction line rather than production line perhaps. He smiled for a second at the thought.

He did a circuit of the grassed area outside and could hear music playing inside the building, presumably as the current service finished. It was the song "My Way": why, oh why, he wondered did so many people elect to go out to such a cliché? He and Penny had joint wills, now out of date for some two years. For the umpteenth time he resolved to do something about it and update his wishes. Maudlin thoughts, though he cheered himself up slightly by imagining alternatives to "My Way" for the music and composing little phrases in his mind that he would specify for printing on any service sheet that might be used at his own funeral. It was surely an opportunity to plug a favourite piece. His favourite artist was the diminutive jazz singer Stacy Kent; there must be something she sang that would suit. He loved her version of "It's A Wonderful World", though that too was perhaps too popular a song for him to think it appropriate. Perhaps "I'm a lucky so and so" would suit; he would not want people to be too gloomy. His somewhat morbid thoughts were cut off as the doors behind him opened. He watched as forty or fifty people came out of the now completed service. It took a little while as groups of mourners chatted in hushed voices and flowers were inspected, but quite soon everyone began to disperse.

The service for Abigail was the next one scheduled. He went to the door. A handful of people gradually assembled and began to exchange words. He spoke briefly to an elderly couple who knew Abigail and her husband some years ago, a work colleague of James, still in touch with Abigail, though "I have not seen her for some years", and people who were neighbours, though none seemed close. Eleven people including himself - it did not seem many, though she was of an age where many of her contemporaries might well have pre-deceased her. Someone asked him what his connection with her was and he almost found himself saying "I found her body", settling instead for his being a friend and neighbour.

Gradually people made their way inside. Perhaps inevitably they spread out amongst the seats making the room look even emptier than the numbers themselves decreed. Hanging back by the entrance, he looked across to the driveway from the road and saw a taxi drive in. Miriam got out, wearing her police uniform and presumably having come straight from the court hearing she had mentioned in her message. Just in time.

"Thanks for coming," said Philip and they exchanged a brief word of greeting as she reached the door and then went in, sitting together in the second row. The presiding officer stepped forward and cleared his throat; the service was under way.

The last time he had been here, the only time in recent memory in fact, was for Penny's funeral. That had been a very different affair; a large number of people had attended. Penny was a popular teacher at a local school, and her funeral was very much a celebration of her life. He would never forget the little group of children who had come representing the school, all in uniform and each carrying a posy. Remembering the occasion was painful, but he also felt it had constituted an appropriate send off.

Some minutes on and it was clear to Philip that this service was awful. Well, he thought so anyway. It was no doubt well-intentioned but it was also proving to be utterly soulless.

It was as if the subject of it was a cipher and it in no way represented Abigail personally, much less her character. The only comments made about her were brief and impersonal. The service was also very short and soon it was clearly coming towards the end. Any moment there would be a final musical number of some sort, the coffin would disappear behind the thick, red velvet curtain and the small group of mourners would all go their separate ways. Done and dusted.

"Is that it?"

Philip realised that he had said the words out loud.

"Oh, God, I said that out loud. Sorry ... no ... No, I'm not sorry ..."

He addressed the man who was officiating. "With your permission, may I say a few words?" He did not wait for any comment or reply but stepped out into the aisle, turning so that the tiny group were all in front of him.

"I'm sorry," he said again "I had not planned to do this and I'm not really qualified to do it either, but all this has seemed so impersonal. I didn't know Abigail for long, just a few months, but she was a lovely lady: lively, interesting and busy in her own way though she could not get around too much recently. I liked her and I am sure others did too. I know she had had some sadness in her life. She lost her husband much too soon and then had the mystery of her son Michael disappearing to cope with as well. He should be here, he should be doing this not me, but I don't know if he is even alive. Maybe no one does. If he is alive and could be located then he could at least help sort out her affairs, but it seems he can't be found. If anyone knows anything about his whereabouts ..."

His voice faltered, he paused and cleared his throat, but even given a moment as he paused no one in the tiny group gave any sign of knowing.

"Anyway, I just thought someone who actually knew Abigail should say a word. She was a lovely lady and I was lucky to know her even for a little while, and besides every life deserves to be celebrated. Sorry again, that's all."

He turned, nodded a thank you to the official, who had stood impassive and unspeaking while Philip spoke, and sat down. The official said no more but made a sign to the back of the room and music began to play, something classical, though Philip couldn't identify it. He imagined it being the default standard; surely no great element of choice was involved in its selection. The heavy curtain in front of the coffin started to close driven by an electric motor the slight hum of which sounded loud in the quietness of the sparsely populated room. The sound continued for what seemed like long moments and then stopped as the music played on and people began to move out.

Philip was embarrassed now. He turned to Miriam and muttered, "At least they aren't playing 'My way', I'm so sorry, I made a fool of myself," as they made their way out. No one spoke to them, and thus no one cast any light on Michael's whereabouts, though he did receive a few smiles and nods. They walked towards Philip's car. The hearse he had seen earlier was gone and a knot of people were already lining up ready for the next funeral.

Miriam stopped just short of the car. "Well done you," she said. "That was such a nice thing to do, speaking up like that." She took his intervention as a sign of a caring nature. She liked that.

"It was only a few words, it was utterly unprepared, but then I didn't intend it, it just sort of happened, it was ... I don't know ..." His voice tailed off.

She put both hands on his shoulders and said simply, "It was fine."

Then she leant forward and gave him a kiss on the cheek. It was the first time she had done that. He immediately felt better.

☞

He had driven them back to Maldon and dropped her off outside the police station; on a yellow line too. They had arranged to meet up in the evening. "After a funeral we need something a bit brighter," she said. Adding "Come to my place about 8.00, I'll cook - I've got stuff in the fridge that will do us nicely." She gave him the number of her flat.

Back at the library Philip realised he was a little later returning than he had predicted. Froby was at the door of her office and spotted him as he came in. She beckoned.

"Where have you been? I thought you were due back an hour ago."

"I was at a funeral, I'm afraid I underestimated how long it would take; the traffic was bad. It was at the crematorium in Chelmsford. I did note that I would be out on the chart."

She was determined to score a point. "It was the old lady you found dead wasn't it?" she said, not waiting for an answer, "I don't know why you bothered to go. As I understand it you hardly knew her."

"That's hardly ..." he contemplated a spirited defence of his attendance, but thought better of it. "Okay, my apologies. I'll get on. By the way I was thinking though, as I drove back to Maldon, if we were to have some sort of dedicated technology area we could give it a special name, maybe that's something to think about. It would lend itself to announcements and updating."

Philip turned away quickly, before she could respond; he did not want to have the contact prolonged. She really was the end, and so insensitive. Bureaucracy and insensitivity combined to make an unappealing mix. And she couldn't say

106

the simplest thing in a straightforward way: she would not see Michael as lost, she'd call it locationally challenged.

With relief he saw a mother with her two children - Suzie and William he remembered - regulars whom he knew slightly and went over to help the kids choose books, grateful to be onto something worthwhile.

"Hi, kids" he said "what can I find for you today?"

Search over, their beaming faces as they carried off some new "finds" cheered him up. Then his mind turned to Froby again: she was impossible, what insensitivity, how rude – even if he was late it was hardly the end of the world, the library had seemed to be functioning well enough without him as he came in. No harm done surely.

He had half hoped to get the top post himself when Froby's predecessor had retired. He'd applied, but so had a good few other people and his experience and the concept of promoting from within did not seem to count for much. Miss bureaucracy-loving-number-cruncher had won the day. To say she was a book person was like saying Attila the Hun was into knitting and her management style was seemingly based on an unthinking when-I-want-your-opinion-I'll-give-it-to-you approach that made him want to put a good management guide on her desk, but he knew she wouldn't like that – or read it - and he also knew that she would guess who had done it. He sighed and tried to banish such thoughts from his mind as Margaret called to him from behind the counter and he saw a queue had formed. He went across to give her a hand.

On the way home he bought a bottle of wine at the Marks & Spencer food shop at the top of the high street ready for the evening. He was still not sure how much of his relationship, though that was hardly the word, with Miriam was down to the continuing saga following Abigail's death. But for the moment if that kept them in touch then so be it, he was not about to complain. Give it a little time he thought; certainly dinner at her place was a step forward.

107

There was some post on the doormat at home; in recent years it never came before he left for work. He opened it up: finding a bill, a circular and an official looking envelope that turned out to hold a reply from the office of the Treasury Solicitor. He wondered what they had to say. The answer proved to be "very little". It was a stark acknowledgement of his letter about Mac and a comment to the effect that the information was noted and that they would contact him again if it proved necessary. And that seemed about as likely as Froby asking him to recommend her something to read. Clearly they thought that the information he had provided had no relevance, and for all he knew they were right. No help there then. He still had hopes that something might come to light to assist in finding Michael - and Mac too, for that matter.

He sat at his desk, sent a couple of emails and idled away a few minutes logging into Amazon and seeing what recommendations they had for him. Then he found himself thinking again about Abigail. Her situation, or rather the situation following her death, was becoming a bit of an obsession. But there must be something else he could do – surely there must. Maybe Miriam would have an idea. Miriam! For a moment he had quite forgotten the time. He rushed upstairs to change and set off up the road, the wine and a pack of beers in his trusty satchel.

CHAPTER TEN
En route to a journey

I went to the boat again today. He wasn't there. The boat seemed different somehow, there was no washing on the line, and just a tarpaulin hung over the boom and lashed to the sides of the boat. As before the door to the cabin was closed. I climbed on board and looked in through one of the windows. But there was nothing to show that anyone was living there, nothing.

As I walked round back along the path to the car park, a woman came out of the boat moored opposite "Starcounter" on the near side of the canal. She must have seen me on board the boat. She asked me if I was Mrs Croft and, when I said I was, she handed me an envelope. It had my name and address on; she had promised to deliver it but handed it over now on the spot.

It was the key to the cabin - I recognised it at once though the tag with the two stars on it had gone.

There was no note. It appeared he was gone. Oh my God, now what?

1997: Maldon and elsewhere

The email reply had been brief but specific and enthusiastic. It ended: Great to have you on board. All set, see you soon. Michael had been busy and he had also been thorough. He reckoned he had thought this through. He had continued to ignore his mother's various messages, convincing himself that things between them would all be easier after a few weeks away and bridges could be mended then. Besides time was pressing and he was committed to the trip. He packed - he had comparatively little stuff on the boat, his winter things were at the house - clothes, toiletries and so on in a case and his lap top and a couple of books in a small carry-on bag, sorted out his banking so that he could access things while he was away and booked a flight to Singapore.

He had some savings. He had worked for almost two years, and by living at home since school, he had had few expenses. Sam might have changed things, perhaps being with her might even have made him get what his parents called a "proper job", but in the event things with her had gone nowhere. They had got on fine for a while, but they had wanted different things. The final straw had been when she accepted a party invitation for them and he had ducked out to go to the sailing club AGM. He could remember her being furious and saying: "No more, all you think about is bloody boats" as she stormed off. He still had a pile of her CDs in his room at home.

He worked to keep the travel costs low. Even the taxes on long haul flights these days were expensive, but with a last minute booking and a brief refuelling stop in Dubai booked on line he had kept the amount down. After all he was not trying to make a profit on the trip, simply to take a break in a financially manageable way. He had booked a hotel in Singapore online too. His passport was up to date: next stop Heathrow.

He had no second thoughts. It was only for some two weeks and he had convinced himself it would provide time for both him and his mother to cool off. Later, when she'd heard what he had done and seen some photos of his trip, she would understand. He wanted her to understand, but he wanted to pursue his life his own way too. He was sure that ultimately it would all be all right.

Heathrow was not the easiest destination to reach from Maldon: it necessitated a taxi to Witham, a train to Liverpool Street then the London Underground and a change on that too. He met the taxi outside the pub, and after casting a backward glance towards the boat, he got in. He'd arranged for the boat's key to be got to his mother. He did want that to be safe.

"Witham station is it?" the driver asked.

"That's it, yes."

"Off somewhere nice?"

Michael was non-committal. "Holiday" he said as the car pulled away. His tone seemed enough to put the driver off chatting and they proceeded in silence as Michael thought about the coming trip.

What an adventure. He had crossed the Channel a few times, to France and to Holland, but this was going to be a bit more than that, a real ocean voyage and a bigger boat than he was used to sailing in. The famous line from the film "Jaws" flashed into his mind – "We're going to need a bigger boat" – and he chuckled to himself. Initially he could hardly believe what he was doing; now, as the voyage got nearer and he was actually on his way, he was really looking forward to the experience and beginning to believe it was real. The driver half turned as Michael chuckled but as he was just pulling up outside the station he did not ask what was funny. Michael thanked him, handed over the fare, grabbed his bags and went to buy a ticket.

After a couple of hours spent mainly staring out of train windows and imagining the sea he arrived at Heathrow, checking in at Terminal 3 and watching his bag being swallowed into the bowels of the airport's labyrinthine baggage system. Security took up some time and once through that he mooched round the shops in the busy lounge aimlessly but bought nothing, then as his flight was called he

112

went quickly back to WH Smith and bought two guide books, a small one about Singapore and a larger one about Thailand and its islands; the latter had a good section about Phuket in it. Clutching the books he hurried to the departure gate.

On the plane he found himself sitting next to an attractive girl about his own age. He had to squeeze past her to get to his seat and noted her long blond hair and legs and short skirt. She took in his suntanned good looks and they introduced themselves. They chatted a little: her name was Jo and she was joining her parents at a condominium they had borrowed on the coast in Malaysia; she was flying via Singapore and had arranged to spend a few days in the city en route.

"Me too," he said when she told him about the time she would spend in Singapore. "Maybe we could meet up there, have a meal or something?"

She smiled; there was definitely a connection there.

"Sure, let's do that," she said.

The flight was more than twelve hours, the stop in Dubai just long enough to get off and stretch with a walk round the terminal. Jo followed him out and they got a cup of coffee and chatted.

"Hotels in Singapore cost the earth," said Jo, explaining that it had been difficult to decide where to stay and that she would find something when she arrived.

"I'm at Robertson Quay Hotel" said Michael grinning, and adding "it's near Clarke Quay which looks a nice area: by the river, bars and restaurants and Chinatown's nearby too. I'm there two nights. We can share if you like! That would save you some money."

She smiled back but only said "We'll see."

They slept on and off as the flight progressed, ate an unappetising meal, served at an inappropriate time - its taste rendered bland by the lower oxygen levels typical of airliners - and watched a perfect example of the dire films usually selected by airlines. Michael flicked through the guide books he had bought. He found details of his hotel in Singapore - there was a picture of the unusual round building - and he passed the book over for Jo to look at.

"That's it," he said, tapping the entry with his finger, but she only smiled again and offered no comment.

Singapore airport is said to be one of the finest in the world and they quickly found that efficiency takes on a whole new meaning there. Less than half an hour after the plane's wheels touched the ground they were through passport control, had retrieved their luggage and were on their way into town.

"Share a taxi?" Michael asked in a brazen attempt to put off their parting. It worked.

Later, having travelled together to his hotel, they dumped their bags and ate brunch at a nearby cafe; it was late morning. Then they stepped out into the heat - there seemed as much coming up from the pavement as down from the sky - and walked along by the river. The city spread around them, huge buildings towering high to create its unique skyline, it was a long way from pictures Michael remembered from school: a Singapore of shops, houses and houseboats. Not so many years back this whole river area was like a housing estate of boats.

It was hot in the midday sun; "hot with a capital H" as Michael put it, and they walked slowly, dodging into a shop or hotel with air conditioning every now and then to cool off in the unaccustomed heat and humidity. Michael found an Internet café where they lingered over cold drinks and he sent an email to Jonathan French, his skipper to be, saying that he had arrived and was ready to meet. Jo went on the computer and reassured her parents that she was safe. They

114

idled the afternoon away and finally they walked more purposefully, winding their way to Chinatown for an early supper.

They picked a place to eat in the open-air food court more or less at random and sat on simple plastic chairs in a space hectic with people, activity and the noise of people chattering and dishes clattering and with the smells of cooking food emanating from the various food stalls all around. The food was excellent and both had a local Tiger beer to wash it down; they found that the highly taxed beers cost almost more than the food. They had coffee and cake in a small café on the way back towards the hotel, now both struggling to keep alert as the day went by and jet lag very much began to take its toll.

Nothing more had been said explicitly about Jo sharing Michael's hotel room. That they would do so had just sort of been accepted by both of them, and once back at the hotel they took turns in the bathroom, Jo emerging wrapped demurely in a robe and crawling into the room's one big bed. Michael grinned to himself as he took his turn in the bathroom. His first night in Singapore promised to be special. Back in the bedroom he climbed in beside Jo only to hear a sleepy jet-lagged mumble.

"I'm absolutely pooped ... I really can't keep my eyes ..."

She was asleep. In the silence that followed Michael too was gone in seconds. In the morning they re-introduced themselves, so thoroughly that they then slept some more. Then, realising the time, Michael was leaping up and rushing for his appointment with his skipper to be. They arranged to meet later.

"Well here she is."

Jonathan French was about thirty, tall, fit and suntanned. He shook Michael's hand and led him along the dock and stood pointing down at the boat. She may have seen better days, but she was, Michael thought, a beauty, and just a lick of paint would work wonders. She was called 'Footloose' and was, he guessed, some forty something feet long. Her teak deck was a rich, dark colour, her equipment was tidily stowed and she looked as if she would sail well.

Michael couldn't wait to take the helm.

"She looks great, but what's all this about?" he replied.

It became clear that although Jonathan worked in a financial role in an enterprise of his father's in the city, sailing was his passion and one he supported by buying and selling boats as a sort of side line. Michael thought it sounded a good way of life.

"I've had an offer for her. Guy came to see her here in Singapore but he lives in Thailand and will only do a deal to buy if I take the boat there, well to Phuket as you know. I've no problem with that, it will be a great trip but I didn't fancy doing it on my own. So welcome aboard. How's the Blackwater?"

"The river's fine. When were you last there?" Michael was conscious that his selection had been, in part at least, because Jon too had once sailed the Blackwater.

"It's been a while. I've lived here for some years. My father has few links to the U.K. now so I rarely go back, especially as my job allows me time to indulge my sailing and do some dealing in boats too. I need the money for this one. I've got my eye on something more upmarket and the finances of buying and selling get complicated."

They had climbed down to the cockpit, chatted for a while, and Jon, as he told Michael to call him, brewed up some tea in the cabin and showed Michael around. Inside the boat was neat, tidy and well-kept and equipped. Jon allocated him a bunk.

"Think you can cope with this?" he asked.

Michael thought for a moment. He liked Jon, they were already getting on well, and he did not want to deceive him. "It's a larger boat than I'm used to, to be honest, but I'm sure I'll cope. I'm a quick learner, at least where boats are concerned. I've sailed since childhood and have crossed the Channel a number of times and done journeys up and down the coast too."

"We'll be fine, I'm sure. Are you all set to leave in the morning as planned?" Jon was now business like.

This was indeed what had already tentatively been arranged and Michael, now he found that finalising the arrangement allowed another night with Jo, was happy to agree the timing. He said it was no problem and they agreed when to meet and that each should bring along certain supplies.

"See you at midday then." Jon grinned at him. "It's going to be a great trip."

They shook hands and parted, Jon ducking back inside the boat and Michael climbing back to the dock and returning to the hotel hoping the time remaining in the afternoon and evening would be fun before he set off into the unknown.

It was.

It the morning he and Jo went their separate ways, each vowing to keep in touch, yet, despite their liking for each other, both knowing that realistically that was unlikely.

In the cab he took to get back to the boat Michael found himself thinking about home. And, as he did so, he suddenly remembered the funeral. He cursed so long and loudly that the driver, an elderly Chinese, threatened to turn him out.

How could he have forgotten, and more to the point, what did he do now? He hadn't thought, he had been too upset and angry and then things had just been moving too fast. He couldn't give up everything here and fly straight home again. No way. For all he knew he was the last person his mother wanted to see anyway. He calmed down, somehow persuading himself that it would be better to leave everything as it was for now. He could barely get back to England in time to attend anyway, indeed he did not even know the exact date, but it must be soon and ... he persuaded himself that it was just better to see her later. In his heart he knew he was being selfish, putting himself and his adventure first, but it did not stop him resolving to join Jon on the boat as planned.

Once his taxi had dropped him off he made his way to the boat. Jon waved him aboard and they quickly unpacked and settled in, then Jon was showing him the ropes – literally – and they worked together to get the boat ready for the trip. They agreed on how to operate the boat jointly: they would make some stops en route, but otherwise would keep sailing, sharing the watches at night. Michael's initial impressions of Jon as someone both competent on boats and pleasant to deal with were positively reinforced. It all boded well and they were soon ready to go.

An hour and a half after he had climbed aboard, the tide was right, and they cast off and headed out to sea.

CHAPTER ELEVEN
Discoveries at dinner

It was a good funeral, I think – if you can have such a thing as a good funeral. The service was nicely done and James's older brother Martin gave an address that was just right – sad at James's passing yet celebratory for the life he had led. We had a good marriage I think, yes we did and certainly many people do much worse. He was a good man. I miss him so much and I know I always will.

I have been so caught up with the funeral arrangements that I have not thought much more about Michael. He's not been in touch and, though I did wonder at one point if he might just turn up unannounced for the service, there was no sign of him. He must be really seriously upset to simply ignore the funeral. I worry that something's not right, something's happened to him and whatever it is it stopped him from coming. I hope he's okay and I hope I hear from him soon.

There is still so much to do. The will and money matters to sort out, but James was always highly organised and I don't need to worry about anything there. The house is going on the market; I can't live in this great place now I'm on my own. I need something manageable, and preferably somewhere that lets me walk into town easily; luckily I can buy something as soon as I see the right thing as James's investments were in part in my name and money is immediately available. When the will's sorted out some money goes to Michael too. But where are you???

Philip arrived at Miriam's place on the dot of eight o'clock. The flat, tucked away off the high street, was small but modern and nicely finished and it was tidy too; either she had tidied up for him or she was better organised than he was. She welcomed him in with a kiss on the cheek and got him to pour them both a drink.

"Good day?" he asked.

Miriam had never talked much about the detail of her work, saying it was mostly "just routine". There's routine and routine, thought Philip, and her job must undoubtedly have its moments, certainly if nearly being stabbed was anything to go by. Probably there were things too that she could not talk about to a member of the public; she wasn't going to say "We suspect that oddball living down your road of poisoning his wife" now was she? Certainly not all of it could be good, he thought further, remembering her being held up at a road accident when she had missed an appointment with him. He knew a pedestrian had been killed and the driver responsible had fled the scene and was still to be found; that sort of thing can't be any picnic.

"I was mainly in court again today; and mostly my time was spent sitting around waiting. People say they want the police to be out and about but they also want wrongdoers punished and you have no idea how time-consuming the legal process can be. Today was typical – a young lad caught vandalising a car, just the sort of behaviour we want to stop, and yet it has taken ten times the time it took to arrest him to get him to court and see him given a small fine. Sometimes I wonder ... anyway, bear with me – the food's coming up."

She disappeared into the small kitchen, refusing Philip's offers of help and appeared with what proved to be an excellent chicken pie and accompanying vegetables. The table was already laid and she served Philip first.

"Do start before it gets cold," she said as she went on to serve her own. He helped himself to vegetables and tucked in.

"Delicious ... sorry." He excused himself as he spoke indistinctly with his mouth half full. Penny had been the cook in their household and since her death Philip was always pleased to find a meal actually set in front of him. His sister was very good; although she lived down in Kent and was busy with two small children, she invited him regularly. He got on well with both her and her husband, but, since Penny died, there was always a slight feeling of 'looking after poor Philip' about their meals together. His own cooking was rather rudimentary, though it was both improving and assisted by the kind of food sold in the Marks and Spencer food shop that had opened recently in the town and was located just where he came through to the high street from the library on his way home.

"What about you? What about your day?" Miriam asked.

"Sometimes I think that I'm in the wrong job. That Froby is wilfully bureaucratic; you know I told you she's bringing in more computers?" He ploughed on without waiting for a reply. "Well, now she's got it into her head that a radical rearrangement would enable her to label the whole area in the left hand corner as a 'Technical Interactive Computer Zone' - TICZ for short for goodness sake; it sounds like a biting insect or an unpleasant skin disease and it hardly trips off the tongue. The only books available soon will be e-books: people will be able to borrow them but they will come primed for self-destruction after three weeks or whatever. Perhaps we will have to have the 'Mission Impossible' theme playing as background music when they are checked out. I don't know where she gets her approach from. But I'm hoping what she wants may prove a step too far. The Library area guy is due to visit soon, and we'll see what he makes of it all. I'm hoping that her current plan is so over the top that it will prove her undoing. At least I've got a school presentation to do tomorrow. I enjoy those, though Robo-librarian will probably want to cut back on such things too soon if she gets her way."

"She's obviously not your favourite person. Robo-librarian sounds about right" Miriam chuckled. "Though I recommend that you don't introduce your colleagues to that name - it might be said out loud and make matters worse. I can't tell you what we call the Inspector in the station on occasion, though I guess he's okay really. Isn't there anything you can do about Froby, your view must count for something?"

"I'm hoping there may be ... we'll see." Philip changed the subject and continued, "Much more important, I met the current owner of what was the Croft's boat at the Heybridge pub the other day, it's called "Starcounter" remember, and it's still moored at Heybridge Basin. You know, in the line of boats along the canal. I had a word with him and his son, it's the son who uses the boat these days, and he used to know Michael, the son that is. He couldn't really help, but he found me an old mate of Michael's who works nearby and when I spoke to him he said that he thought he'd gone overseas for a job, out east somewhere, something to do with boats. But oddly he was sure Abigail knew about it, so it still does nothing to explain the complete lack of contact or the fact that so far as we know she had no idea where Michael went."

They ate in silence for a moment then Miriam said, "I guess it might lead somewhere, at least someone knew something. We'll see. Incidentally, I meant to say this again - I thought it was so nice of you to speak up like that at Abigail's funeral."

"Oh, don't remind me, it was so blooming embarrassing."

"No, don't think that, it was good." She paused, then continuing, "Are there any other developments?"

"Not really. I had a totally bland reply from the Treasury Solicitor - you know you suggested I write to them to say about Abigail mentioning this Mac person. They didn't seem much interested and it doesn't sound like I'm likely to hear any more from them either. But there is one other thing actually."

He got up and went to retrieve the bag he had carried the drinks round to dinner in.

"Well, two things in fact." He first got out a package wrapped in coloured paper and handed it over.

"First of all there's this, I felt bad about our spending the evening of your birthday together and I didn't even have a gift for you, though, in my defence, it was a slightly unexpected invitation." He paused. "One I was very glad to receive, of course!" He gave her a broad smile.

She opened the package to reveal a book: the latest Patricia Scanlan novel.

"That's really kind. Thank you so much."

"I always like giving books for presents; well, not least because it's the only thing I can wrap up! I cheated too. I know what sort of thing you borrow from the library, though I ignored the crime ones – coals to Newcastle, I thought."

"This is fine, she's a favourite author of mine, and I'm sorry about the birthday evening, it did get me out of a hole, but it wasn't totally that - we are getting on well aren't we? To be honest with you I haven't got to know too many people around here so far. As I told you I've only been in the town not quite a year and it's been easy to lose myself in work, you know, funny hours and all. I've only taken a few days off. To be more honest I left my last posting after some difficulties ... another, more senior, officer was bullying me after I'd turned down his romantic overtures. Frankly he was thoroughly unpleasant. Some people call the police pigs: in his case he deserved it. I couldn't face a fuss and making a complaint though, however much in the right you are about anything like that, challenging it still looks bad on your record, so I just put it down to experience and in for a transfer. I thought a small town like this would be a real change."

"I'm sorry, that's just not on. And is it – a change, I mean?"

"Oh yes, in all sorts of ways. And, work apart, I don't know why I haven't gone for a more rural area before. I was brought up in the country, down in Kent, but I moved to London as soon as I started work. I love it round here; the walk we took at Goldhanger for instance was a treat. Wasn't the recent television adaptation of 'Great Expectations' filmed near there?"

"Yes nearby, it was done at Tollesbury, I think, and there was a shot of a coach crossing the causeway to Osea Island at low tide too. You ought to see the causeway; it's been there since Roman times. We can do that walk again, if you like. Last time I went along the river path all the way from Heybridge I saw kingfishers in the culvert below the sea wall. Some people see it as a rather bleak landscape here – all the mud flats when the tide is out, but I love it and the salt marshes are fascinating."

They moved on to dessert. She had made trifle. "Proper pudding," she said. "For a treat. My mother always said that trifle was only any good if it made a noise like a cow taking its foot out of the mud when you serve it. And ... there you are!" She spooned it out with a satisfactory squelch and it indeed proved to be good.

Dessert finished he got up to help clear the table; they moved the dishes into the kitchen, although Miriam insisted on leaving the washing up for the moment saying that she would do it later.

Standing up Philip remembered that in the bag he had brought the drinks and her present in there was something else. Just as he had left home he had slipped the photographs and notebook he had found amongst Abigail's library books into it; he had never looked at them properly and he had brought them along, perhaps still fearing that conversation might flag between them and that having it to hand might be useful as a talking point. He was still feeling his way with Miriam and still feeling desperately ill equipped so to do. He explained to Miriam about the book and they agreed to have a look at it together.

"There didn't seem to be anything useful there," he said, once when they were back in the living-room. "But you never know and besides, you should be good at spotting clues."

She ignored the crack and the book, asking first, "What's in the envelope?"

"That's just old photographs. They seem to be from a holiday in Scotland by the look of them. One of them has Dunoon written on the back: it's a small town on the Clyde – near where the American nuclear submarine base was at Holy Loch. I don't think they help much."

"Let's have a look."

He remembered reading about how the area surrounding the town was affected when the naval base closed and most of the Americans moved away. He pushed the envelope of photos across the table to Miriam.

She shook the photos out of the envelope and spread them on the table. They were typical holiday snaps, probably fifteen or sixteen of them. He remembered the one of Abigail on the pier, the others were scenes of mountains, sea and lochs; the weather had clearly been good and Philip wondered

126

what time of year it had been. They did not look recent; indeed Abigail looked a good twenty years younger.

"They seem to be from some years back, I wonder why she kept them," Philip said.

"She may have had stacks of photos in the house for all we know, the question is why did she keep these particular ones here inside this book? Let's look at that."

The book was neatly written in the hand Philip knew from Abigail's letter to him, but it was not a recipe book, despite the entry about cheesecake; it was a journal. Not a diary: there were no dates and the entries ranged in length from a few lines to a page or so. As they read them it appeared that they were just random jottings, small streams of consciousness when the mood took her. Perhaps writing the entries had made her feel better. First they flicked through from the back; nothing else fell out. In fact most of the book was empty but the last few entries were about Philip and her thoughts on meeting him.

"I don't know how I missed this," Philip sounded contrite. "I thought it was just recipes."

"She obviously liked you," Miriam observed, having read a number of pages. "In fact," she turned a further entry back into the past, "she seems to have restarted writing entries in the book when she met you. And I'm sure she would have sent you that letter, you know. She really hoped that you could help."

"I still wish I could."

They turned to the front of the book. The entries there were clearly from an earlier time and were jottings relating to the death of her husband and also to the row with Michael and his subsequent disappearance. They appeared to be a continuation of entries made in some earlier book, though any indication of date was consistently absent.

"It is sad," said Miriam "and it must have been such an upsetting time for her. She either gave up hoping Michael would return - she may even have thought he was dead - or perhaps she just stopped writing about it."

"Yes; or both," added Philip.

Miriam started to pull the photos into a pile ready to return them to the envelope when something caught her eye.

"Wait a minute, this one isn't a photo," she said, pulling one picture out of the pile. "Well, it is a photo, but it's been sent as a postcard. Look, the stamp shows it was posted in Thailand."

The picture showed a marina, with the figures of two men, one older than the other and both clad in shorts and a T-shirt, sitting on bollards on the edge of the quay, a building of some sort behind them to the right and boats moored on a quay to the left; a mass of masts showed in the background. Both men were wearing sunglasses and sun hats.

"I am pretty sure that's Michael, though it's not completely clear," said Philip.

Miriam got up and fetched a magnifying glass from a drawer and Philip looked again, muttering, "Part of your Sherlock Holmes kit, I presume."

He gave her no time to respond but continued. "Yes, that's definitely him. Despite the sunglasses I recognise him from the picture in the local paper, you know, when he disappeared. He looks happy enough. What does the message say?"

They turned the card over again and peered more closely at the somewhat faded writing, Michael had certainly not inherited his mother's neat handwriting, but they could still read the brief message.

Dear Mum

I'm sorry. I needed a break. I'm in Thailand –
Phuket – I took a job helping sail a boat up from
Singapore. It was marvellous, I'll show you photos.

Back soon, well fairly soon. I'll write properly
and tell you more when I know where I'm staying. No need
to worry.

Love you ... M

Philip looked up. "So he was definitely there in Thailand, presumably having sailed from Singapore and, by the looks of this, his mother knew that. I notice he didn't mention the funeral, probably couldn't think what to say having missed it. He would have to have said something in a letter though, wouldn't he? If he did write again, I wonder what happened next."

"Yes, but I'm not sure about the letter, and I wonder why he didn't email her, she had a computer. But look here at this card." She tapped it with a finger. "It's been redirected by the post office. Abigail must have moved house after her husband died; she mentioned the idea in the notebook. If so, then if Michael did send a letter it may never have reached her. There's usually a time limit on redirection, you pay for a month or whatever, and letters from overseas can take forever. By the time it got here the redirection period might well have finished."

"The post can take an age here," said Philip, knowing that the local area had come high in a national survey of bad postal delivery only recently. "You could be right, that would explain a lot; well it would begin to. You should be a detective - oh wait a minute, you ..."

He was cut off as she slapped him on his arm.

"Have you got a bit of paper?" he asked.

She went to fetch a pad and he looked again at the photo under her magnifying glass, particularly at the building behind the central figure. On the wall was a painted sign, it said:

BLUE LAGOON MARINA – Phuket

Boat mooring – boate repairs – boat sails

He wrote the name down, also writing the words "sails" and sales" and thinking that English spelling had not been the sign-writer's strong suit.

"It looks like the sort of place he might have got work. Do you think he simply stayed on there?" he said.

"It's a long time ago, but I suppose it's possible. If he did he would never see any advertisements that the Treasury Solicitor's office might have put in the newspapers. I've no idea, but I guess you could ask. Let's see."

Miriam switched on her computer and entered the words Blue Lagoon Marina Phuket into the Google search box, and clicked. Amongst a number of entries that were listed she found a place that consisted of a hotel, apartments, a marina and a boat repair yard. There were pictures and many of the boats shown were clearly worth a lot of money; at least one was listed for sale at over a million US dollars.

"This must be it," she said "I'll send them a message."

She typed a short note.

Hello from England – I wonder if you can help. I am trying to trace an Englishman called Michael Croft. I have reason to believe he might work on your site – repairing/refurbishing boats or sailing too. I'm not sure.

If you have any knowledge of this person – he's around 40 years old – I would appreciate your reply. Thank you.

She clicked send.

"Now, we'll see," she said, turning round, but Philip had gone into the kitchen to do some rapid washing up as she typed. He emerged and agreed: they could only wait and see.

"Good heavens, is that the time?" Miriam exclaimed suddenly, going on to explain that she was on an early shift on the following morning then off to attend a short course.

"Right, I'll be off, thanks so much for dinner and do let me know if you get a reply to that email."

Philip picked up his bag and headed towards the door, and as Miriam came to show him out he forced himself to have a small moment of confidence. As they parted he stood close and lent forward to kiss her. She moved towards him and then, just when their lips were about to touch, he let out an involuntary giggle. She moved apart abruptly.

"What on earth?" Her face expressed total mystification.

"Oh, I'm so sorry. I had a sudden flash of you in uniform and me being clapped in irons for assaulting a police officer." He giggled again then realised he had probably spoiled it all.

But she grinned. "Don't be silly. I'm not on duty and besides ..." She leant forward and they kissed. Evidently he had not spoiled the moment at all. It was a good moment.

CHAPTER TWELVE
An unexpected turn of events

A post card, he sent me a postcard. The little ... but he must be okay. He's in Thailand. He says he's just sailed from Singapore to the island of Phuket and got paid for it. Is that possible? He might have bought a stamp a bit sooner then, but thank God he's safe even if he's on the other side of the world.

The stupid, silly b ... no, I can't write that, though I'm sure no one else will ever read this. He says he'll write properly and give me an address and he did say sorry, I should think so - though I'm sure we must both share some of the blame. It's going to be okay, I can't wait to hear more - come on postman, come on. But just wait until I see him, he's going to get a piece of my mind and no mistake. A letter now please ... and soon.

1997 Thailand

Now ashore Michael and Jonathan had taken a two bedroomed apartment overlooking the marina. It was part of a timeshare property but Jonathan had been to the marina before and knew someone who owed him a favour. A week's rent had cost very little and the cost was split between them. Michael, who would probably stay longest, had had a free period of accommodation on the boat and was also being paid a bundle of cash for his time.

Now with the boat safely moored they could relax and ease their tiredness. They sat under an awning at a nearby food court enjoying a Singha beer; it was served ice cold and the glasses had been kept in the refrigerator too, to help stop it warming too quickly in the heat.

"I've sent the buyer an e-mail to say we've arrived so I should be out of here soon," Jon said.

133

He was due back in his Singapore office, with some 'big deal' in prospect and his evidently impatient father chasing him to return. Michael had the accommodation booked for a week and thus planned to make the most of a break - there were great beaches nearby and a whole island to explore. Only after that would it be time to return to England, reality and whatever his mother had in store for him. If he was honest he was not keen to make the return with troubles awaiting him.

"Let's get something to eat," said Jon, sipping his beer and picking up the menu.

&

The voyage had been a revelation to Michael. 'Footloose' was a bigger boat than he had ever previously sailed in: with an experienced skipper from whom he rapidly began to learn a great deal and a totally different environment, not least the hot climate and warm sea, it all made for an exhilarating experience.

As they set off Michael was somewhat apprehensive. From Singapore to Phuket is about six hundred miles as the crow flies and 'Footloose' was no crow he thought to himself. It was many times further than he had ever sailed before, though not as far as it would have been had he pursued his idea of sailing round the whole U.K. coastline. But as the Chinese saying has it, a journey of a thousand miles starts with a single step. They would progress step by step, each leg of the voyage manageable in its own right. And so it proved. The weather was good, the sailing was a pleasure and they found they got on well, taking turns at the helm and with Michael picking Jon's brains about the boat, the sailing, the route and the area.

Jon had a route and ideal stopping places in mind; it was, after all, a journey he had undertaken several times in the past.

On the first two nights they moored in isolated coves. Michael found the night skies amazing and told Jon how his father had loved them. They had a good load of supplies on board and cooked supper in the cabin, retiring to their bunks early. Setting off again at first light, they made good progress.

Along the way they stopped at a marina on the Malaysian island of Langkawi. This was very much a holiday area and ashore they ate at a local restaurant, then spent rather too long in one of the nearby bars, cold beer following cold beer almost unnoticed in the heat of the evening. Michael woke up in his bunk, the sun shining on his face, to find that he had no very clear recollection of how he had returned to the boat. As he lifted his head from the pillow it seemed as if someone was hammering multiple needles into his skull. He groaned, lowered his head again, pulled the covers over his head to blot out the sun streaming in through a porthole and returned to his slumbers. It was long past midday when he finally woke. Jon was crashing about ahead of him and then he heard the shower running; Michael assumed that he must only just have woken too.

For the first few hours thereafter Jon spoke only a single sentence. "We'll stay here today and move on tomorrow." As they were both in a similar state it was certainly not a question of the skipper admonishing the crew. They gradually revived, a process aided by a dip over the side, and by mid-afternoon were sitting drinking coffee in the cockpit.

"This is the life," said Michael.

Jon snorted "What do you mean, you felt as bad as I did."

"No, not last night's overindulgence ... or this morning - definitely too much beer. I mean the voyage. The boat's great, the voyage is great and it is great too to get away for a while. I am so grateful that you picked me for this."

"I've sailed since I was a small boy," said Jon "and I guess I'm lucky to be able to live and work in a part of the world where it's possible to spend so much time afloat. Once I started dealing in boats too that added to the fun, though the plan is for me to continue learning the business from my dad and gradually take over from him, doing more and more as he does less and less. I'm making the most of the sailing while I can. Perhaps it's crazy to sail all this way just to sell the boat, but it's fun ... so why not, eh."

Jon paused and went below to refill his coffee mug. When he came back he drank with considerable concentration for a moment then continued, "What about you? You can't potter around on that river of yours for ever you know, nice though it may be. There's a great big world out there and with your talents at sailing you could find all sorts of work in all sorts of places."

Michael considered this. Jon was no doubt right. In some ways the world was his oyster but first he had to finish this voyage, get things sorted at home and then, maybe then, make some decisions that would take him forward more constructively than in the past.

He simply replied "I guess so, but it's where to start. That's the question. Let's get to Phuket first, eh? What time do you want to set sail in the morning?"

"Oh, after a whole day off, at first light I guess. Now do you think I can trust you to have supper ashore again tonight without descending into another beer fuelled drunken stupor?"

Michael reacted fiercely, "You led the way, you ..." then he saw that Jon was joking and they both laughed. He'd been dead right earlier: he had been so lucky to be picked for this trip. He went on thinking just that all the way to Phuket.

⚑

After a meal at the marina, and with the voyage over, the two of them had fallen in with a crowd of tourists at a bar on the nearby beach. There is something about eating and drinking in the open air. Cold beer followed cold beer and at midnight Jon was heading arm in arm to an apartment with a young Australian girl in a tight T-shirt and shorts that made her legs look like they went on forever.

"See you in the morning," he said over his shoulder. Michael couldn't be sure, but it sounded as if it implied that he wanted to have the apartment to himself overnight, so Michael finished his beer and went back to his bunk on the boat.

They had not sailed through every night, more usually finding places to moor or anchor and continuing in the morning. If they did sail on then they both took turns on watch. Only on one night was there a problem. Michael was on watch and to begin with all was well. The night sky was awesome, the Milky Way arching above the boat in a vast swirl of brilliant light. Every night Michael thought of his father. How he would have loved to see this; he would have been pointing out constellations and describing the wonders that the sight indicated, telling Michael about the distances involved, about double stars and nebulae, and about stars dying in gigantic supernova explosions that seeded the universe with all the materials that built planets like earth. Even as a child his father had always regaled him with such things. "You're stardust," his father had told him. "Every single atom in your body was created in an exploding star."

He looked up: it was quite a thought. Ever since those times he had always found clear night skies to be one of the great pleasures of his sailing. He missed his father and still felt bad about the funeral, not for his dad - he would know nothing of what went on - but for his mother. He was still telling himself that time would make it easier to heal the rift when they saw each other again. Although he well knew everyone died, it still did not seem fair; his father had yet to turn sixty.

He had been a successful man. The city institution for which he worked would also miss him. He had rarely talked about money. They lived in a nice house, four bedrooms and a lovely garden, and he imagined they were relatively well off, certainly when his father had pushed him to go to university and he had used the now considerable cost as one of his arguments against it, that had been quickly brushed aside. Just once, he could not remember quite when or why, his father had told him that there would be money for him when he went. The comment had been linked with one about "being sensible" and had been said a while before they argued about what Michael should do with his life. Now he wondered what exactly that had meant.

As he sailed on gradually the stars disappeared above as the sky darkened, the wind rose and the waves too. Sailing was exciting in such conditions and he felt he was coping well; the boat was well equipped to be sailed single handed. But it was not his boat and Jon had specifically asked to be called if the weather changed significantly. It had certainly done that. It might just be a passing squall but he called Jon anyway. Jon had pulled on a waterproof and climbed from the cabin into the cockpit looking somewhat tousled; he looked around and suggested a minor change to the configuration of the sails, but he did not take the helm.

"You're doing fine," he said. His confidence in Michael had grown over the past days as they had worked the boat in tandem. They sat together in the cockpit as the boat rushed through the waves, the sound of the wind and sea strong in their ears and salt spray on their faces. The squall proved to be a short lived affair, the wind dropped back a little and Jon returned to his bunk. Only later Michael found that in the initial manoeuvring a small amount of water had splashed into the cockpit and his laptop computer, precariously balanced on a shelf above, had fallen and spent the night on the floor, making it soaked and useless. He mentally heaved a sigh of relief that he had it insured; meantime he had no doubt lost what was on it.

Soon the island of Phuket was in sight. The last miles of the journey made for easy sailing and the boat performed like the trooper she was. She was a pleasure to sail and Michael felt in his element; he wondered if he would ever be content with something as small as "Starcounter" again. Jon radioed ahead to the marina and they were soon edging into a designated berth on the quay. Michael looked around him in awe: some of the boats around were motor yachts, a few of them the sort of thing that cost as much as a supercar. The world economy might be in a mess, but here at least there were apparently people with money to spend. It reminded Michael of the old saying that owning a boat was like standing under a shower tearing up ten pound notes. A profusion of sailing boats were moored up too and the air was filled with the characteristic sound of wire slapping on metal as the light wind caught the stays and knocked them against aluminium masts. It was a common sound heard everywhere boats were moored and, despite the exotic location, it reminded him of home.

Once safely secured and with the sails stowed away neatly they climbed out of the boat and up onto the quay, Jon clutching a camera. To begin with the ground seemed to them to sway alarmingly after so much time at sea and it took both of them a moment to find their land legs. For Michael especially, just finishing his longest ever voyage, it meant a few rather disorientating minutes.

"Let's record the moment," Jon said. Then more loudly he called across to what appeared to be a holidaymaking couple heading along the quay towards the hotel.

"Can you help us please?" He waved the camera and they paused and came across. "That's kind. It's all set up, just press here."

He indicated the shutter button. The man duly took the picture as they sat on bollards, their backs to the marina. The couple accepted a proffered thank you, passed back the camera, and resumed their walk.

Then Jon led the way across the wide open yard, an area where a number of tall, huge wheeled cranes stood ready to straddle boats and lift them bodily out of the water and where some boats already stood on dry land undergoing various sorts of repair and maintenance work. Sounds of hammering, drilling and sanding gave the area a busy feeling of industry. At one point as they walked through the area a pressure hose was turned on and the edge of an arc of spray caught them before the hose was got under control. The man holding it was Thai: he smiled and called out something in his own language, which they assumed to be an apology, though they had not been made very wet.

"Boat maintenance is big business here," Jon explained "Thailand is a much less costly place than Singapore or even Malaysia to have work done. People bring boats here from all over the region. But what we need now is a beer, then we can take our stuff to the apartment; that will be more comfortable for a few days." Jon went first to the bank, then bought a pack of cold beers in a supermarket. They carried them back to the boat and drank sitting on deck in the sun. Jon produced Michael's money in cash in Thai Baht, thanking him profusely for his help. Michael secreted this away in his shoulder bag thinking that the whole trip had been a wonderful experience, they had got on well, the boat had been a dream to sail and he had learnt a great deal to boot. It had whetted his appetite in a big way; if he was previously keen to work with boats, he now knew for sure that this was what he wanted. He wanted to make it up at home, but was resolved that it would not be to the exclusion of such ambitions.

Michael took a long swig from a bottle and looked around; the sky was clear blue, the temperature was hot, the sounds and smells around him heralded something new - he was in another world. It looked good and the voyage had been a great success. Michael remembered how he had sat undecided in the pub in Bradwell, trying to make up his mind about the trip. It had been touch and go for a while, but impetuousness had won out in the end and he now felt it was a very good decision.

Once they were ensconced in the apartment they had both began to set to with various chores. Michael wrote his mother a card, saying little, and using the photo of himself and Jon by the boat which they had got printed off the camera in the nearby supermarket. He couldn't face a telephone call so started writing a long letter too, hoping it would help sort things quickly once he was back though, for the moment, he rationalised that time and distance apart was helping that aim. He was unable to email her as her address was lost with his computer. He wondered if it might be cheaper to replace this here rather than when he got home.

"Just off to get stamps and things," he said to Jon as he went towards the door.

He got stamps at the hotel, flirted with one of the girls on reception and arranged to use their address for any replies that arrived before he left. He added the address to the letter, sealed it and dropped it, the card to his mother and one or two other postcards he had written, in the post box by reception. He took the bundle of dirty clothes he had bagged up in the apartment and set off to the laundry which Jon and he had seen just along from the supermarket. He dropped off his clothes; they just asked his name, there was no system of tickets or receipts – "I remember you, no problem," said the smiling girl at the laundry. He then went to the supermarket and, having bought a few supplies he visited the bank located just next door. Here, keeping a little of Jon's cash aside to see him through the week, he paid most of the sailing payment into his account using an arrangement he had set up in England. He then checked his balance, inserting his card into the ATM and printing out a slip from the cash machine. He took one glance at it and his eyes widened in amazement.

At first it just confused him. Despite having clicked on "English" as the language choice as he started, the balance was shown in Thai Baht and the figure was in the millions. It took him a moment but wrestling with the exchange rate still did not make it right. He repeated the calculation several times. In pounds it might not be millions, but while he had been at sea a sum of something like £100,000 had been paid into his account.

CHAPTER THIRTEEN
A plan and a plan

It's a year since he went, a whole year. The only word I ever had was that dratted card, never the promised letter. I can't contact him without an address and apparently he doesn't want to contact me. Not attending James's funeral was just the last straw - if he wouldn't do that then I should really not expect to hear from him. I can't go through life expecting every day to hear something *from him, it's just too upsetting. I won't think like that, I should just forget ... but I know I never will. Where are you?*

Despite queues at the library counter, Froby had dragged Philip off to her office to discuss what she now thought of as her grand reorganisation - for an hour. She was becoming obsessed. Philip's deadline for what he thought of as the great book cull was on hold. "We'll get everything sorted and make one big move to make the change," she said. "If necessary we can close for a day - or two." Oh joy. He had flirted with the idea of raising the matter with the Area Manager, who was due to visit that very afternoon, but thought it better to let matters run their course. It might just make matters worse if the idea was not squashed and if Froby knew he had tried to scupper it; his future position would not be helped one tiny bit. Besides he had been working on the matter in other ways and was hopeful that, as a result of his efforts, her plan would not come to fruition.

Meantime, the normal business of the library continued apace: a lady he didn't know wanted to find books at a particular reading level for her young grandson; Mrs Worthing, a regular, checked again for the new Patricia Cornwell she had ordered and he patiently explained, again, that books ordered could take quite some time to arrive, especially when it was a new title by a popular writer that was wanted by a large number of people and she was down the queue; and Mr Denton, a daily visitor to the newspapers and magazines, wanted to know why someone had cut half the pages out of The Guardian. Philip sighed inwardly but resisted saying it was probably to remove all the misprints that paper was renowned for containing. Instead he apologised and resolved to write a note to his colleagues asking that everyone kept more of an eye out for "phantom article choppers". Silly question of the morning was someone asking "If I take out a book of crossword puzzles, should I complete them in pencil or can I do it in ink?" Philip explained patiently that they did not keep such books and the customer had left clearly disappointed.

When the Area Manager arrived he went first to the counter where Margaret was on duty.

"How's things going?" he asked. He knew all the staff by sight and made a point of speaking with those with whom he crossed paths during a visit.

"Fine," she told him "We're getting all set for this big reorganisation, though it's..." she paused, looking perplexed, then continued, "Well, it's quite ... elaborate."

"What do you ...?" He was about to ask exactly what she meant, but continued "... No, never mind. Is Miss Frobisher in the office?"

There was no need for Philip, who had heard this exchange, to say anything now; the cat was well and truly out of the bag and he did not doubt that Froby would fill in all the details. He just hoped that her grand plan was something that would not meet with official approval, and wondered if she had adopted any of the suggestions he had been progressively making. He crossed his fingers for a moment as he went to his next task, while wishing he could be a fly on the wall at the coming meeting. He hated Froby's mad plans and he just hoped that he'd been able to do sufficient to change things.

The manager headed for the office, intent on finding out what was going on. He sighed inwardly. Miss Frobisher was very much not his favourite person, indeed he had been one of those on the selections panel who had voted against her. He still found it odd that a majority had favoured her appointment. His monthly meeting with her was not his favourite thing either; he found it hard to warm to Miss

Frobisher. He had never called her anything else; in fact he would have had to turn up her personnel file just to remind himself of what her given name actually was. She projected a protective air, clearly at pains to be thought of as efficient, but seemed indifferent to anything else, certainly to a more friendly working arrangement or any small talk. She peered at him over her steel spectacles, which he privately thought made her look like a prison warder, opened a bulging file and cleared her throat.

"Maybe now we can get to the other matter I mentioned when you arrived," she said when their routine business was over. "We need to keep moving forward and I have devised a plan that I think will jump this library not only up to date but into the future. Perhaps I can summarise the main elements involved." She smiled. It was, he thought, the sort of smile favoured by Bond villains about to order someone's death.

Despite not knowing what was coming next, he already instinctively dreaded hearing what those 'main elements' were, but he nodded his head a fraction. He was pretty sure that nothing would stop her now until she had got it out.

"Well, rather than just adding a few more computers, I want to create a dedicated technological section. It will need some moving around of things, but the effect will be worth it. I shall call it the Technical Interactive Computer Zone, TICZ for short. It needs a striking name, don't you think? And that seems good to me."

She did not wait for any comment, continuing, "We would have the computers there, of course, make it the centre of our Wi-Fi facility and add printers and scanners as well and also perhaps other equipment, binding and labelling machines perhaps. It would be necessary to upgrade the seating - ideally we need some proper office style chairs - and to make it really attractive we could put in coffee machines and a slot machine for snacks. I am working on whether to have additional cards for library members wanting access, ideally swipe cards that would automatically open a barrier between the new area and the rest of the library and help keep the TICZers and the ordinary members separate."

Her list went on, her requirements going from the bizarre to the ridiculous and the obvious cost rising as she spoke. He inwardly raised an eyebrow, then raised it some more. When she proposed a fruit machine as "an essential feature to appeal to the young" he opened his mouth to comment, but she ploughed on seemingly without drawing breath. When she had told him what she proposed to call the 'zone', he had stopped her, though it took two attempts. He hardly believed what he had heard. The "Technical Interactive Computer Zone", TICZ. What on earth was she thinking?

"This is, well ..." he paused to consider the most appropriate word "it's ... well, it's very ambitious isn't it?" he finally said slowly, with considerable emphasis on the word "ambitious".

"Well, thank you, of course it is; we can't stand still, can we? What was it Henry Kaiser said? 'You can't sit on the lid of progress. If you do you will be blown to pieces.' And we certainly don't want that now do we?" She gave him a triumphant look and took her spectacles off to polish them with a large bright pink cloth she took out of her desk drawer.

He could hardly believe she had taken his comment as a compliment. He had meant too ambitious, too ambitious by half and hardly appropriate either; she was contemplating so many bells and whistles that the next thing she would want was an increase in staff numbers.

He held up a hand saying "Hang on, this is a lot to take in. Do you have a written proposal about it?" He prayed she had not taken it so far and that just his asking for one would delay things for a while.

"Yes, of course," she answered crisply and produced a smartly bound report from the file in front of her and passed it across. He should have known. He thanked her, though feeling the very reverse of thankful, and found himself thinking that if she was blown to pieces his life would become a great deal simpler. He flicked through some of the pages, noting they went as far as a page 47 a few pages from the end. How long did it take to prepare something of this absurd length he wondered? What else had not been done while her attention focused on the details contained within the report's no doubt verbose profusion of many words? He nearly asked a question, quickly thought better of it, then biting his tongue he got to his feet.

"Well, let's leave it there for now, shall we? I'll certainly have a look at it," he said turning briskly and opening the door. "I'll see you next month. My secretary will phone as usual about a date and please ... please do not spend any more time on this until then." He gave her proposal a little wave as he spoke.

Froby returned her glasses to her nose and spoke up. "I wonder, perhaps we should schedule an additional meeting to consider this, do you ...?"

This time he interrupted firmly: "We'll have to see. Leave it with me and I'll let you know." He was well pleased with his choice of words. There was an old saying that if someone says 'I'll think about it and let you know' – you know. And it's not good news.

He walked through the library quickly avoiding eye contact with any of the other members of staff. He did not know how much they knew of her plan and did not want to get into any further conversation about it. Once outside and heading for the car park he sighed and whispered, "Oh my God" quietly to himself as he exhaled.

Philip had seen him leave but found his face unreadable. He wanted desperately to know how the meeting had gone, but clearly he would have to wait.

CHAPTER FOURTEEN
Something to consider

I'm staring at a blank page. No time for a real entry today. I have just realised it is the reading group at the library soon. Philip said he would run me there. What a good idea joining was, I've enjoyed attending – just time to collect my thoughts and put my coat on.

1997. Thailand.

Michael looked again at the bank print out. It still showed the huge figure; he was stunned. He couldn't take it in, so much so that he dropped the slip, scrabbled to pick it up again and, even though it still said the same thing, he put his card back in the machine and repeated the check. The result was still the same. He was apparently £100,000 better off than when he left England. For a moment he could not believe it. It was an error, an absurd error, it must be. But then he remembered his earlier thought: his father had always said he would get some money after his death and he knew that some of his parent's savings had been held in his mother's name. Presumably following his father's death some pre-existing arrangement had triggered an immediate transfer and in due course her funds would be swelled again later when the estate was finally sorted out.

His mind racing, he retrieved his shopping and walked over to the little café and sat down under an umbrella at a metal table outside. One of the girls serving came out to him and he ordered a coffee. He was still shocked. He must have looked it too as the girl who delivered his coffee noticed and asked "You okay?"

"Yes, fine," he replied. "I'm probably just tired, I've just sailed all the way from Singapore."

"Wow, very long way. You good sailor? Boat very big? How long you take?" Her clipped form of English sounded attractive to him. She looked attractive too and her wide smile was a treat to behold. He was the only customer at present and she sat down at his table, smiled again and it was clear she expected some answers.

Michael didn't object, and he was still too fazed by his surprising bank news to bother to embellish the story of their voyage to impress her; he just described the trip straightforwardly. She remained interested throughout his description. When he had finished his coffee, paid the bill and got up she immediately wanted to see the boat.

"Which boat you sail? Please show me," she entreated.

She beamed that smile again and Michael couldn't resist. She shouted something in Thai to a colleague inside the cafe, doubtless a comment about holding the fort or some such and they walked through the marina to where the boat was moored. Michael helped her on board and showed her round. She proved to be a fanatical and knowledgeable boat lover. Her family, she explained, had a small sailing boat as she grew up. "I sail very much," she said simply. They exchanged names, hers was Poy, and he discovered that she had just finished a degree course in business administration at a university in Bangkok and was working at the café part time while she decided what to do next.

An hour later, having promised Poy that he would meet her back at the café and that they would go for dinner together, Michael was heading off to the apartment to tell Jon he wouldn't be there for supper. As he let himself in he found Jon on the phone. Michael waved at him, saw that the conversation was likely to go on and so went to shower and change - he was still getting used to the heat; this country seemed to demand that you take a shower several times a day – and headed out again signalling with an invisible knife and fork gesture that he was going to eat out. Jon waved acknowledgement - he was still on the phone.

Poy was sitting at the same table outside the café; she had changed and her long black hair was tied in a ponytail. She greeted him warmly and walked them to the entrance to the marina.

"Need wooden bus," she said, and in due course she was waving down a bus which along its length had all the windows framed in wood like an old fashioned Morris Traveller. They made their way to Phuket town and Poy confidently selected a restaurant in the picturesque old town, where the architecture was predominantly Chinese in style. She was stunning and Michael was mesmerised, what's more she knew and liked boats – they got on famously as they chatted primarily about his voyage. She did the ordering, consulting with Michael about what he liked and chattering to the waitress to make sure it was delivered just so.

After dinner and a return bus journey, he left her back at the marina, where she had rooms set above one of the shops near the food court, and was back in time to have a nightcap bottle of beer with Jon on the balcony with a view of the marina spread below them.

"Have you been in touch with home?" Jon asked.

Michael hesitated, muttering that he had written home but could not yet face a phone call, and ending, "I must give it all more time, I'm sure that's best."

But then, overwhelmed by his financial news, he told Jon about the money.

"It doesn't make up for losing your old man," said Jon, "but it sure is nice, and it gives you so many options – suddenly you have a lot to think about."

"A lot more, you mean," Michael said.

Both still tired from the voyage, they repaired to bed.

In the morning Michael was disturbed by banging and crashing sounds outside his room. He tried to ignore them, pulling the sparse covers round his ears, but a sudden shout added to the noise.

"God damn and blast!"

The shouting woke Michael completely and he stumbled out of his room. Jon was crashing about in the kitchen area, his computer screen glowing on the worktop, and his cursing getting worse - and worse

"What on earth's going on?" Michael asked.

"It's the buyer, he was supposed to collect the boat today – and make the payment for it too. It was all set. Fixed. Now the bastard has reneged on the whole deal. He's walked away.

Last night it was all fine, now suddenly it's not - I'm buggered."

Michael said a brief "Sorry", though feeling that saying so hardly covered things. After all the boat must be worth tens of thousands of pounds and he knew Jon had another deal dependent on it. Jon shook his head, running his hand through his untidy thatch of hair.

"What a bloody mess, I have to be back in Singapore the day after tomorrow and the boat is only booked into its mooring here until then. If I leave it here, then how do I sell the thing? If I sail it back, then when ... it's hopeless. I need another buyer ... like right bloody now!"

"Do you know what happened?"

"Oh, something to do with the money; he'd freed it up for the boat then some business deal went down and the money's been sucked into that. But it doesn't matter why he can't complete, he can't. He won't."

"Might the position change?"

"I don't think so, no. I wish. I so need this deal to complete."

There did not seem to be anything useful to say. Jon dialled a phone number and Michael excused himself,

"Give me a moment, I must shower," he said, explaining also that he had arranged to meet Poy for breakfast.

Michael shaved and showered and got dressed. He was to meet Poy at the same little café, where she was on duty this morning. He went out onto the balcony where he could see that Jon was sitting head in hands, his mobile phone on the table.

"Look, I'm sorry; I'll cut this short and be back soon. We can talk some more then. I'm sure there is something you can do. I'll help if I can." Jon snorted dejectedly.

Michael slipped out without waiting for Jon to answer and ten minutes later he was sitting in the café ready for breakfast. Poy looked as attractive as ever and was clearly pleased to see him. She quickly organised some breakfast for him, saying "I eat already", and sat drinking coffee with him while he explained what had just happened.

"I must get back promptly, my friend has had bad news; he brought the boat here to sell it and now the buyer has had second thoughts. I need to help him if I can, see what can be worked out. Can we meet later?"

"Can do, am here till four in afternoon."

"Okay, I'll be back before then." He excused himself, paid the bill, and made his way back to the apartment. Jon was still sitting on the balcony, now with a cup of coffee. His mood had changed, radically changed. And it soon became apparent why.

"There is a way round this. I've had a great idea. Just great," he said, continuing without pause. "I'll sell you the boat – at a special price of course – it will sort the matter here and now. She's made for you, look at how you sailed her on the way here! Don't tell me you didn't enjoy it."

"You're mad. I couldn't buy her!" Michael laughed out loud, it was ridiculous.

"But you can, you must. You have the money, you told me about your inheritance, surely its arriving right now is a sign And you have just spent days on end telling me that you want to work with boats, that sailing's your life - she's not just a boat for you, she's a business, a livelihood, a way of life. She can be home too for a while, if you want. You can give sailing lessons, take tourists on trips and do work in the boatyard too if that helps financially; you told me you're a skilled carpenter. You can do it – seize the moment, let's face it you'll never get a chance like this again. Not ever. You really won't. You bloody well know it."

He thrust a file into Michael's hand, saying "I can forego any profit to get this sorted. Just look at the details. It's a bargain, the deal of a lifetime, of two lifetimes." He spoke with enormous enthusiasm.

Too shocked to speak, despite his overwhelming reservations Michael found himself taking the file. He had sailed the boat. He already knew her well. He sat at the table and flicked through the papers it contained. A factsheet explained that the boat could sleep six or seven people and was well equipped. She had a good galley with a gas cooker and even a refrigerator; she had a toilet with a basin and shower, with pressurised hot water; but he knew all this. He had experienced the excellent headroom below deck and used most of the equipment. Everything functioned well. He read on. He found that the boat was originally built in the eighties in East Anglia up the coast from where he lived. "She's a British export," he said to himself. He wondered what had brought her here. She had been well looked after, the navigation equipment was modern and the current in-board diesel engine was a replacement fitted only a few years back. She was a damn good boat. She sailed well, he certainly knew that. And Jon was right: she could also provide him with a home, a source of income and a whole new life style, he thought. What was more it could be a way of life he had dreamed of, albeit one which his parents had labelled as not being a proper job.

"I know she's great and all that but she's on the wrong side of the world," he said. He closed the file and pushed it across the table towards Jon, who opened his mouth to interject, but Michael went on, "No, it's ridiculous. It's not possible. I can't buy a boat." Michael sounded firm but already he found himself thinking that maybe, just maybe, he could. Even the name, "Footloose" appealed to him. He had said no, but he knew that he meant that he would think about it.

CHAPTER FIFTEEN
The only action possible

Philip hadn't seen Miriam for a few days, partly because she had been away attending a course and partly because he had had a date in his diary to visit his sister down in Kent, a journey made utterly unpredictable in duration because of the Dartford Crossing, the toll bridge and tunnel across the Thames between Essex and Kent and a part of the notorious M 25 ring road. Despite this, he always enjoyed his visits there. His sister's two kids were fun and had him down as a good reader and a regular source of new books. He had been dragooned into a session drawing elephants and, following a good lunch, after which he could happily have dozed off, he had read them a story. He still had the Madrigal books in his bag from the last school visit he had done: he read about a Halloween party at which Madrigal's cat Sootin had got stuck under a white sheet and been mistaken for a ghost. He left with the kids' shouts ringing in his ears.

As his sister kissed him goodbye she whispered, pursuing a recent theme "You're always welcome to bring a friend." She made sure that the word friend was heavy with meaning.

Miriam had phoned him just briefly while she was away to say that she had received a short reply from someone at the boat marina in Phuket. It was not good news.

She read it out:

```
Sorry, I don't know the name you mention, but this
is a busy place, both the marina and the island -
there are many people working in the yard, plus a
mass of small businesses and boats running trips to
the islands for tourists. Your Michael might well
be here even if I just haven't come across him.
```

The message was signed by a George Schultz, a German or American perhaps; certainly it seemed to be testament to the fact that at least some foreigners worked in such a place.

Now he had picked Miriam up in the high street and they were again driving to the pub in Goldhanger where they could also take a walk before having an evening meal.

"We ought to go to a proper restaurant again sometime, not just a pub. Let's fix something; my treat," said Philip, conscious that he wanted to impress.

"Oh, this is fine. I enjoy the walk here. Maybe we'll see those kingfishers this time," Miriam replied.

Philip parked the car alongside the wall of the pretty village church and they set off through the churchyard and across the fields; there would be plenty of light in the evening sky for a while yet. Philip had been busy on the Abigail front. The one piece of evidence they had unearthed was that Michael had been in Thailand, specifically he had been on the island of Phuket; the photo he had sent to Abigail proved that. If he had moved on then he might be anywhere. But, following the reply to their email, the fact that one local person out there didn't know him hardly proved anything.

158

Philip recalled the old saying 'absence of evidence, isn't evidence of absence'. It seemed to Philip that there was only one way to be sure: he had to go there. It was Abigail's fault. There was something about her, something about her plea to him, even though it was not sent, that hooked him in. He couldn't spend the rest of his life worrying about this. If it was possible he wanted to find out where Michael was, to actually find him. He had to do something and then, successful or not, he could put the matter aside knowing he had done all he could.

This was, it seemed to him, one thing he certainly could do.

He had not taken a holiday since Penny died. He was long overdue for a break and having spent less money than usual over the last two years he could for once well afford it. He supposed he was lucky, at least financially. He did not earn a fortune, though he enjoyed his job, finicky Froby and her obsessive push for ultra-modernity apart that is, and he had inherited the house he lived in from his parents and had no mortgage. He and Penny had regularly put money aside for holidays together while she was alive and he still had a standing order going into the holiday fund savings account.

As they walked across the fields he broached the subject with Miriam.

"I thought I might go there," he began.

"Go, go where?"

"To Thailand, to Phuket ... to that boatyard."

"But what about the email? They said they didn't know him," said Miriam sensibly. He knew it was true. It was nothing if not a long shot.

"I know that, but it was just a single person saying it, and he did say it was a busy area so there might be ... I know I've got a bit of a thing about it all, but the worst that can happen is that I have a break. I've not taken any holiday for two years. I know it sounds silly, but I can't let the matter rest. I feel I must actually do something tangible. There might be a clue there, Michael might even still be there, but whatever happens I could then feel I had done everything possible to follow up Abigail's plea for help. Then I could put it aside."

"Well, it's up to you and I can see it would get it out of your system, but do think about it carefully, won't you. Take a moment. Now, you promised me kingfishers."

"Well, not promised exactly, but ..." They chatted about other things until they reached the pub and, as before, ate a pleasant meal together. Philip raised the question of his idea of a visit to Thailand again during the meal, but could not draw Miriam to say much about it. She just repeated her initial reaction, saying "You must think about it".

Rightly or wrongly he felt she was not dismissing the idea, but only being protective. After all, such a trip could be a huge disappointment and he was sufficiently honest with himself to know both that he was being very optimistic if he believed he could find Michael and that there were actually very few grounds, if any, for any optimism at all. If he could have read Miriam's mind he would have seen he was correct.

By the following morning he had decided: it was the right thing for him to do. He would book the trip and go. He would find out about Michael once and for all, even if the answer was a negative one. Once at work, before doing anything else he went and logged the leave he needed into the library's staff record system. He was so overdue to take leave that even Froby could surely not object to it being somewhat short notice. All he had to do now was to book a flight and hotels and ... okay, he thought, so it needed a bit of organising.

He got organising.

The next day he was not on the rota for the library and he had time to check things out. He walked to one of the travel agents in the high street and after waiting for a clerk to become free, ran through some of the options. He quickly discovered that a package made little sense and concluded it was better to sit at the computer himself and book online, rather than in front of someone else doing pretty much the same thing and seeming to do it painfully slowly.

A couple of hours later, as he sat at his desk in the study, he had a thought. He was unsure how good an idea it was, but he did it anyway. He phoned Miriam and left a message:

Hi – good morning, it's Philip. Sorry, I know you're working. I just wanted to say that I've decided to go. I know you said consider carefully, but I just feel it's something I have to do and get out the way. And here's the thing, I have done some thinking – it's - I wondered perhaps ...well why don't you come too? At least think about it ... please. I'll get you a ticket. And ... who knows he might just still be there! Bye.

He regretted it as soon as he had done it. It was far too early for this sort of thing. Besides she was busy, surely she was busy - she would never say yes, never in a million years. Would she?

CHAPTER SIXTEEN
Plans, travels and a surprise

I know I'm getting older, aches and pains and a bit more difficulty getting about are normal enough at my age but I'm usually fine. I can't remember the last time I even had a cold. But the other day I had ... well what did I have: "a turn". I came over all light-headed and had to sit down for a while until the feeling passed. It was like how you can feel when you stand up too quickly, but more than that

– and when I hadn't just got up. The feeling passed after a few minutes and I found a cup of tea cleared it completely. But tea helps anything. It happened again this morning so I think I might ask the doctor about it.

I rang for an appointment and they offered me something almost three weeks ahead; I might be dead by then I told them, but evidently if I telephone at eight o'clock in the morning I can get an appointment for the same day. What a crazy system. If they have slots tomorrow why not give me one? It means they have to deal with another phone call tomorrow just as I do, and they also had to spend time explaining it all to me today. It's no wonder the NHS has not got any money - it's all being spent on admin.

Anyway I'll telephone again in the morning and we'll see. It may be *nothing, I hope so - I can't remember when I last went to the doctor.*

Miriam's return message had said no. Well, she'd actually said that she would have loved to, and she said she had ample holiday allowance to take, but ... something about a court thing that she couldn't duck. She was probably just being kind, Philip thought, and letting him down politely. He could offer to delay the trip, though he couldn't remember what the conditions on his ticket were, but then thought that it would be just too humiliating if he did that and then found that she said no again. Forget it. It was all decided now and he had to go.

He had fixed a flight, now he treated himself to a couple of nights in a Bangkok hotel on the river, one his friend Richard at the council had stayed in the previous year when he and his wife had holidayed in Thailand, and he had arranged a domestic flight to Phuket after that and accommodation in a small hotel on the beach and not far from the marina for ... he had left this open ended and would have to decide how long to continue searching once he got there. He sent Miriam a copy of his itinerary with a note saying that he had to get the whole thing out of his system and hoping to see her again very soon once he was back. Unable to think of the right words, he did not mention his invitation for her to accompany him to her again.

One evening, just before he was due to depart, he met Richard at the pub down at Heybridge Basin for supper. They sat outside overlooking the river, though the tide was out and no boats were moving. Water trickled into the lock through leaks in the old wooden gates. Richard and his wife had been to Thailand the previous year and he had offered advice about the trip, not just recommending the hotel in Bangkok, which Philip had booked even though it was, by his standards, quite expensive, but also about getting about, the sights to see and a reminder to buy nothing without bartering and to avoid eating the smallest chillies which were, Richard assured him, always the hottest.

"You'll love it, never mind about this Michael character, it's a great place for a holiday. Bangkok is fantastic: though you need to plan what you do; don't end up spending hours in the traffic, the city is incredibly congested. But you'll be staying near the river and many sights are easily accessible from there – you can travel in style along the river. Also the hotel has a shuttle boat that goes across the river to the nearest Skytrain station; that's great, cheap and easy to use and you can look down on the traffic from high above the streets."

He was enthusiasm personified about it all and had even brought some photographs. Philip looked at temples with soaring red and gold roofs, markets and the beach where his friends had ended their trip. He tried, somewhat unsuccessfully, to forget Miriam's message declining to accompany him but he also kept thinking about Phuket and what he might find there. Or not find. But the photo of Michael leading him there had been taken so long ago, he had to realise finding him now was a longshot, a very long longshot, and not allow himself to succumb to any unreasonable optimism.

"The food there's great too. Have you eaten Thai food?"

Philip was miles away.

"Philip ... where are you? I said the food's great and I wondered if you had eaten it before."

"Sorry, just thinking ahead about the trip, and yes, in fact I had a Thai meal not so long ago, at that restaurant at the top of the High Street. Do you know it?"

"Yes, we went there soon after the holiday. It's good, though it's not the cheapest place you could eat at, but I always thought of you as more of a pub grub man or ... hey wait a minute, going to a place like that, I bet you were with someone. Am I right?"

"It was just a friend, I ..." Philip's voice tailed off into silence; he certainly wasn't about to get into discussing the situation with Miriam just after she had declined his proposal about the trip to Thailand.

"Just a friend, eh? Okay, I can see you aren't going to say any more, but I hope she's nice. You deserve it. You've had a tough time. Talking of deserving it there's one thing I wanted to tell you. I've thought about this, it's really none of my business and I shouldn't even know about it myself, but ..." Richard paused.

"What on earth are you going on about?" said Philip.

"Well, promise you won't repeat this, and promise you won't say I told you about ..."

"How can I tell anyone if I don't repeat it?" Philip interrupted.

"You know what I mean. Anyway I thought long and hard about this and I think you should know even if the outcome is disappointing."

Philip interrupted him again, his tone now impatient, "For goodness sake, what is it? Get to the point will you!"

"Okay, the thing is ... your old lady left you some money, or rather she intended to leave you some money. My colleagues found a codicil in her house, you know a sort of extra addition to her will, but sadly there is still no sign of any actual will ... and, as I understand it, that makes the codicil invalid. Sorry. No money then, but they say it's the thought that counts. Seriously she must have really valued what you did for her and, now she can't tell you herself, I thought you should know that."

Philip's eyes widened and his face registered considerable surprise. "But I didn't even do much. I only knew her for a few months. But I did like her."

"Never mind, she obviously liked you and was grateful for what you did. Don't you want to know how much money it would have been?"

"Well, if what you say is right then there's really no point is there?" He paused. "All right, go on then, how much? I assume you know the amount if you're saying that."

"It was £10,000, no less."

Philip was shocked. He was sure Abigail must have been comfortably off but, even so, it was still a lot of money, way beyond his immediate expectations, but there seemed no more to be said about it in the circumstances. So he settled for a simple "Right", his voice trailing off into silence at the end of the word. They ate their meal and talked of other things, then walked back along the canal to where Richard had parked his car.

Richard left Philip with a cheery "Have a good time - and good luck!"

꘎

On the morning of his departure he got up early and packed his things, most of which he had laid out the night before. He ate a quick breakfast and waited for the taxi he had ordered to get him to Heathrow.

He had had a busy last day at the library, including a difficult exchange with a woman who had insisted it was wholly reasonable that he should look after her two children – a rambunctious pair of about five or six years old – for a few minutes while she "popped over the road to Boots", where apparently she "only needed a few things and would be back in a tick". She took the politely put news that they were not in fact a crèche badly, quickly got belligerent and

167

threatened to cancel her library membership. Philip was strong on the library being a community service, but wondered if perhaps there were some local residents who might benefit others by not using the library. She was one member he would be glad not to see for a while, though it seemed odd knowing he would be away for more than just a day or two; he had not had a long break for what seemed like an age.

Back home at his desk he switched on his telephone answering machine and put a paper weight on a pile of personal papers. As he did so he noticed the letter from the Treasury Solicitor's office amongst the bills, circulars and other detritus of his filing. After their unenthusiastic reply to his mentioning Mac he had forgotten all about them. No one there knew about the photo he had found or that it seemed to suggest evidence of Michael being in Thailand, and he wondered for a moment if he should tell them, but decided, sod it, they did not seem to find the information he had given them of any use, let them wait, maybe there would be something useful to tell them when he got back. Right now all the evidence, if you could call it that, was tenuous at best. If he found out no more on his trip it would change nothing. But just in case he pushed the letter into his flight bag so that he had the contact details with him as he travelled if he needed them. Was doing this an act of wholly unjustified optimism he asked himself? He didn't know. A car horn sounded in the road outside and he grabbed his bags and went out to find the taxi.

The journey to Heathrow, not one he did more than once in a while, was stressful. On London's infamous ring road, the M25, the traffic was appalling, with stretches where road works limited the traffic to fifty miles per hour – well, through which even going as much as fifty was impossible - and many places where the traffic stopped altogether. He began to think he would be late, but despite the traffic they arrived at Terminal 3 with a little time to spare before check in began. He found his way - there were people everywhere -

168

and a small queue had already formed at the designated counter. He checked in in due course and went through airside.

It all seemed to take an age and, once through, he avoided the shops: he already had a book, a paperback rather than a heavy library tome, so he sat drinking coffee and wondering: perhaps the whole venture was just plain stupid. At that precise moment he was pretty sure it was and almost regretted his impulsive decision to go, but he consoled himself with the thought that this was his first real break for an age. In the last couple of years he had to admit to himself that he had been in something of a rut, but now this Abigail business had given him something fresh to concentrate on. Whatever happened he would see some sights and get a bit of sun. He and Penny had always enjoyed travelling together, never that elaborately but on a well-planned basis and usually to a destination where there was something to see rather than just a beach. Their last holiday together had been to Venice. Recalling it gave him mixed feelings: it was a lovely holiday, but it also brought back sad memories as it was the last such trip they made together.

Nevertheless, her death was a while ago now, and the hurt had faded. He still found himself wishing that Miriam had decided to come too; he could not remember how long it was since he had embarked on a holiday journey alone. He nearly phoned her, though he knew her phone would be switched off as it always was while she worked, but he stopped the thought; he still felt her saying no to joining him might well be a rejection. He had thought things were going well between them. The evidence was that she enjoyed his company and then there was the kiss in her flat, which was surely a good sign. But even so her decision had dented his sparse confidence and now he still wondered about it a little. He would no doubt discover on his return, and then they'd see. He certainly wanted the outcome to be favourable.

The time soon passed and he was finally on the plane, and in the air.

He heard a rustle of silk at his side.

"Can I get you a drink?"

The hostess, dressed immaculately in a colourful uniform, smiled down at him. Thailand was famous for that – the land of smiles it was called. He thanked her and ordered a soft drink; soon a meal was served. This was dinner he told himself, putting the setting of his watch forward to Thai time and settling in for the long flight. He settled down and found that he slept much better than he thought he would. Breakfast was served an hour and a half before landing, but he ate little; he just wanted the tedious flight to be over and to get to the hotel. He filled in his landing card then dozed briefly again and was then startled by the announcement that they were about to land.

He disembarked and found a long walk ahead to passport control, but he was amongst the first passengers off the plane, it was still early in the morning and the queue when he arrived there was not too bad. He shuffled forward, watching passengers presenting their passports and having them checked by the rather military looking officials in glass-fronted boxes ranged in line across the huge, lofty steel-strutted hall. Each passenger had to remain still as a small camera recorded their entry into the Kingdom. It must create quite a portrait gallery, thought Philip: he recalled hearing it said that if you ever found that you looked like your passport photo then you were too ill to travel. Add a measure of jet lag to the mix - the time here was seven hours in advance of home - and in such circumstances no one was going to look at their best. He chuckled to himself and, looking ahead, estimated that it would take some ten or fifteen minutes for him to get to the front of the queue. He opened the zip on his flight bag and reached inside for his book. He stood reading, pushing his bag forward a little along the floor as the queue shuffled slowly forward. Reading engaged him and he was startled when suddenly someone touched his arm and a voice spoke over his shoulder:

"Philip, there you are, I was towards the back of the plane, I was worried I wouldn't catch you before you went through, oh, and ... good morning!"

He spun round in amazement to see Miriam smiling at him. He was virtually speechless.

"How ... What ... I mean, how lovely, but how?"

Miriam hugged him and gave him a kiss.

"I really thought my coming would be impossible. I was in court in London the morning of the flight and went straight from there to the airport. I only just made it. I got allocated a seat close to the back of the plane and only reached the gate when most passengers, including you, were already on board. You were on the other aisle as I went by – your head in a book, what a surprise. You didn't look up and I was being hurried along by people behind me. When I got to my seat I fully intended to get up and speak to you once we were airborne, but the plane seemed full and if we couldn't organise seats together standing in the aisle felt as if it would waste the moment - so then I thought this would be the best moment to spring the surprise. Anyway, after all that, I do hope you're pleased to see me."

The queue had been edging forward as she spoke and Philip just had time to say "Yes, not half!" and then had to usher her forward to have her passport stamped.

He followed in his turn and they went together to find their cases. The carousel number for their flight was displayed on screens above their heads. Both of them changed some pounds into Thai currency, Baht, and when they had claimed their suitcases they hurried to find a taxi to take them to Philip's hotel. The driver was a young man, impassive behind dark glasses, wearing a tee-shirt and jeans. The boot contained a huge, cylindrical tank of liquid gas fuel and had room for only one suitcase. With the other propped on the front passenger seat, they climbed into the back and were soon heading off out of the airport. Remembering Richard's advice, Philip checked that the taxi driver had switched on the meter. He had.

As Miriam slipped her arm through his, Philip could hardly believe what had just happened. If she had meant to surprise him, she had certainly done that.

"You … well, what a surprise" he said. "But what a very good one!"

CHAPTER SEVENTEEN
Arrival and explorations

The doctor says it should cause no big problem, but there is a weakness in my heart. It's one of the reasons I get breathless and can't walk too far. I feel fine really, but I guess I am getting on – age sort of catches up with you unawares. I'll need to take some pills and have a check-up regularly now, but all being well he says I should be good for a few more years yet.

I can't complain really. James was the one, unfair he died so young. But I must be realistic. I know it's something that might just cause problems at any time. I have loose ends I'd like to settle. I will finish that letter to Philip. I'm sure he'll help. I'll send it, I really will, before it's too late. I'm sure Mac would think that's right.

They swept along the broad expressway that started the journey into the city taking in the alien scenery they passed; twice the driver pulled up to pay at toll points. Richard had briefed Philip about this – you had to make sure a taxi into the town took the fast route, well faster. Bangkok's traffic was notorious and if a taxi driver thought a passenger would not be prepared to pay the toll fee then they would go another, slower, route. After about forty minutes they were off the expressway and onto ordinary roads and progress became slower.

There was traffic of all sorts: cars, trucks, taxis and also tuc-tucs, Thailand's ubiquitous people carrier; these looked like motor bikes at the front with a flat platform at the back for the awning-covered passenger seat. They were noisy, the unique rat-a-tat-tat sound no doubt giving them their name. Like the numerous motor bikes that swerved in and out of the traffic many were loaded to absurd levels. They saw one with six people on and an uncountable number of packages too.

Motor bikes often had a man on the front and a girl on the back, mostly the girls sat side-saddle, and a few carried more than two people. They saw one bike on which the passenger was doing her eye make-up as she went along and several talking animatedly on mobile phones. Other bikes carried massive cargo, including piles of fruit, dead chickens hanging from poles and in one case a tower of eggs stacked on trays behind the rider with the whole pile rising higher than his head.

This last one had them both pointing and laughing with Philip saying, "Omelettes to come, I think," as they sped past.

Miriam was wide-eyed at it all and replied, "It makes Maldon High Street seem a little tame, doesn't it?" Philip nodded.

The roads were lined with shops and buildings of every description, the pavements were busy with people and wheeled stalls: some of them were effectively mobile kitchens selling food and sending smoke up into the sky. Fascinated by the vibrancy of all this they found another quarter of an hour had flashed by and then, before they knew it, they were at their hotel, the taxi driving up a steep ramp to the reception entrance on the first floor and a smart doorman hurrying forward to open the door, see them in and look after the luggage. The heat hit them as they stepped out of the air-conditioned taxi. The hotel lobby area was cool, large and stylish, with décor that was distinctively eastern and restful; once inside Philip found a seat for Miriam.

"Let me have your passport and I'll sort out rooms; I need to book a second one," said Philip, some of the implications of her surprise arrival only now just dawning on him.

"That's ... right, yes, okay." She sat on one of the sofas dotted around, opened her bag and handed over her passport.

"You wait. Back in a moment, though we are probably too early to get into our rooms straight away. I'll sort things out and then do you fancy breakfast? We do need to persuade ourselves it's morning."

"Fine."

Like Philip, Miriam had eaten little on the plane and was now feeling distinctly hungry.

Philip went across to reception and was greeted with a smile by one of the reception staff, a lady who, exotic to his eyes, was dressed in a beautiful silk outfit, which nevertheless seemed to constitute a uniform here. He had been right, it was still too early to get into rooms, check-in time was not until the middle of the day, but they were able to have keys at 11 o'clock – "Bit early, no problem," he was told. He was able to book a second room; much as he would have liked to share he felt he could not just assume that Miriam would too and it did not seem to be a question to broach in public in the hotel lobby. The porter would look after their luggage for the moment. He went back to Miriam and explained.

"Okay, but I feel I look dreadful. I must look such a sight after the flight," she said.

"Not at all, you look great. I'm worse, I'm sure, unshaven and travel-worn. You can shower when we get rooms, meantime let's catch up and have a good breakfast. Do you want a quick stop off first? It's this way." He pointed in the direction the receptionist had indicated.

The restrooms had wooden figures on their doors to differentiate between men and women. Inside he found a burner warming lemongrass oil and sending a pleasant yet unfamiliar smell into the air. They met up outside and Philip led the way down one floor to where the receptionist had explained that a buffet breakfast was served in a room alongside a terrace and by the river.

Before they sat down they walked across to the wall of the terrace, which overlooked the water. Sunlight sparkled on the surface. The river – the Chao Phraya - was wide and fast, with many boats heading up and down. These ranged from tiny one-person boats to a barge "train", a string of seven or eight huge heavily loaded barges being towed in line behind what seemed an absurdly small motor launch as the water lapped their gunnels. The city's skyline of towering buildings ranged along the river banks towards where the river flowed out from the city to the sea.

"What a river. It's stunning isn't it?" said Philip.

"Sure is. And so different too – I've not seen a yellow-brick road, but we're certainly not in Kansas anymore!" Miriam smiled, continuing, "And although our being here has a serious purpose, this might just be fun too."

They lingered over breakfast, the biggest buffet spread either of them had ever seen. They both ate well, going back for a second helping of fresh cooked waffles, something that, as Philip said, "is sadly not on my regular breakfast menu."

After breakfast they explored their immediate surroundings, first circling the pool area before going back indoors. The hotel had several restaurants and behind the hotel was a shopping plaza, two floors of shops: some smart – selling jewellery and silk carpets and the like – some just routine – a discount fashion shop, various restaurants, even a Boots the chemist. Spread along the central aisle of the lower floor were arrayed a variety of market stalls, selling everything from soaps and oils to bags and bangles. Beyond the U-shaped shopping centre was an open area for parking and more market stalls.

They looked at the menu outside a small Thai restaurant beyond the market stalls. It looked simple, but very pleasant.

"This might be somewhere nice to eat this evening, get us into the local food; more reasonable than the hotel too, I expect," said Miriam. Both of them were thinking that after a huge buffet breakfast they would not need to eat much more until the evening.

Soon it was the time when they could get into their rooms. After they had unpacked and cleaned up they met back on the river terrace and sat watching the view.

"Let's work out a short trip," said Philip. "We want to make the most of our time here. What do you fancy?"

Miriam thought for a moment and then said, "The Grand Palace seems to be the top attraction. Let's go there and then do something different tomorrow."

Philip agreed. "It's just along the river," he said.

They took the hotel shuttle boat to the other side of the river, where they hired a long-tail boat, a long, low, narrow craft with an awning above, a huge outboard motor and a long "tail", a pole with the propeller on it at the rear, the latter evidently able to avoid the greenery, water hyacinth, great clumps of which dotted the river and moved along with the current. Their boat took them up river to the landing stage near the famous Grand Palace, top of the list of must-see sights in the city. The low seats meant that the boat was not the most comfortable thing in the world, but it went at a great rate, throwing up clouds of spray and leaving slower craft far behind in its wake. The river scene was vibrant, giving them a first taste of this exotic city, and the journey was exhilarating.

"Richard said that we were bound to be told the palace was closed and to ignore what is just a tout's ploy to get people to take a taxi ride to a nearby shop," said Philip. No sooner were they off the boat than this proved to be the case as various drivers came forward from tuc-tucs to persuade them away from their goal. They stepped out, moving quickly to leave them behind, soon slowing as they found that moving slowly and steadily was essential in the humid climate. Inside, they found that the palace grounds were extensive and both beautiful and interesting. They knew that Thailand had long been a monarchy, indeed the elderly king is virtually revered by the population and the royal history quite clearly included lavish expenditure on real estate - the palace buildings and grounds were stunning. They paid to have a guide show them round and found that the uncharacteristically fat Thai lady, Jackie, who was pushy enough to get the job, was a delight: enthusiastic, well informed and funny. She paused at one point asking if they wanted the happy room.

"What's that?" asked Miriam.

"Make you happy, make you unhappy if you need and cannot find," she explained: she was describing the toilet! Their guide smiled broadly at their momentary confusion, then waited patiently for them to re-join her.

At the end of the tour she told them how to locate the right waterbus to get back to the pier they had started out from.

Back at the hotel they spent some time relaxing by the hotel's pool. The low-rise hotel was in three blocks surrounding the pool and gardens in a large U-shaped garden area facing the river. The water in the pool was warm and they both swam, then lazed under the palm trees surrounding the pool. Suddenly Philip panicked:

"Heavens, what about your onward flight! We need to get you a ticket to the island."

"Not necessary," replied Miriam. "I booked it with the London leg. You gave me a copy of your itinerary, remember? I just booked the one you are on."

She then produced from her bag the Patricia Scanlan book Philip had belatedly given her for her birthday, prompting Philip to comment, "Fancy bringing a huge hardback in your luggage."

"It's a holiday remember, I have to have something I am really looking forward to reading for that. Never mind the weight. I'm sure this will be good. Besides it was a present." Miriam opened it as she spoke, but before they settled to reading they talked together of their coming visit to Phuket and Philip tried his best to sound matter-of-fact about it.

"It's a great place to go, I think, so even if we don't find Michael, then we should have a nice break." But secretly as the visit got nearer he was keeping his fingers more and more tightly crossed.

He continued: "Abigail really was such a dear. I'd like to think we could do something for her, even now. I discovered something really surprising about her just before I left. My friend Richard heard tell of it - he works for Maldon Council. He probably shouldn't have told me, so do keep this to yourself. She left me some money, well ... that is she didn't ... well, I mean she wanted to. I'm not putting this very well. They found a codicil to her will. It's quite recent - it had to be, I hadn't known her long - but ... anyway, as it turns out it has no validity as there's no sign of any will. No will, no money for me."

"Well, it's still nice to know what she thought and I'm glad to hear that you know what she intended, even if I have to arrest this Richard for betraying Council secrets when we get back. You obviously meant a lot to her. Do you mind me asking, how much would it have been?"

"£10,000, no less – and that would have been very nice, though I did little enough for her really, so the amount also seems absurd. But anyway as it turns out I get nothing, just my friend arrested."

Miriam let out a low breath. "Wow, it's a tidy sum, or would have been. What a shame."

They had an early supper in the Thai restaurant they had found behind the hotel, after which they were both flagging from the long journey and the jet lag. Tired, and with drinks with the meal accelerating their desire for sleep, they arranged a time to meet in the morning and opted for an early night. It had been a pleasant day and Philip could still hardly believe what Miriam had done. The memory of the moment that they had met in the arrival hall would certainly stay with him for quite a while.

Miriam woke first. It was early, but despite the time change she really felt it was morning and she couldn't wait to see more of her new surroundings. They had arranged to meet for breakfast at eight o'clock, but Miriam was up and dressed and walking through the garden at the back of the hotel before seven o'clock. She found a chair under a small pagoda-like structure on the river's edge and sat watching boats come and go – everything from the classic Thai long tail boats to water buses, sweeping along at speed, and the huge barges towed in long lines behind seemingly too small motor boats. The sun had yet to reach its full heat and it was still comparatively cool; the early morning light shone on the water. She revelled in this new place. They had a whole day for sightseeing before setting off to Phuket, but first she had a small 'errand' to run. She had thought long and hard about it; it seemed right and the exotic location and atmosphere gave her an air of excitement. Emboldened, she went up to the reception area before meeting Philip for breakfast.

"You're looking bright-eyed and bushy-tailed," he said, when he found Miriam already seated at a table just inside the breakfast area. "What time did you wake?" He kissed her on the cheek before he sat down.

"Soon after six - still getting used to the time, I guess, though I feel fine. I've been sitting watching the river. Come on, it's a buffet, remember – we have to help ourselves."

They ate a hearty breakfast and set off for the day's sightseeing. Philip suggested several visits he felt they would both enjoy and which would allow them to go on their way to Phuket feeling they had at least seen something of the city. Again Philip dwelt on Miriam's mindboggling surprise appearance at the airport, wondering just what it boded for the future. Meantime, he was just happy at the prospect of their spending more time together. It promised to be a good day.

CHAPTER EIGHTEEN
Taking a break

Meeting Philip has made such a difference to my life – and all from that silly whistling trick. I see him regularly and his visits are as important to me as the books he ferries to and from the library for me. He has given my reading habits a shake up too; he's recommended titles I would never have come across or selected – the one I'm reading at the moment is very good.

It paints such a clear picture of life just after the First World War and the heroine, who gives her name to the book, Maisie Dobbs, is both totally believable and a clear creation: a strong woman character. I love a good mystery, and this is that, but it has a light touch too – difficult to describe, which is just what I told Philip I enjoy.

It's the reading group this week too, another book to finish, I have enjoyed going to that. I don't think he realises just how important he has become to me; though they are so different he reminds me just a little of Mac.

"We could try to change flights and move straight on to Phuket if you want," offered Miriam, but Philip immediately rejected the idea.

"No, we have the whole day for sightseeing," said Philip, putting down his tea. "It would be complicated to change things and besides it's so nice just to be spending time with you. We deserve a break so let's just enjoy the day   "Fine." Miriam had made no attempt to change his mind and Philip became quickly convinced that her offer had not been made just to be nice. They had both enjoyed having another leisurely breakfast in the hotel. Philip always found that the completely different start to a day on holiday, and the lack of any rush compared with a normal working day at home, was one high amongst its pleasures.

For a day they could put all wondering about what lay ahead once they reached Phuket on one side. Miriam knew little of Thailand and was happy to let Philip, who had at least had the advantage of chatting to Richard about it, make suggestions as to what they should do. It was Saturday and so Philip felt that an obvious choice was to visit Chatuchak Market, Bangkok's famous weekend market. Despite his eagerness to get to Phuket and possibly to Michael, Philip was also keen to spend time with Miriam getting to know her better. At breakfast he had made things clear.

"Right, I promise to stop going on about Michael and what might happen in Phuket for a bit and concentrate on exploring somewhere new. This is supposed to be a holiday, after all."

"I agree, and I'll remember you said that," said Miriam, adding, "So, what's next?" She was evidently expecting Philip to take the lead.

"I have just the place for you – fancy some shopping?" he said, going on to explain about the market.

After checking directions at Reception and then a pleasant run in the hotel shuttle boat - a junk-style craft with a rounded awning to keep the sun off its passengers and seats around the sides for maybe thirty or forty people - that gave them twenty minutes or so to take in the scenery, they went ashore and climbed the steep steps beyond to the Skytrain station. They bought tickets, finding the necessary coins for the ticket machines and expressing fascination to each other about the sensible system of reusable plastic tickets which would be sucked away into the ticket machine as they disembarked at their destination. Having double checked that they were catching a train going in the right direction, they

185

set off. The carriages were quite full of people, but they were air-conditioned and the train progressed quickly. Looking down on the busy streets it seemed it was very much the way to travel.

"What a great service," said Philip "I know the city is too low lying for an underground railway, but just imagine the chaos on the roads while this lot was being built. Just as well it turned out so well."

They had to change to a different line at Siam Square, where the station led out into huge multi-story shopping centres, but this was easily done and they were soon at their destination. Before going down the steps to the market they looked out across the huge area of the market.

"Just look at that," said Miriam. "It's unbelievably large."

"The guidebook said there were around six thousand stalls spread over an area the size of five football pitches ... and that looks about right," replied Philip as they made their way down the long flight of steps. Once at ground level they picked an entrance at random.

The covered aisles between the stalls were narrow and it was low too in places - they had to duck regularly to miss goods hanging up on display in front of stalls - and the grid of little "streets" was not entirely regular so it was difficult to keep track of where they were. People around them seemed to move slowly, weaving between each other with no pushing and shoving. Sometimes stalls selling similar things were located together, but mainly there was no total order. It was clearly a popular spot and there were plenty of people buying and selling. Miriam quickly fell into shopping mode and began to investigate the various wares. Stallholders sometimes lacked good English and this prevented them answering at length. But other people helped, and there always seemed to be someone on a stall nearby who spoke sufficient English and who rushed over to assist. Richard had told Philip that prices here were definitely less than in the city itself, and certainly things seemed good value – though bargaining was expected and they found that this brought prices down still more.

"This is truly amazing: if I had thought of the largest market imaginable, doubled it and doubled it again ten times, then ignored any order that might have come to mind, invested it with a measure of chaos, an appealing hubbub and some exotic smells then I might have begun to get close. In fact when I read about this place I hadn't imagined anything even close, so it's all utterly surprising!" And the surprise sounded in Miriam's voice. Philip was pleased. He hoped very much that Miriam would enjoy the day, and the whole trip.

The stalls sold a bewildering range of goods, everything from fresh food and fruit to antiques, household products, textiles and clothes. They wandered, they got lost, they looked at everything and Miriam spent what seemed to Philip like an age comparing the colours, designs and styles of a variety of goods. One stall holder seemed endlessly patient, unfolding scarves and holding them up until a final decision was made. Then the process began again with bags to find a match that Miriam found acceptable. Finally she bought a silk bag and several scarves; several because as she explained the price was better that way.

"You mean you spent more than just one would have cost!" said Philip logically, thinking that it was an unarguable fact of life that men and women shopped in totally different ways. The wandered on.

Almost everyone they saw in the market was Thai, though just a few tourists and other farang mingled with them. At one point they overheard a thirty-something couple, a Thai girl and a European man, apparently arguing.

"You go. Go away, go away," she said emphatically, waving her arms about, and initially he protested. She persisted and explained: "Go away while I buy, do not want farang price."

He duly wandered off and hid while she negotiated on her own and no doubt made a better purchase.

Philip said, "Maybe we should recruit a Thai helper to get the best prices." Some things were not solely for sale either: you could choose the fabric for curtains, for instance, and come back to collect them when they were made up in the size and design you specified. You could buy some oddball things too. They saw Siamese fighting fish in what looked like sweet jars, and there were a variety of animals, not just those you might expect, like puppies, but also wild birds, reptiles and snakes – the latter drawing a shudder and a gasp from Miriam as she rapidly moved on.

"I'm not surprised it's so busy, you can buy anything here," said Miriam. "And it's not just tourist stuff."

"I bet it includes some things that are illegal though," said Philip, adding, "Where's a policeman when you want one?"

Miriam smiled and replied, "I'm certainly out of my jurisdiction here, thanks very much, and off duty too."

She took his arm. As they walked on they found that those stallholders who could speak English called out a variety of suggestions to them: "Happy hour – buy one, get one free" – "Best price this year" – or they just named what was on offer: "Tee shirt", "Many scarf, all silk", "Shirt for you". On the other hand, at a small number of stalls they saw no business was being done and the owner was curled up sound asleep in a chair behind their display. Well, it was a very warm day. It was hot work just walking up and down the aisles.

"What about a drink?" asked Philip. Miriam agreed.

"Let's see what we can find," Philip said.

They made their way to the far side of the market, and found an area where stalls were selling food and drink. Most stalls had no seats, but as they walked further on they found one that did. A cold drink was welcome, and they perched on two miniscule child-size stools for a while and indulged in a little people-watching.

Presently Miriam noticed that a young man, sitting at a table a little way off, seemed to be looking at them. He was drinking a coke and reading from the top of a pile of newspapers and magazines.

"Look over there," she said in a stage whisper. "That guy's clearly watching us, maybe we're being followed."

"Or perhaps you're paranoid," replied Philip. "Or do you see potential crime everywhere? Though I guess we would be easy to follow," he added, "we do rather stand out, you know. There are not so many foreigners here."

As he spoke the young man got up and came over. "Please can you help," he said smiling, "I want learn English and have problem." He held out a magazine with many words ringed in red ink. "What these words mean, please?" he asked.

Not a gangster then, he just wanted to practice his English. Philip signalled that he should sit down. Gop, as he said they were to call him, presumably in lieu of another impossibly long name, was a student at university studying some sort of science subject, but he explained that he wanted to travel and ultimately to work abroad and he knew he must learn good English if he was to do that. They spent half an hour or so chatting with him, and helping him to define the ringed words in his magazine to extend his vocabulary a little, before he went on his way with a cheery goodbye.

Revived by a cold drink and a break, they walked around some more.

"It's hard to imagine that there's another such market anywhere in the world with a better range of goods or a more beguiling atmosphere," said Philip.

"I agree," said Miriam. "I just wish I had more space in my luggage. So many things are too large to take home. I love the ceramics, the furniture, the baskets ... it's a great place. You're a good guide you know, I can't think of anyone better to be in Bangkok with. This is fun."

"Thanks for that," replied Philip. "But we can't stay here all day long, there are other things to see. You ready to move on?"

"Okay." She said, reluctantly, preparing to leave this shoppers' paradise.

"Richard told me of a place that makes for a less obvious visit; it's called Vimanmek Mansion. I looked it up and it does seem interesting. So, after seeing the Grand Palace, which is probably the most popular place to see, are you up for visiting something a little more off the beaten track?"

"Sure. Is it far?"

"Not really and again it's within reach of the river so we can begin with a boat ride, but let's be sure. We'll go back on the train to the river first."

As they reached street level from the train, Philip took Miriam's hand and guided her to a taxi, speaking to the driver without her being able to hear.

"Where are we going now?" she asked, but he only shook his head and said "You'll see."

After only a few minutes they pulled into a hotel forecourt. Philip gave the driver some Baht and they climbed out.

"Well?" Miriam wanted an explanation.

"This is the famous Oriental Hotel," said Philip. "I'm told it's well worth a look and we can get directions at the desk."

They took a few minutes to look at the stunning reception area, hung with huge lanterns, and then walked through to the famous Authors' Lounge, a cool, elegant space filled with white wicker furniture, and outside onto the river terrace.

"Goodness knows what it must cost to stay here," said Philip. "But it's certainly something to see."

The people at Reception were very helpful and a smartly uniformed young man confirmed that, from the hotel, Vimanmek could be reached by getting a boat along the river to a spot a few piers further upstream beyond the Grand Palace. Then they would need to take a taxi for only a manageable distance to complete the journey to the Mansion.

"The boat yesterday was fun, but it was hardly the most comfortable form of transport in the world. Let's see if we can get something else." Miriam was in practical mode.

After further consultation at the desk they were assured this was possible and a little while later they were at the public pier alongside the hotel and stepping into a short, awning- covered boat in which there were real seats rather than low benches. It had a plump, hump-backed look, very eastern in style.

"This is just great," said Miriam. "It's slower than the long-tail boats, but you have time to take in the view. It's more comfortable on the bum too!" She smiled and they both watched the activities ashore as they went along. The river was well used and a profusion of boats were around. More than one long-tail boat went by them in one direction or the other throwing up a shower of spray that had them ducking for cover.

"Just one thing." Philip spoke slowly, then hesitated "About Michael, I mean ..."

Miriam silenced him with a withering look. "You promised" she said with finality as they were both distracted by the boatwoman manoeuvring to a halt alongside a similar boat coming down the river in the opposite direction. It had another woman at the helm and as the two engaged in a chat they saw their lady collect a wicker basket containing what proved to be her lunch from her friend. If they understood her explanation correctly - she spoke little English - the two took turns to prepare food, then had to make sure their different journeys up and down the river coincided so that they could meet and neither one went hungry.

Miriam approved of the arrangement. "What a neat idea," she said. "Trust a woman to think of that."

Philip ignored the quip.

They arrived at the appropriate pier, clambered back on shore, found a taxi, and soon they were pulling into the grounds and walking to the Mansion. It was a striking building: large, imposing and incredibly pleasing in warm, weathered teak wood; it was three stories high and had an attractive red-tiled roof.

"This is lovely," said Miriam, pleasing Philip by suggesting that his research might be leading to a successful outing. They paid the minimal entry fee - such things seemed really inexpensive in the city - walked up the steps to the imposing entrance and had to wait five minutes for the next scheduled English language tour. Evidently no one could walk round alone here, they discovered, so information came as part of the deal.

"It's reputed to be the largest teakwood structure in the world," said Philip as their guide arrived, a lady dressed in a plain, almost military-style uniform, and they joined a group of English speakers on the next tour.

Their guide was a stickler for detail and her description soon showed that the place proved to have a curious history.

From 1906 to 1910 when he died, King Rama V lived in Chitrlada Palace. Ahead of this being completed he needed somewhere else to live for a while and arranged for the Munthatu Rattanaroj Residence in Chuthathuj Rachathan at Koh Sri Chang in Chonburi to be dismantled, brought to Bangkok and reassembled. It must have set someone a few problems as it is a building of considerable size. So it was re-erected in Dusit Gardens in 1901, this being an area of orchards and paddy fields, which the King had bought earlier, in 1897, and had laid out as gardens. Someone in the group asked about the cost of so doing but the guide simply smiled and said "Not known".

"Moving the entire building" said Philip, "what an undertaking, I bet it cost a bomb, but I guess what the King wanted he tended to get"

Miriam voiced agreement, then took the opportunity to whisper to Philip "You know I'm not going to remember any of these names."

The guide continued, telling them all that the King then lived in the building for five years until his new home was ready. Curiously during this time, apart from the king and his family only women were allowed in the Palace. For a while thereafter the Mansion was kept up well. Queen Consort Indharasaksaji lived there for a while after the King moved, but she too moved on following the King's death, with the Mansion then being used only as a storage place for items surplus to Royal requirements.

"Most of us make do with a loft or box room for such things, but royalty are evidently able to store their junk in much greater style," said Philip. "Imagine this whole building serving as no more than a large cupboard."

The guide continued her information download telling them that thereafter the place went right out of the Royal minds – "Some much forgetting," was the way she put it. Only in 1982 did Queen Sirikit rediscover the place, though

193

no particular reason was given as to why it should suddenly have come to mind again.

"Perhaps she finally needed something being stored here" said Philip, "when I broke my teapot a while back I had to retrieve an old one from the attic."

Miriam giggled and shushed him as the guide continued, explaining that then, with the current King's blessing, the Queen arranged for it to be renovated and turned into a museum commemorating King Rama V by displaying his personal photographs, art and handicraft items. She saw it as a showcase of Thai heritage, open for all to see and to view its collection of silverware, ceramics, crystal ware, ivory, pictures and artefacts from around the world. Other items were displayed too, and such included an old manual typewriter because, the guide explained, "It was first machine to use Thai alphabet."

"It must be a special machine," said Philip. "If I remember right then the Thai alphabet is some 45 letters long."

They found it was a fascinating place. First, in terms of the individual items displayed, much of it, like tableware from England and France, from overseas, and secondly as a building. It boggled their minds to think of it being dismantled and moved to its present site. Unlike so many such places, which have been set up as museums in a way that makes it difficult to imagine them in use - in this case as a home – they found it seemed very real. As they went along the corridor that ran round much of the outer edge of the building, once an open veranda to protect the rooms from the sun and heat, the sensitively made arrangements were very much apparent.

"You know it's very easy to imagine life going on here when it was a palace." Philip commented, prompting a nod and a smile from Miriam. He found her smile pleased him enormously.

The rooms they were shown through still looked much as they must have done when the Mansion was occupied. There was a music room, an audience chamber and other public rooms as well as the Royal apartments, which were housed in the octagonal part of the building. All was set out pretty much as it used to be, right down to the King's bathroom.

"It's as if he was here yesterday," said Miriam. "Though he does seem to have taken his toothbrush away with him."

The wooden building itself was impressive, and the guide pointed out how it was constructed entirely without nails using only wooden pegs to pin the timber together.

"I suppose that helped make it easier to dismantle the building in order to transport it across the country," said Miriam, "though the more we see the more enormous that task seems."

The overall look of the place had an elaborate, western influenced style. The shining teak floors showed the result of regular polishing over many years. They had a rich sheen that looked as smooth as a mirror, and everywhere the view outside was of beautiful gardens. In the early nineteen hundreds this must have been a tranquil spot.

"What about a drink next?" said Philip and Miriam readily agreed; after the tour they had lingered, first strolling in the grounds, then wandering slowly in the heat until this was the obvious next step.

"I wonder if Michael came here or did any sightseeing in Bangkok," said Philip as they sat in a small cafe. "As far as we know he had not travelled much and he was young; this place must have been a culture shock."

Again Miriam quickly diverted him. "I dare say, but remember you promised to forget all about that for today. That was a good tour, wasn't it? Imagine a time when the King could simply snap his fingers and an entire building

195

could be moved half way across the country on a whim. It's mind boggling."

They reviewed their day to date and, after a snack, they were ready to move on and again Miriam wanted to know what was next.

"I thought we might go and see Jim Thompson's house," said Philip, "it seems appropriate given our mission," he explained. "That's the name of that shop in the hotel lobby. What do you mean?" Miriam queried.

"Well, you know how much you love the Thai silk we've seen?"

Miriam nodded enthusiastically.

"Well, Jim Thompson was an American businessman who was first to set up silk production in Thailand on a large scale commercial basis. His house is a traditional Thai wooden place, very typical of how people lived here years ago, well people of means anyway, and it's now a museum."

"Sounds interesting, but why is it so appropriate for us?" Miriam queried.

"Dare I say this after you vetoed my last attempt to mention Michael? It's because the man simply disappeared. He was visiting Malaysia at the time and one day he went out for a walk in what was a wild area, jungle almost, he never came back - and he was never found. To this day no one knows what happened to him, he may just have got lost and died of exposure or it may have been foul play of some sort."

"Okay, I see what you mean, but let's hope nothing similar happened to Michael. You've been at that guide book again haven't you?" Miriam smiled and they set off to find the museum.

It was a real luxury for them both just to have time to wander without routine or worries about work. Jim Thompson's house proved a successful visit too, so too for Miriam did the shop alongside it, which was full of exotic silks: scarves, blouses and shirts, purses and much more. They took a break in the café before moving on and failed to resist a scone.

"This isn't very Thai, is it?" said Philip.

"Well, let's have a Thai meal this evening," Miriam replied and they set to planning the rest of their day. Philip agreed, thinking as he did so that not only was their sightseeing going well, but how much he was enjoying their simply being together.

↦

Finally they had caught the Skytrain again. When they reached the stop by the river they returned to the pier and waited for the hotel boat that would take them back to the hotel.

"I wonder what our chances are of finding Michael are?" Philip queried as they waited for the boat. He drew breath as if to go on, but Miriam held up a hand in mock horror.

"No, not yet," she said, "we agreed today was for us and it's not over yet, there's still ... no." Whatever she was going to say next was stillborn and, despite Philip's entreaties she would say no more. The arrival of the boat and another trip along the busy river put thoughts about Michael out of Philip's mind for a while.

Twenty minutes later the boat tied up at the hotel jetty. Just entering the hotel was enough to make them feel special: doors were held open, greetings exchanged and smiles splashed around with great abandon. The day's sightseeing done they found they had time to change before going to get some dinner and they went up in the lift towards their rooms together. Along the 3rd floor corridor Philip stopped at his room door. "See you in half an hour in the lobby," he said restating the dinner arrangement they had made earlier and inserting the key card into the door of his room. Miriam's room was further along the corridor and she walked on leaving him to go inside. The rooms were very well appointed, beautifully decorated and, as expected, provided a real treat. With Miriam having appeared unexpectedly as she had Philip had no qualms about having followed Richard's recommendation and booked this particular hotel, it was an unashamed treat for them both; though left alone he would no doubt have gone for something less expensive.

As he pushed open the door he could see that Housekeeping staff had visited and the room had been made up while they had been out sightseeing. But he immediately saw also that something inside had changed. The room looked different: opposite him in the space at the foot of the bed stood a suitcase; it was not his.

As he wondered what was going on he felt Miriam come into the room behind him. She put an arm around his neck and spoke close to his ear.

"I went to reception before breakfast and arranged for them to cancel the other room and move my stuff in here during the day. They thought it was a great idea, smiles galore it caused, so I hope you approve too. Do you have some space in your wardrobe?"

Philip was lost for words, but he turned towards her and, with only a tiny hesitation, he put his arms around her, drew her close and they kissed. As they parted he still said nothing, though his smile spoke volumes and hers warmed his heart.

"It seemed to me that it would have taken forever for you to suggest this. It is alright isn't it?"

Still stunned, Philip managed a brief, "Oh yes, yes of course." He resisted adding a "Not half!"

"Right then, I'm going to unpack properly – how long do we have before dinner?"

It was not really a question and she went straight on without pause, "However long it is I'm sure we can put it to good use, don't you think?"

Philip could only agree.

A while later as they both set off to get some dinner they had big smiles on their faces; Miriam was well pleased with her decision and both of them felt that the intervening time had indeed been put to very good use.

CHAPTER NINETEEN
More than a boat

I'm decided. I'm going to leave Philip some money. I won't tell him and anyway with luck he won't get it for a while, but I'll make the arrangement. How much is right, I wonder? A nice round figure of some sort, I'll think about it. It needs to be enough to act as a clear thank you. I won't need to redo my will, just a simple codicil will do the trick, I can't get Philip to type that up, that would give the game away and no mistake. I'll need it signed too. I've made some notes and I'll get it organised, then it can be put away safely with my will.

Now that I think about it I've no idea where my will is. I must think about that too.

1997 Thailand

Michael repeated his earlier comment: "I can't, I can't just buy a boat, certainly not here, not now, it's ... well, it's mad."

Jon was not going to let the matter rest: "I've not known you very long but I do know how much you love the sea, boats – everything to do with sailing, on the way here you didn't just sail "Footloose" you bonded with her, you made her your own."

"Well, I suppose so, she's a great boat that's for sure, but still ..." Michael's voice tailed off and he looked uncomfortable.

"She is. And that's not all. I have spent a good deal of time chatting with you on the way here, you know. As I understand it you've been marking time for a couple of years, working here, working there and spending your spare time sailing the family boat."

Michael protested: "I suppose so, but it's not so bad, it's fun and I like it."

"I'm sure you do, but it's not going anywhere is it? Would you truly call it a real job? Or a career? No? I don't think so – be honest, you know what you want to do in broad terms, but

201

you are not only nowhere near to doing it – what's more you have no real plans to get anywhere near doing it. Well, do you?"

Jon put a clear challenging emphasis on the last two words. Michael opened his mouth to protest at this blunt challenge, but Jon shushed him, his needling question clearly rhetorical, and continued apace.

"It's true, you know it's true, or everything you have been telling me while we made our way here has been nonsense. Now just think about it: you've nothing planned to get you what you want, you've no ties, the thing with Sam came to nothing so you said, and yet this gives you exactly want you want. It gives it to you in a moment: a job, well not just a job, the job, your own business, the way of life you want, a new start and a new home. You'd live comfortably here too, the cost of food is low, the climate's good, you don't need many clothes – come on, is this an opportunity or what?"

Michael was silent for some moments, as Jon just looked at him. He could see the sense of it, Jon was right to say it was a real opportunity, one that would never come again, but he still hesitated, it was also such a big step, a huge risk and not least a surprise; it was not what he had expected to happen on what he had seen simply as a short break. He knew there was an urgency involved too. Jon had to get back to Singapore, whatever he did about the boat he was clearly open to a deal right now while he saw Michael as his only immediate option, though another solution could come up, it seemed unlikely to do so at time soon.

"I don't know ..." Michael's paused, turning to put the kettle on and adding "Want a coffee?"

His question brought a brief "Okay."

Rattling the mugs Michael continued. "Anyway what would it cost?" He saw the question as much as delaying tactics as anything else, but Jon was quick to answer, he had clearly been thinking about the matter and saw the question as a step forward.

"I'll let you have her for what I paid for her," he said naming a figure significantly less than Michael had imagined "You can see the invoice I have for her purchase. It's more important for me not to have a loose end than to make a profit and, as you know, I have to get back to base. Besides I would really like you to have her, the other guy proved to be a complete jerk and 'Footloose' would probably just have sat on a mooring most of the time with him."

Michael found himself imagining. "She would need a little work, I'd have to spend some money on that if I was to use her in the way you suggest, and I'm not sure I would know how to go about getting the hires and so on I would need, not here. I know damn all about this place, after all."

Jon immediately interjected, "It's no problem, listen, you could ..." But Michael silenced him, this time interrupting firmly. "No more please - at the very least I must think about it, how long have I got."

"Tomorrow morning, don't give me more time to find an alternative arrangement, it is the opportunity of a lifetime for you and I know you would regret not taking it. Always."

Michael excused himself, asking as he did so for the key to the boat and promising to take another look at her later.

He left Jon in the apartment and went out, the bright sunlight blinding him as he emerged from the stairwell. It was a beautiful day, there was a warm breeze, there was not a cloud in the sky and, although he loved his home, it did make this seem like an ideal environment for a sailing business. He walked round the marina and climbed on board the boat and opened the cabin door. He went down into the cabin and got a can of Coke out of the refrigerator; it spat a little foam at him as he opened it. He took it up from the cabin then he sat in the cockpit, his mind racing. He took a gulp from the can.

There were a hundred good reasons not to pursue this course, it was a leap in the dark, but he also recognised that what Jon said was true. He was in a rut, he had no real plans, he was free-wheeling in a way that led to nowhere of any real substance or permanence. His way of life passed the time pleasantly enough, but it presented no challenge and he knew it would begin to bore him if he didn't get more. Taking the job of crewing "Footloose" was the first real decision he had made for ages; maybe it was time to make another.

A shout interrupted his brooding: "Hello, 'Footloose' – how you today?" He looked up, shading his eyes from the sun, and saw Poy standing on the marina dressed in shorts and a yellow tee shirt looking down at the boat. She looked bright, attractive and, to his eyes, exotic. He smiled and she asked him, "Have drink for me?"

"Sure," he replied, signalling that she should come aboard.

She clambered lightly down the steps to the jetty and swung a leg over the rail to get onto the deck. Michael dug another Coke out of the fridge and passed it over. To begin with her presence was a pleasant distraction and they chatted inconsequentially for a while, Michael happy to put thoughts of the boat out of his mind, but when Poy asked what he would do next he found it all came out. He had already told her Jon had a problem, now he explained how it made a problem for him too.

"He has to sell the boat – quickly - and he wants to sell it to me. But it's just too much," he said. "I see the opportunity, but I'm still not sure. The boat needs a bit of work too, it would have to look just right if I was to hire it out for trips, training days and such like."

Poy asked about it, "You can do?"

"Can do what?" asked Michael.

"Work to make boat right," Poy replied.

"Oh, yes, what needs doing is no problem, I work on boats all the time at home and the cost shouldn't be so very much. But I don't know this place. I've no idea how to set up and run a boat business like this and find customers or even if that would be possible here - or about my status here as a foreigner. And, what's more, there's no time, he wants me to decide by tomorrow morning! If I say yes I may be in all sorts of trouble - and if I turn it down I may regret doing so for ever more."

"Not easy," Poy sounded sympathetic. "But maybe if you had help the problems go away, you more sure of making success. Right?"

"What do you mean? " Michael asked and found her smiling at him enigmatically, her face full of enthusiasm.

"I can help?" she asked.

"You ... how?"

"I need job, I know boats, I know this place, I know how all work, have business degree! Can be assistant. Can also crew and find customer – hey, I cook good too!" Her enthusiasm was visibly growing. "You cannot miss this, with me too can make this good, make money, no problem."

Michael certainly hadn't foreseen this, he liked Poy, he had hoped to see her more in the time he was to spend here, but it had never crossed his mind that she could be part of this sort of venture, much less the answer, that she could make a pivotal difference to something so important. Furthermore he hardly knew her, she was attractive certainly but he had no knowledge of her capabilities.

"No, buying a boat would be difficult enough, employing someone would be downright bloody impossible," he said,

205

and at that moment he really meant it, he thought it was all crazy, impossible and he could not do it.

"No not right, I show you," Poy said.

"Show me what?

"Show you sailing, we take boat out right now, no problem."

"That's crazy too, besides it's not my boat."

"Okay, nearly your boat. Come on, can do, can do now!"

She beamed, but her look also indicated steely determination. Michael found himself carried along by her enthusiasm. A short sail would be no problem, it would give him time to think and besides Jon had given him the key and knew he was 'having another look'; now doing so would take place away from the marina. He said nothing, but slowly began to make the boat ready for sailing and found as he did so that Poy was soon busy alongside him. She seemed to know exactly what to do and soon "Footloose" was under way, the sails ready to raise and the diesel engine running smoothly and carrying them passed other moored boats out of the marina towards the open sea. Once out of the channel they raised the sails and the boat caught the wind and picked up speed.

An hour later they had dropped anchor off a small island, a spot that Poy clearly knew and had directed him towards, and Michael found himself looking round. The place was idyllic, the weather was still wonderful, not a soul was in sight along the tree lined beach of pure white sand and, he could not help thinking, surely there must be tourists that wanted to come on a trip like this. He found himself miles away when Poy brought him away from his thoughts by saying, "Race to beach". She quickly stripped off her shorts and tee shirt to reveal a striking yellow bikini and, before he could react, she had dived over the side and was swimming strongly towards the shore.

Michael grabbed his swimming shorts from the bag he had in the cabin, changed quickly, checked the anchor was secure and then followed her. Once he caught up they walked a little way along the beach, and then sat under the trees at the shore to get some shade.

"Well, what you think now? Sailing okay?" Poy asked.

Okay it certainly was, Poy was not used to a craft of the size of "Footloose" but she certainly knew her way about a boat, she had great confidence too and when Michael had let her take the helm she did well, demonstrating a real feel for the boat. She was clearly a fast learner; anything Michael suggested had been quickly taken up. She had proved to be very competent crew.

"Fine, you know your stuff. Look we better get back, Jon might think the boat's gone missing."

They stood up and walked back along the beach, stopping opposite where the boat was anchored Michael took her hand, "Thanks for coming," he said and attempted a kiss. She pulled back.

"You captain - cannot kiss crew," she laughed, and grinning at him she waded quickly into the sea and struck out for the boat. Michael followed her and they climbed aboard over the stern, dried off and got ready for the return trip.

The sail back was exhilarating. The boat went well, she really was joy to sail, and Poy continued to demonstrate both that she knew her stuff and that she looked amazingly good in a bikini. Once safely moored back at the marina, Michael found his mood changing. This seemed not only like a great opportunity, but something that would be good in so many ways, if only he could do it.

"Well?" Poy looked enquiringly, "showing okay, I sail very good okay, you buy boat now, yes?"

"Wait a minute, it was fun yes, and you certainly handled the boat well, but ... I still don't know, how could I employ you, I'd have no customers to begin with, no income?"

"We work out, no problem, you first pay me nothing, we share profit. Soon!" Again her enthusiasm grabbed him and he found himself wondering: in his mind 'it's crazy' was turning into 'it's possible', no was becoming maybe.

Once ashore they went to the food court together for a late lunch. Poy went into the café on her way to explain her absence to her colleagues, telling Michael when she caught him up "I say I go for job, they know I look". They ordered fried rice, vegetables and chicken and cold Singha beers. Michael could not stop himself imagining working with the boat, with Poy, having his own business, having the freedom and the sailing for which he longed. The many practical reasons to decline Jon's offer began to recede in his mind, though doubt still remained in pole position.

They finished their meal and Poy explained she must do a few hours in the café. "I promise to think about it," Michael said as he left her. "Maybe you are right – can we meet for breakfast tomorrow, early, before I tell Jon what I've decided."

"Sure," she replied, and then grinning at him she added "only if you decide okay."

⚑

There would be numerous details they must work out. A payment would need to be made, Michael had decided to go for a discount on the already unbeatable price on the basis of helping him undertake the work needed on the boat, he reckoned he was in a strong negotiating position and there was no sign that Jon had another option waiting in the wings.

He also had to finance living until the business side was up and running and he did not want to allow all his funds to disappear.

Once he heard from home he would make a quick trip back, but he hoped that, once bridges were mended there, his mother would be pleased for him. He even allowed himself to imagine her visiting and seeing what he was up to, and approving of it. Somehow though, he allowed the situation here and now to outweigh thoughts about home. Meantime, documents would have to be exchanged, bank arrangements made, insurance and a longer term mooring found and, not least, some customers sought out and signed up too. He could be a boat owner, a businessman and a resident overseas - all in a moment.

Michael went from lunch to the nearby bank and his queries were referred to a larger branch in the town. He set off to find the bus and spent some time in the town.

When he saw Jon later in the day, despite his badgering questions he refused to be drawn.

"I'll let you know in the morning, I promise. I am checking things out, I am thinking, but I do need to sleep on it."

In fact he hardly slept at all. He spent some time in the small hours sitting on the apartment's balcony, staring out across the marina, and drinking coffee that made it even less likely that he would sleep. At one point he walked slowly round to the boat and stood looking at her bathed in the light of a three quarter moon. Later, as the sun rose, the dark of the night moving quickly to light in the way characteristic of locations near the equator, he still felt unsure.

Finally he slept.

He was sitting outside the café before it opened for business and ordered some coffee when the first member of staff arrived and began to open up. Coffee will be coming out of my ears soon, he thought. Poy joined him there half an hour later. They exchanged good mornings and Poy sat opposite him and waited expectantly. When Michael said nothing she posed the question.

"Okay, we make business together?"

Michael still said nothing. In the long moments that followed his mind remained in a whirl, there were so many reasons why he should say no, it was mad, it was crazy, it was way out of his comfort zone. He had never even lived away from home, well not counting the short time on the boat in Heybridge, never mind run a business, yet he could see so clearly the way of life buying the boat would give him. Perhaps he could make it work he thought, but he still remained less than totally convinced.

"You think it not work?" Poy had a habit of posing questions that were not quite phrased as questions, though the tone usually made her intention clear, as it did now.

"I'm honestly not sure."

"You want it?" It was another question.

"Well, yes, I guess I do, but I'm still not sure." At home maybe, he thought, but out here he just didn't know.

"You want it, you make it work – we make it work. Can do, no problem."

She smiled at him in a way that shot enthusiasm into him as if by injection. And in that moment he knew. The decision was made.

He had to give it a try.

Twenty minutes later they were both in the apartment sitting round the table with Jon.

"Who's this?" said Jon, looking at Poy as they sat down. "I have decided to go ahead," replied Michael, seeming to ignore the question and finding his voice shook a little despite his recent certainty. "And I already have an employee to help."

"Partner," Poy said sternly, "I business partner".

CHAPTER TWENTY
Door to door enquiries

Philip found me another new author last time he came and I've just finished "Italian Neighbours" by Tim Parks. It's about his life, living in Italy. Not the sort of book I usually read, after all my travelling days are over. I'm not likely to ever go to Italy again now, though I have fond memories of Florence. But I loved it. It was amusing and it painted such a real picture of Italian ways. Philip told *me there are a couple of sequels and that Tim Parks has written novels too. He's very much another author to add to my list.*

I still can't find my will even though I had a good old hunt for it. No matter I'm sure it's safe somewhere.

Thinking he was to be travelling alone, and having, by his standards, gone wild with the budget in Bangkok, Philip had booked into a small hotel in Phuket, one set by the beach, yet no great distance from the Blue Lagoon Marina. After their time in Bangkok, time that had been better in every way than Philip had ever dared to hope, they flew to Phuket. A short flight, an hour or so, a comparatively small airport, and once disembarked an easy taxi ride brought them to the small hotel with none of the grandeur of the large Bangkok hotel they had just left. Here the atmosphere was distinctly informal. Despite this being their first visit they were welcomed at Reception like old friends. The young man who took their suitcases called Philip "Boss" and the lady who ran the hotel, which only had about twenty rooms, checked them in herself.

"This is nice" said Miriam, surveying their room, "just look at all those coloured silk cushions and it's got a lovely view of the garden."

Philip smiled to himself; he very much wanted Miriam to like all this.

After they had unpacked they ventured out for something to eat. The area behind the hotel ended with steps going down to the beach, and the seating area around the pool was well tended and neat, with some chairs sheltered from the hot sun by trees. A handful of people sat round the pool area which was located alongside a small dining area.

"This seems very comfortable," said Miriam. "A pretty good choice from a simple scan of a few pages on the Internet, I'd say. Look at those orchids, they seem to grow here like weeds, can you imagine?"

They sat with a view of the sea and ordered some food. They were both really getting into Thai food, and enjoyed a late lunch before going back to reception to check out exactly how to reach Blue Lagoon Marina and being told that the buses that ran outside continued past the marina which was about fifteen minutes away.

"No problem. Very near. Take wooden bus, only a few Baht, get off not supermarket, few metres more."

The manager was happy to help and she added that buses "come in own time" but they were, it seemed, evidently regular. Any bus would do for the journey they wanted, all went the right way.

They waited in the road between five and ten minutes and then saw a small single deck bus approaching, its sides open to the air, painted blue and with a very obvious wooden frame to its superstructure. They had been told that there were no formal bus stops, all they had to do was flag it down to board and ring a bell to alight. Its cost was indeed only a few Baht and a few minutes later they found themselves walking into Blue Lagoon Marina.

The place was of some size. After walking down the entrance road for maybe a hundred metres they found an area of small shops to one side: a bank, a supermarket and a small café amongst them. Nearby, in a row of shop houses, a small food court was still serving lunch, a number of people sitting under an awning at simple plastic tables and chairs. Still ahead of them was the hotel and apartments and to reach there they had to walk through an open area ringed by boats, all presumably brought ashore to undergo some sort of work. Cranes and equipment dotted the area. Beyond was the marina, a multitude of masts rising into the air indicated sailing boats, though there were also some motor yachts in evidence moored amongst the throng of craft.

They walked further in.

"It's quite a set-up," said Philip. "Looks like plenty of places Michael might be, but plenty of places to hide too. Or he may have moved on."

"Don't worry. If he's here I am sure we'll find him. If not then another possibility is that he was here and we'll find someone who knows where he went. If we don't find him here, we might learn something about how to track him down."

"Yes, but if he stayed in Phuket and he moved on from here then that might have been years ago." Philip sounded dejected, imagining a trail gone cold. He was hoping for the best but not wanting to increase any ultimate disappointment by raising his hopes. Realistically finding Michael was a long shot after all.

"Let's be systematic about it," Miriam became business-like. "We'll treat it like door to door enquiries, let's take different directions, there are places right round the marina to check. If we do that then we can meet up back here at that café in, what, an hour, a bit less, and if we've had no luck we can see how far we've got and decide what's best to do next. It looks like it will take several circuits."

"Yes, Sergeant!" Philip agreed and they set off, each taking a section of the marina around which were set shops, agencies for selling boats, pictures of the various craft for sale filling their windows, and an assortment of other businesses selling tours, clothes, souvenirs and boating gear. The first place he went to check was a boat selling agency. A girl jumped up from a desk as he entered eager to greet a potential buyer. She did so in pretty good English too.

"Hello, I wonder if you can help me." Philip began realising he had little idea how to continue.

The girl came forward grabbing a portfolio of information about boats as she did so, and Philip continued.

"Sorry, I'm not interested in buying a boat, I'm afraid. I'm looking for someone who might work here at the marina. An Englishman, about my age, his name's Michael Croft. Michael Croft." Conscious of the possible language problem he repeated the name saying it slowly and clearly, then continuing "Do you know of him?"

He did not go into details, thinking that to start by mentioning he was going back nearly twenty years would not help, what's more the girl would hardly have been born then. Though he did add that Michael might have been around for a while, it would not help either if people thought he was looking for a new arrival.

"Many people at marina, what he do?"

Despite his lack of interest in buying a boat, the girl was evidently prepared to help. But of course Philip didn't know the answer to her quite reasonable question, he found himself waffling.

"Well, something to do with boats, obviously, I think, probably sailing boats. He's a craftsman too, a carpenter, you know, he works with wood." The girl looked puzzled and he mimed sawing wood, thinking how utterly pathetic it all must sound. Nevertheless the girl gave it some thought, but then concluded that she could not help. "I not know, sorry," she finished.

Philip came out back into the heat, the office had been air conditioned, and stood at the rail that ran round the edge of the marina. He had a notebook in the shoulder bag he had brought to enable him to carry a bottle of water, the case for his sunglasses and other bits and pieces. He got it out and drew a rough plan of the marina. He noted the name of the business he had just been into in place on the chart and put a cross beside it. He would record where he had been. If he found any places that were closed or where someone suggested he returned to speak to someone else then he would have a clear note of it. To cover everything here might well take some time.

Fifty minutes later he had talked to about fifteen people without success. Some had dismissed his enquiry briskly, others had been helpful but knew nothing, and a couple he had made a note to return to, one had promised to think about it and in an outlet selling marine varnishes and paint he had been told that it would be better to talk to the boss – "Not here now." He returned to where they had started their search and headed toward the café, as he did so he saw Miriam coming the other way. She waved, but even before she reached him she gave a slow shake of her head.

"I found no one who knows him," she said as they sat down at a table shaded by an umbrella just outside the café and ordered cold drinks. "I assume you're the same."

He nodded and, pushing her sunglasses up from her eyes to rest on her head, she continued. "But there are a good many places here – how many did you speak to?"

Philip consulted his notebook. "Fifteen, but two might be worth another word," he said.

"I did about the same. We are not done yet, so don't despair." Miriam tried hard to sound upbeat.

When the drinks arrived she put the question to the waitress, who went inside and asked her colleagues but returned to say no one knew the name. Miriam's experience had been much like Philip's, though she reported having had one false alarm.

"In one shop I was told the name was known, they said it was a few doors along – I chased along there but the place was called 'Mitchell Craft' a boat brokerage of some sort not a person; they didn't know Michael there either."

It was proving difficult to describe Michael, their only photograph was many years old, and, though most people had been helpful, his name had rung a bell with none of them. Like Philip, Miriam had one shop that was worth returning to where the owner was due in only later in the day. They sat for a while, enjoying the shade, then finished off their drinks and headed off again to make a further circuit with a second rendezvous agreed to be made at the café in an another hour or so.

"I'm looking for an Englishman who works somewhere on the marina, about my age, his name's Michael Croft."

Philip must have repeated his question thirty or forty times now. Once he thought he had something, an assistant in a boating gear shop thought it rang a bell and called a colleague out from the back of the shop, but there was no luck there either in the end. Another person directed him to Mitchell Crafts which Miriam had come across earlier. This time there were no establishments to which it seemed worth returning. Feeling increasingly dejected, he made his way back to the café and ordered another cold drink. He was again first back, but this time when Miriam joined him after only a couple of minutes he saw that she was smiling.

"You have something?" he asked.

"I might, I just might, have a lead." She deposited a pile of leaflets on the table, obviously picked up from the places she had visited.

"Well, don't keep me in suspense," Philip wanted to know at once about anything indicating even the smallest chance of success.

"A drink first, please" she waved to the waitress.

"And also a question - back at the beginning when you first started to check a few things out after Abigail's death, when you first came across Michael's existence, do you remember if he had a middle name?"

"Why on earth ...?"

"Just answer the question, sir, I'm a police officer," she said sternly but with a grin; a moment of levity was welcome.

"I'm not sure, I think perhaps he did, but what it was I'm not sure, do you think he might be using that?"

"Not exactly, it's just that ..." but Philip interrupted her.

"Hang on a minute." He held up a hand and puckered his brow in thought. "Yes ... I do remember now I think about it, I am pretty sure it was Andrew, yes, I'm sure of it. But how does that help? For goodness sake spit it out!"

She rummaged amongst the pile of brochures as she continued, "I think we're looking for Mac."

"Well that would be good too, but we've no clue even as to who he is, much less where he might be now ... Hey, wait a sec, I see it now. You mean the initials: MAC. Michael Andrew Croft. He might have used the name Mac, or at least been called that by his mother and maybe others too. If he used it routinely way back then he might go by that name here too. You clever girl – that's brilliant!"

"You see I told you that you were doing the right thing getting into bed with the police!" She grinned again and continued, "You need a detective with you, you see. And I found this. It's what triggered the thought."

She took a small leaflet from the pile on the table and pushed it across to him. Below a picture of an attractive-looking sailing boat positioned afloat centre page with an island in the background was printed:

A GEM OF A SAILING BOAT AVAILABLE FOR:

TRIPS TO PI – PI AND ISLANDS

SNORKELLING

SAILING INSTRUCTION

CHARTER

LONGER VOYAGES BY ARRANGEMENT

"FOOTLOOSE"

The business was called Mac's Sails. On the reverse side were other pictures, the boat – "Footloose" - under sail, the boat anchored just off a beautiful beach and a shot, taken down below the water, of fish swimming above a reef. There was no picture of her skipper, but there was a mobile phone number.

"It must be him!" Philip was instantly ecstatic.

"Well wait a minute, it looks possible, good even, but there could be other explanations so it's not actual proof yet. It looks as if this Mac doesn't have an office round the quay, there's only a phone number printed on this and the leaflets were in a rack at an information point, but I bet one of the tour places here acts as an agent for him. Let's walk round again and see."

"We could ring the phone number on the leaflet," said Philip, maintaining his enthusiasm.

"Perhaps, but, think about it, maybe better not. Don't you think this should be broached face to face? I think a little caution is in order. If we see him, we'd know at once if it was the right person, you have that photo from the paper."

Philip thought for a moment. "Okay, I suppose you're right. I guess a bit more checking first can do no harm."

With Philip having agreed her plan they finished the drinks they had ordered and set off together on another circuit. There were, they found, a number of tour shops. It seemed that trips to the smaller islands nearby in a variety of boats were pretty big business. People of whom they enquired at the first two outfits to which they showed the leaflet said they knew nothing of "Mac's Sails". But at the third someone said they knew who he worked through and directed them to a fourth, a small shop front and office called All Tours. They went inside.

"Ambitious name" said Philip. "Do you think they could arrange us a round the world cruise?" But before Miriam could respond someone came forward to help and quickly confirmed that they indeed took bookings for him, but even so there was still not complete certainty.

"He just Mac" the girl in the shop told them. "I not know full name. Today he sails, gives lesson, sleeps on boat, back mid-morning tomorrow."

They thanked her and promised to return, but said nothing of what they wanted.

Philip's impatience showed.

"Oh God, so near and yet so far, it might be him – or not, but it seems we'll just have to wait I guess," he said.

"Well, so be it," Miriam replied. "Let's make the most of our time for the moment then, this is supposed to be a holiday too, you know. Besides there must be something we can do to fill our time."

221

She smiled at him roguishly and they headed back to the hotel.

ꕤ

After a spell in holiday mode, when they returned the next day they found the "Footloose" was already there, secured at a mooring almost opposite the All Tours office. A sandwich board stood on the stern displaying the services of Mac's Sails, but no one was visible on board. Philip was no expert but it seemed to him to be a great boat: it was a good size, and was clearly well equipped and very well kept. He imagined customers would regard it as just what they were looking for.

"It must be him." Philip pointed to the name painted on the stern that abutted the quay alongside a floating pontoon just below the solid path. "Look: the name has two little stars painted next to it, just as 'Starcounter' does back in Heybridge. He obviously kept that idea going."

"That does seem an unlikely coincidence, more likely it is more evidence. I wonder where he is."

Miriam turned to lead them to go back to the office, but at that moment a figure ducked out of the boat's cabin, locked the door to it behind him and made to come ashore; he was carrying a cylindrical canvass duffle bag over his shoulder and, as he looked up to the walkway and the tour office, it was clear even from a distance that they had found the right man. He was older than the photo of course, but he was still suntanned, still had the same head of tousled brown hair and appeared to be a clear match to the old photograph. Philip stepped forward as he came up the steps from the pontoon.

"Excuse me, are you Mac, Michael Croft?"

"That's me," he replied brightly. "Wanting a sail are you?" Unsurprisingly he had assumed they had approached him as potential customers.

"No, not that, my names Philip Marchington and this is Miriam Jayne. We are here on holiday from England; from Maldon in fact, we hoped to find you - it's about your mother."

"What!" He looked shocked "It's been years since I heard anything from her; you might say that we are estranged."

"Yes, we know that, there was something of a row, wasn't there?"

Philip realised he had never given any great thought to this moment. He had thought long and hard about the prospects of finding Michael, but hardly considered what he would say if he did find him at all. He supposed he had thought it would all be straightforward. It was quickly apparent that was not to be.

Now he found Michael suddenly looking angry. "You could say that. I don't want to talk about it. It's long forgotten - she ignored me when I tried to put things right, now it's too late ..." For a moment he seemed on the point of saying more but ended abruptly saying "Just clear off and leave me alone. Whatever it is, I don't want to know."

"Wait a minute. We're only trying to help ... we ..."

Michael cut him off. This time he spoke angrily, "Well you're not. I said I don't want to hear it and I don't, now go, just go."

He turned abruptly on his heels and stormed off away from the boat and strode briskly away from them along the quay. It seemed that they had found their quarry, but in other ways it looked like their mission was a failure.

"Well that's not what I expected, let's follow him." Philip took a step forward in the direction Michael had taken.

Miriam put a restraining hand on his arm. "Wait a moment, he's obviously shocked at anything about his mother raising its head after all this time, goodness knows what feelings he now has about things back then - if we charge after him and tell him that she's dead it may well make matters worse. In fact it seems to me it likely would – and believe me in my job I know a little about breaking bad news. Let's leave it a while and try again. When we speak next time at least he will already know we offer a link with his mother of some sort."

Reluctantly, Philip agreed with her. They checked in the office where they were told that "Footloose" apparently had nothing booked for the next few days. They left a note, giving details of where they were staying and saying also:

We apologise if the sudden mention of old difficulties stirred up bad memories. It is not our intention to cause distress or to make any sort of trouble. We have news of your mother that we are sure you would want to hear (she is not aware of our contacting you). What you do with the news is entirely up to you.

Please let's meet and talk. We will eat lunch at Blue Lagoon Food Court tomorrow and the next day. Contact us at our hotel or find us there - you will not regret our meeting.

They put their names and the details of their hotel at the end.

"I just hope that this does the trick," said Philip. "On reflection I guess you're right about not pushing him too hard, but we are not staying here for ever, are we? We'll soon be back on the other side of the world and unable to do anything. I suppose, failing all else, we would just have to write him a long letter or let the authorities contact him."

"I would hate the news to have to be broken to him in writing, especially officially, fingers crossed he will meet us tomorrow." Miriam realised how important it was to him that everything now ended satisfactorily. She squeezed his hand and continued, "Don't worry until tomorrow, then we'll see what's what. One thing at a time, at least we've found him. Did you really expect that?"

"I don't know. I hoped to but I did know it was always a long shot."

The next day, having heard nothing, they again visited the marina. Arriving as planned at lunchtime they ate a wonderful meal at the food court and paid an unbelievably small amount for it. They lingered over two large Singha beers but, although they kept their eyes skinned all through the meal, of Michael there was no sign. So then they walked to where "Footloose" was moored. The boat was still there, silent and locked, but the lady at the tour company swore she did not know where Michael was – "Not know, not see" – and more than two hours after they arrived at the marina there was still no indication of him being around. They waited a few more minutes and returned, somewhat dejectedly to their hotel.

It seemed that for the moment at least they had no option but to wait.

CHAPTER TWENTY ONE
News from here and there

With some small prospect of finding him I find I can't stop wondering what happened. Where has he been and why did he never get in touch? Whatever went on all those years ago, he was young and I'm sure it was in the heat of the moment that he first left. I wonder what sort of life he has had. I hope he's been happy, though of course I must be realistic: it's possible he had something happen to him

... he could be dead. He could have been dead for years.

But let's pray not. Once Philip is on the case, maybe we'll find out. I do hope so.

The next morning dawned bright and sunny again. After about a dozen unfinished comments starting "Do you think ..." from each of them, both Philip and Miriam vowed to say nothing more about Michael until lunchtime. Instead they concentrated on being on holiday – together. They had got up late. They swam in the hotel pool and went for a long walk along the beach, if nothing else they were getting to know each other better. Philip said a little more about his wife's death, about his love of books, his job at the library and his disappointment at the direction things there were taking of late. Miriam was sympathetic, she had had boss trouble too after all, and together they invented a dozen drastic fates for Froby

Miriam suggested arresting her for gross bureaucracy, insensitivity to library members or failure to read sufficient books. Philip smiled at the thought. "Maybe I'll go back and find her sitting immobile at her desk with an 'Out of Order' notice hanging round her neck like one of her precious computers," he said. "We need them of course, but we need books too, though it's a question of balance and I think she has it all wrong. We certainly don't need her constant nit picking and bureaucracy. I wonder what the Area Manager made of her grand 21st century book obliteration plan."

"I guess you'll find out soon enough, sadly this holiday won't last for ever."

"You're right, I will, but I have been working on something of a plan of my own too. We'll see." Philip smiled, but shook

227

his head when Miriam wanted to know what he had been up to, saying simply only, "Not yet."

After several days not thinking about England in any way, they both sat down to check their emails; the hotel had two computers in the lobby. Miriam took only a few minutes and left saying she would see Philip back by the pool when he was done. He moved down the list of incoming messages in his Inbox, he found some spam, as ever, some newsletters and invitations he had invited including a regular one from what he would always think of as Waterstone's. He looked at the new name, Waterstones, for a moment, wondering how they could possibly drop the apostrophe with a total distain for grammar and tradition. But he was not going to worry about that now and in any case he was surely too young to be a grumpy old man, he thought, though perhaps, if he was honest, he was happy to be in training to become one.

There was a message from his sister asking him to go for lunch the Sunday after he would be back in England and asking too, as she was beginning to do all too regularly, whether there was "someone you would like to bring with you". Why did married friends and relations always want to match-make any of their single friends, even when they were, like him, bereaved? It had been a while, but ... anyway this time he might just surprise her. He resolved to check the date with Miriam and wondered if he could persuade her to turn up for Sunday lunch in her police uniform. He could imagine his sister's face if that happened and the rest of the family too for that matter. Better still maybe they could drive down in a police car and arrive with flashing lights and sirens blaring. The kids would adore that, and would certainly demand a ride. He smiled inwardly at the thought, and scribbled a note to remind himself to ask Miriam and, all being well, put the date in their respective diaries. He could reply to his sister once that was done, he smiled to himself again and clicked on the next message which he saw was from the library service; even the pathologically officious Froby didn't usually worry members of staff who were on holiday and, after all, there was precious little he could do about, say, a damaged or overdue book from the other side of the world.

But it was not from Froby as he first expected. It was a missive from the Area Manager and it was about her.

The note apologised for his being contacted during his holiday and insisted that this was exceptional but that he would want to know the news. Lucky he wasn't a banker, he thought, such people were probably contacted on the hour, every hour and had work to do as a result even when in the furthest flung holiday destination. After a good deal of gobbledegook about targets, objectives and phrases like "serving the community", "core reading skills" and "literary values", he found the key paragraph. It said:

```
… so it is the view of management that Miss
Frobisher can be more suitably deployed at the main
Chelmsford Library and she will be moving to her
new post at the end of the month. Continuity is
important and thus I am asking you to take over as
Acting Head of the Library with immediate effect on
your return to work. It seems that the skills and
values that you demonstrated so clearly at the
interviews when the last appointment was made are,
in fact, just what is needed at this time. I am
confident that you will deal proactively with the
challenges ahead and look forward to working with
you.
```

Philip was stunned, delighted, so much so that he could not think straight for a moment. If he was honest with himself he had been worried about both where Froby was taking the library and how wherever it might prove to be would affect his position. He read the paragraph a second time. Even in the world of libraries Philip noted, business-speak crept in; he was sure he was up to the "challenges" and that, given a moment, he could even work out in what way a proactive approach differed from simply an active one. The message ended with the words:

Do not worry about this now. Enjoy your holiday; I know it's the first one you have had for a while. We will need to meet to finalise matters when you get back and by that I mean getting the word "Acting" off your job description and making the change permanent. Between you and me the changes that Miss Frobisher wanted to make were just too much, can you believe she wanted to install fruit machines and computer games. We do want to move ahead, but we must maintain a balance and ensure that traditional library activities do not suffer.

It finished by telling him that other members of staff were being told the news in his absence. When he got back to work he would be in charge. Good news indeed. It was amazing: Froby had apparently presented every absurd idea he had mischievously suggested as her own 'considered plan' and gone so over the top that it had resulted in complete rejection. He did not actually punch the air, but looked as if he well might. He was so pleased, not just for himself, but because with the way in which Froby had been operating now not approved, there was hope yet for the library to retain its integrity. He scanned the few remaining messages quickly and rushed back to the poolside to tell Miriam the good news.

He started with the lunch invitation, telling her that he had heard from his sister and that he would love her to join them, explaining that it was down in Kent. Miriam seemed pleased and explained in turn that where his sister lived was not far from where she had been brought up. She promised to check the date. He moved on:

"I also had an email from the area guy at the library."

"They are surely not bothering you with work at his range, are they, holidays should be sacrosanct?" Miriam was outraged on his behalf.

"No, not really, it was exceptional: good news, really good news, so I'm glad they wrote. The dreaded Froby has been moved out, off to some job at Chelmsford: side-lined into a backroom job, I suspect."

"But where does that leave you?" Miriam sounded concerned.

"That's the good news, I'm moving up!" Philip smiled again at the news and also because his tactics had apparently worked.

"That's great, and you are grinning like the Cheshire cat as a result, but does it mean that you are going to have to be the one who must implement her 'grand plan'?"

"Well, that's it actually, it seems her grand plan fell on deaf ears and was regarded as being way over the top ... and after I had been so encouraging about it." He smiled again.

"That grin is growing, what have you been up to?"

"Well I did make a few suggestions. I knew that she would want all the credit if a scheme was approved and it would not come back on me. No one was ever going to ask me how I could suggest something so daft. So I kept suggesting more and more until the whole thing was truly verging on the ridiculous. It seems she must have taken it all on board, to have actually thought these were good ideas and then gone on and presented everything, lock, stock and barrel as her own idea. He said that her written report ran to 52 pages; that's unbelievable! Give someone enough rope and they will hang themselves, they say. I never thought that she would actually take on the idea of a fruit machine - that seemed to me to be risking going too far; but she did. Can you believe it? Anyway her idea seems to have fallen on sensible and decidedly deaf ears."

"You wily old ... anyway I'm very pleased. And I rather like the idea of being on holiday with the Head Librarian. Mind you I'll expect your recommendations of what to read on the beach to go up a notch or two now."

They both laughed out loud. Then suddenly Noon, as they had discovered the manager was called, was at their elbow:

"You have telephone for you," she said. Philip got up and went with her to reception, thinking it must be Michael – after all who else had the number?

"Hello, you are Philip?" It was a woman's voice. Philip could but agree that he was.

"My name is Poy, I am with Mac, Michael. You know his mother, yes?"

"I do, we came hoping to find him. We have important news for him. We really need to meet him. Will he talk to us?"

Perhaps Poy, whose sing song voice told him she was Thai, provided one of the reasons why Michael had stayed here, thought Philip as she continued.

"When he came back, after seeing you - was very upset. I made him talk. We met soon after he arrived here. He never spoke of this. I knew there was some problem in England before he came here, but did not ask, it was good time, not for going into bad past. We set up Mac Sails and we get together too, you know."

Philip was able to squeeze in an "Okay", but she continued apace.

"He has not spoken to mother for many years, yes?" She didn't wait for an answer.

"You must speak to him, but he is unsure, still angry, not about you, about the past. I do not know all the details, but I do know he has regrets, big regrets. I saw your note and worry he will not meet you. He thinks that if you go home then it will all go away, but it needs sorting or it will be too late, you will be far away. I will bring him. Make sure he is at small café near bank. You know, on marina?" Again she did not pause, finishing, "come there too - 1.30 okay?"

This time she did wait for an answer and Philip, deciding against elaborate discussions over the phone, simply said "Yes, sure, we'll be there ... and thank you. See you soon."

He hurried back to the pool where Miriam lay full length on a sun bed reading her paperweight sized Patricia Scanlan novel. Philip explained quickly about the call.

"We have to get changed and go," he said. It seemed they would definitely meet Michael again, but, given their experience so far, they both found themselves wondering if he would he listen to what they had to say.

※

Out of their swim suits, a quick change and they were onto a bus and soon back at the marina. As they approached the café, they saw Michael and an attractive Thai lady were sitting drinking tea from tall glass cups at a table outside; both wore shorts and tee-shirts sporting the slogan "Footloose – the perfect sail".

As they got close Michael spotted them and jumped up. "I told you two I'd much rather not talk about this, just leave us. Please just go."

It was clear that Poy had not told him they were coming, probably fearful that he would have refused to meet them. He glared at Poy, perhaps realising from her expression what had been arranged, but she tugged at his elbow indicating he should sit down again, saying simply "Please. You must listen. It's important." Grudgingly he sat down again and before anyone could speak a waitress interrupted and Philip and Miriam ordered drinks as they sat down. There was silence for a short while then Philip spoke.

"Please let's start again." He searched for a way to get into it all, first addressing Poy and introducing himself and Miriam. Then he turned to Michael. "I'm a friend of your mother," he said.

Miriam took over, her voice firm.

"I am sorry but in fact I'm afraid it's more accurate to say he was a friend of your mother, a good one, but we have to start with bad news and tell you she died a couple of months back. She had a stroke. She died peacefully sitting in her garden; the doctors said she knew nothing about it."

"Oh, God, that's ..." Michael's voice tailed away as he tried to take in the news.

They all sat in silence for what seemed like long minutes. Philip broke the quiet spell saying "She was a lovely lady, we are so sorry."

Then Michael spoke again. "Right, so what's your role in this?" he asked.

"It's a long story, but let me try to explain briefly." Philip described his meeting Abigail, how they had talked regularly and how he had helped her with a few things at home and brought her library books to the house. "She was an avid reader and I work at the town library, it was one of the things we had in common."

"It doesn't really explain why you're here though, does it?" Michael gave them a quizzical look.

"I walk past her house on the way to work. I found her dead," said Philip.

Again no one spoke for a few moments as Michael and Poy took this in. He went on:

"If the weather allowed she often sat in the front garden and we spoke as I went past her house to and fro to work. That morning I got no answer and I found her just sitting in her chair. She looked quite normal but I couldn't rouse her. At first I thought she might just have passed out. I rang the ambulance, but it was too late and later it was clear that she had died of a stroke. I'm very sorry."

"I see." Michael still seemed shocked and was clearly uncertain what to say. He folded his paper napkin up and crushed it in his fist.

"She was a lovely lady, I liked her," Philip continued "But there's more – later I returned some books she had been reading back to the library and I discovered that one of them had a letter tucked inside it. It was addressed to me. It was unfinished, but it was clear that she wanted my help to find someone – you, though it was a little confusing and anyway we thought of you as Michael, her son who disappeared almost twenty years ago. For a while we thought the Mac she had mentioned to me occasionally was a different person."

Michael now seemed to feel some explanation was required.

"We had a row, oh it's so far back, but at the time I suppose I was idling my time away sailing, punctuated by odd jobs around the boatyards, and my parents wanted me to go to university so that I could get a 'proper' job after that, but I just wanted to sail. After my Dad died my mother and I really fell out – we had a big bust-up and I went to live on Dad's boat for a few weeks."

He paused as if remembering, his expression still troubled; he continued to crush the napkin in his hand.

"'Starcounter' is still around, much loved and still kept on a mooring in Heybridge Basin. The son and family of a friend of your father own it," Philip injected into the pause, thinking that Michael would welcome the news.

"Wow, really. I loved that boat."

He paused again and smiled at the thought, then continued: "At the time I wanted to get away, on an impulse I took a job sailing a yacht up here from Singapore. I didn't think it through before I went and then I finally realised too late that I would be away and miss the funeral. The fact somehow didn't occur to me until I had arrived in Singapore; I was unsure, angry and just so bound up in what I was doing. My mother must have been so furious with me, so hurt. When I got here I sent her a card and then a long letter apologising and trying to build bridges – but she ignored it, I got nothing back and ... I don't know, I was angry then and left it. I left it too long. Far too long; I know it's no excuse but there was so much happening here."

He looked from one to the other of them, but neither Philip nor Miriam said anything. After a moment he continued.

"I bought "Footloose", it was the boat I'd sailed up here from Singapore. The owner had a buyer for it but that deal fell through. He offered her to me – it was such a great deal - and ... I don't know, I guess the moment to re-contact home eventually sort of passed. And now she's dead. I feel terrible, but she did ignore my ..."

His voice broke for a moment and Poy, clearly supportive, put her hand on his arm and gripped it tight.

It was Miriam's turn again. "I/m sure you are not the first to let a key moment pass ... in the circumstances ..." she paused, continuing "Anyway, we think we know what happened. We have the card you sent, a photo of you right here on this quay, because she received that she knew you were safe and in Thailand. She always kept it, our finding it's one reason we were able to find you. Anyway, though she did receive it, it had been redirected."

"What do you mean?" Michael sounded confused. He gave his tea an absent-minded stir as if looking for something for his hands to do.

"It seems Abigail ... your mother ... moved house soon after her husband died and after you had gone. She must have redirected her post and while the card reached her we reckon the letter never did. Certainly it seems clear that she never had any idea what had happened to you. She wasn't ignoring you; it seems she just didn't know where you were."

236

"Oh ...oh, my God." As the circumstances became clear Michael looked stunned and rubbed his head with both hands, ruffling his tangle of hair still further.

Philip went on: "We don't know what she did early on. We presume she made some efforts to find you, but that evidently proved fruitless and no doubt time went by with her waiting for you to make contact, time passes so quickly in such circumstances. Finally, she must have given up all real hope. Though, as Miriam said, she always kept that card, then – perhaps because of her heart, she started to have some heart trouble not long ago, she seems to have wanted to make one more attempt to find you. That's where I came in. She wanted my help, though she died before she was actually able to tell me exactly what it was she wanted. The letter she was writing to me was never completed or sent and I only saw it at all by chance because it had been tucked in her library book."

They talked more about what had happened, how Philip had begun to investigate, discovering how Michael had disappeared and their eventual locating of him in the marina.

"He's been nothing if not persistent in his search," said Miriam and, turning to Philip "Perhaps you should be a detective!"

Philip laughed "Oh very funny, you ..." he turned to Michael. "Sorry, it's a private joke. Miriam's a police officer. But there is something else you should know. Your mother apparently died intestate, there was a recent codicil, which indicates that she had made a will at some stage, though that's invalid now with no will found. It means we have to contact the authorities – tell them about you – and we must do it quickly or the house will be sold and the government will take all the money. Will or no will you are clearly her heir. I can start the process if you like, I've got the address of the Treasury Solicitor with me, that's what the government office that deals with this sort of thing is called, and I did have one earlier contact with them. After all they could be wrapping things up without you right now."

"Yes, please do," said Michael, adding "if you don't mind, that is."

"I'll email them when we get back to the hotel. I'll print you out a copy of it and of any reply, after that you can take it from there."

Michael looked pensive, the implications of the situation were really only now beginning to sink in.

"I suppose I'll have to come to England to settle everything up," he said.

His face showed that, for the moment at least, it was not a prospect he welcomed. Philip considered for a moment.

"Well, yes, you might well need to - or on reflection you might well want to, not least there's the house to be thought about, but we are flying back in a few days and, once we are back, we could do some of what may be necessary for you to get sorting things out under way. I'd regard that as the least I could do for Abigail."

"Come on, you tracked me down right across the world that's hardly nothing, but ..." he paused, almost choking, then continued "what a bloody mess, to think that this ... this estrangement was all based on a misunderstanding, a complete bloody misunderstanding – we both thought the other wanted nothing to do with us. It's just – oh, damn, damn, damn, I've been such a bloody fool."

Poy had listened to the conversation silently, now she put an arm round his shoulders,

"You weren't to know, Mac," she said, "don't beat yourself up over it. You made good life here, for you, for us, if you had not stayed on here you would have no boat, and you would have no me either. Mai pen rai."

She finished with a Thai phrase adding to Philip and Miriam "That is Thai, mean never mind, very big never mind."

"She's right in a sense," said Michael "You know I went out to Singapore to help sail a boat back here?" Philip and Miriam nodded. "Well, as I said, when I got here, the buyer fell through, Jon, the guy who owned the boat, had to have the money – he owed it I think – anyway he offered me such a deal. It was a one-off opportunity to have the kind of life I wanted. I had just met Poy and she knew boats and she knew this place too - I had a business manager, crew and helper all in one ... and a beautiful partner in due course as well." He turned and smiled at her. "We've been together ever since. What I did was impulsive, I know that. When I was offered the boat, I had money from my father's will sitting in the bank, and meeting Poy was the final element – without her I might not have dared to do it. I may have been young, acted impulsively and the way things happened clearly caused problems, but I'm glad I did, it's given me everything I ever wanted ..."

"Us." Poy interrupted him.

"Yes, of course, us," he smiled again. "But the situation with my mother ... that's just ... I don't know. I need some time to get my head around it. Look can I buy you both dinner tonight? It's the least I can do to thank you for what you've done. I really am very grateful."

They arranged to meet later that evening; Michael and Poy would come to their hotel. Philip and Miriam bid them goodbye for the moment and made their way back to the hotel, which was to be where they would all have dinner. It was still lovely outside and they sat in the shade taking stock.

"He looked pretty shell shocked," said Miriam.

"Well, I guess it's a lot to get your head around and, whatever sort of misunderstanding there was, and I bet

239

you're right about that letter's failure to arrive, at least he wrote, but he must feel some of the blame. He let it go on too long."

Miriam agreed but added, "He seems a nice enough bloke, but he was young, angry and impulsive and, if the looks he and Poy give each other now are anything to go by, in love too. One can see how events must have just carried him along. It may seem obvious with hindsight, but it's all too easy to let the moment pass, once some time had gone by it must have become more and more difficult to take another initiative, impossible ultimately. Come on, you promised to send that email for him, once you've done that officialdom must put things on hold and just wait for a while, then her affairs can be wound up as Abigail would have wished. At the end of the day, we have achieved that – well you have."

"I guess, though in the event we sorted it together, didn't we? I'm so glad you came, not just because of the business with Michael but ..." Philip's voice tailed off, unsure exactly what to say.

"Okay, I'll go and send that email," Philip continued, getting up as he spoke.

"Right, and don't forget to tell them you are away or they'll be trying to contact you at home."

There was still some while to go before they would be back in England.

CHAPTER TWENTY TWO
Clutter in the locker

It's funny as you get older, your outlook and priorities change. All my best friends have gone, there are so many people I miss, but I've had a good life, so I can't complain. Well, I can – I could have done without an errant son, and James should have stayed with me longer. And even now Mac, I still wonder where you are? But I have a lot to be grateful for and just recently Philip has been a welcome addition to my life, he's so kind, but we get on well, I really do count him as a friend despite the difference between us in age.

He's had a tough old time too, after Penny died. I hope he can move on, he's young, well by my standards he is and I just want to see him happy. Anyway in due course I will be able to give him a little boost. Before that happens though I hope he can give me one.

By the time Michael and Poy arrived for dinner at their hotel Philip had sent an email to the person who had replied to him from the office of the Treasury Solicitor. He explained that he was overseas, but that he had located Abigail's son who was living and working in Thailand.

He emphasised that there was no doubt about it, but he wondered, indeed asked, what proof they would want. Michael had left home intending to be away for only a short spell originally, he presumed he would not have brought things like his birth certificate here with him, though that might well still be in Abigail's house. But he must have his passport. He ended by saying that he could be contacted at home on his return and giving the date on which he got back. It was only a few days ahead now. He also said Michael would be in touch direct and printed out a copy of the message to give to him when he and Poy arrived.

That evening they all ate together alongside the hotel pool and with the sea visible just a few yards away, the noise of the gentle surf mixing with the other night noises of a tropical country as frogs, insects and nameless creatures of the night went about their separate business. Michael seemed to be beginning to come to terms with things, but was still struggling with the implications.

"After all that wasted time, I did not even get to her funeral" he said as they ate. "I always regretted not being at my father's," he continued, "that was an unintentional result of my unthinking and impetuous departure, but if things had been different I would certainly have been there following my mother's death."

Miriam hastened to reassure him. "It was a nice funeral," she said. "Even though, with no relatives located, the local Council had to organise it. There were not so many people there, but I think that was largely because Abigail had outlived most of her friends. There is one thing you should know about. It's a good thing. Philip here spoke up at the service, we both attended and when it was clear how impersonal the service would be he simply got up and said a few words. I thought it was a lovely gesture."

Philip shrugged her compliment away "I didn't plan to do it, but it just seemed right," he said. They all fell silent for a moment, Michael just mouthing a thank you.

They ate in silence for a moment, finally Michael spoke again: "Looking back I owe so much to the original voyage that brought me out here. I know it caused disaster between myself and my mother but there were positive things too. I have never regretted buying 'Footloose', Jon was right – it was him I bought the boat from - it was a wonderful chance and gave me a whole way of life that has suited me well ever since."

"Us," said Poy simply and Michael nodded, smiled and touched her arm.

243

"Yes. She's right." He left his hand on her arm, continuing: "Yes, Poy was a key to the whole thing. And that's something else I missed: the chance for Mum to meet Poy; I know she would have loved her. If I had not met her I doubt I would have done what I did. Thinking back over everything that happened, things could so easily have been different. One night on the journey up from Singapore we were hit by a quite fierce squall. We were fine, but the boat bucked around for a while, we shipped a little water and my laptop was ruined falling into it. I guess if I had still had my email addresses when I got ashore I might have got in touch that way – as it was the lack of those just gave me another excuse to do nothing but write that ill-fated letter. It was so easy to just get on with setting up the boat, the business and getting into life here."

He paused, clearly running things over in his mind.

Then he continued: saying, "After some weeks I did telephone home, but I couldn't get through, I guess she must have had a new number at the new house – I don't even know where she's been living since then, that's ... just awful."

"I'll give you a note of the address," Philip assured him. "It was a nice place ... it is a nice place. She was very comfortable, a terraced house just off the bottom of the High Street between there and the Quay. She could walk into town, though towards the end her hip was giving her some trouble and she found that more difficult to do."

Miriam looked at his troubled face and tried to reassure him. "It's all such a shame, but you can't turn the clock back, and you could say 'if only I had done this or that' about endless things and make no difference. For what it's worth I think she would be very pleased with how your life has been since."

Michael did not look very reassured but she hoped he would feel better in due course.

"Okay, you have been so kind" Poy addressed both Philip and Miriam. "We are so lucky you got involved. But let's think about now. When do you go back home?"

Philip named the date, now just a few days ahead.

"Good, you have time – please tomorrow come on boat. We will take you for a sail, go to nice island, we can swim and I will bring food. Can you meet us at 'Footloose" at, say, ten o'clock tomorrow morning?"

"That would be lovely," said Miriam, and Philip endorsed the sentiment adding "We'll both look forward to it".

In the morning Philip again checked his email. There was a reply from the Treasury Solicitor's office, this time it was more welcoming of his comments and it set the scene for what would now happen. Philip sent a brief acknowledgement, printed out copies to pass to Michael and tucked them away before they set off for the marina; he would pass it on later.

⚐

Later they met at the café on the quay prior to the sail and sat with teas and coffees with the activity of the marina going on around them.

"There are some expensive craft here" said Philip, then indicating an obviously top of the range motor cruiser adding "look at that one, I bet that's worth a bit."

"It's one we could well do without," said Michael.

"How so?"

"It's a Brit" Michael told them "Jake Stonely. I'm sure he's a crook. The word is that he's into drugs, and worse for all I know, but drugs for sure. Not what we want in the marina at all. Come on let's get aboard 'Footloose'."

They got up and headed along the marina. Philip might have lived and had been brought up in a sailing area, but had never been into boats though he had sailed with friends a few times on the estuary near his home and been on a couple of trips on one of the old-style sailing barges that had long been a feature of the town. There was an annual barge race held locally and he had followed this in a boat which was not actually competing. The barges looked stately under sail and in the year in which Philip had done this the wind was such that all aboard had enjoyed a good run. Miriam had never been on a sailing boat in her life. Initially she had been reticent and as she stepped on board the rocking boat she had wondered if this was going to be her idea of fun. For a moment she looked distracted and fell a few steps behind. By the time Philip noticed there was several yards between them. He looked back and saw her turn firmly as if making up her mind about something. A moment later she had strode purposefully up the gangway onto the motor launch Michael had said was owned by a crook. Dumbstruck for a moment he watched as what appeared to be the owner came forward. She reached in her bag and showed him something; Philip could not hear what was being said. He started forward but already Miriam was on her way off the boat. The owner stood for a moment looking down the gangplank, then turned as if storming away.

"What was all that about?" Philip asked when she had caught up and as they all climber aboard 'Footloose'?"

Miriam looked a little sheepish. "Sorry, I know I'm on holiday, but I realised I knew the name" she said "Jake Stonely was notorious in north London for a period before I moved to Maldon. It was well known he was a villain, drugs is right, but there never seemed to be any evidence that could be used against him. Then just when it looked as if there might be, he vanished. Came here by the looks of things, I've no idea of the case, I wasn't involved."

"Whatever did you say to him" Philip demanded, and the others voiced a similar question virtually at the same time.

"Well, I showed him my warrant card" she said "I know it has no validity here, but a few questions about his status and intentions seemed to put the wind up him. I told him I was involved here on a 'joint operation' – true enough about Philip and I and you Michael – but I'm don't think that's what it made him think of. He may find it difficult to carry on fully with whatever he is doing if he thinks the Thai police may be about to descend on him."

Philip was stunned. He was learning more about Miriam all the time, and some of it at least was surprising, He must have looked horrified, because she quickly tried to reassure him.

"Don't worry, I don't suppose he'll even remember my name, besides we'll be gone in a day or two. Anyway he's a blot on Michael's marina and, from what I know of him from the past, I couldn't resist the opportunity to put the wind up him. I'll report he's here when we get back."

Philip was not entirely reassured.

A few minutes later the focus was on the coming sail. Michael and Poy worked together like a well-oiled machine, which doubtless came from their mutual love of sailing and years of practice. In the event Miriam's initial uncertainty evaporated; they both found they loved the trip on 'Footloose'. They were allowed, indeed encouraged, to take turns at the helm and revelled in the sensation of the boat rushing through the water.

Soon they were at anchor just off the beach of a nearby island, and were relishing the delights of a swim in the crystal clear water and then wading ashore and tucking into the picnic that Poy had organised for them all. They sat together on the sand, leaning against a fallen palm tree, in an isolated spot of the unspoiled beach.

Miriam could not disguise her enthusiasm for the trip.

"This is marvellous," she said excitedly. "I thought the beach by the hotel was good, and it's very quiet, but this is ... well there is not a soul to be seen, what a joy."

"It's a popular place for us," Poy told them "We regularly bring many people here or somewhere similar just because it is so isolated. Customers love it."

They chatted for a while then Philip and Michael began discussing what Miriam had taken to referring to as "the Abigail situation".

"I don't suppose it will be too complicated now," suggested Philip "I presume you have your passport and can establish who you are to the satisfaction of the authorities."

"Yes, once I hear from them what needs to be done, I'll have to decide how to handle it. I am happy to visit England, but I can't leave the boat for long – the business won't run itself."

His comment had Poy chipping in quickly. "I can run while you are away – same, same I do when you are here!" and prompting a laugh, though Philip reckoned that it might be true enough. Michael looked after the boat, and Poy might well run most everything else.

Michael continued, asking: "Can you really do some of what's necessary back in U.K.?"

"Yes, of course. As I said, I feel it's the least I can do, liaising with you will not be too much of a problem with email and so on these days, but you might need others involved too, a solicitor for instance to see to the house and so on; I can recommend a local firm I've used if you like. It would be easier if there was a will, of course, and actually there not being one seems odd, Abigail always seemed pretty well organised. I wonder what happened to it, the codicil certainly suggested she had one."

"Yes" Michael paused, deep in thought for a moment. He began "I was thinking, I wonder if ..." but said no more.

They finished eating and went for a long walk along the beach. They still did not see a soul; it was idyllic. Back opposite the boat they packed up and waded out to climb back on board over the boarding steps fixed on the stern. Poy waded with the picnic bag held above her head as if it was something she did every day. Back on board, she started to ready the boat for the sail back, but Michael asked her to give him a minute and disappeared down into the cabin.

He remained down there for ten or fifteen minutes during which they heard sounds of banging and the occasional muttered curse. Finally they heard him say "Yes!" and he then returned topside clutching a large rather crumpled manila envelope and with a triumphant smile on his face. He turned serious again as he spoke however.

"Something else I got wrong," he confessed, "before I left England my mother was trying to contact me at the boat, at Heybridge Basin that is, I said I lived on board 'Starcounter' for a while, and she left various notes on it for me. They all said the same thing, that I was being silly, that I should come home and that we should sort things out between us. I must confess that I stopped reading them after the first few. But this is different."

He waved the envelope.

"It arrived just before I was leaving to come here, it must have got packed in my bag and I only found it amongst my things when I arrived in Singapore. I never opened it. When you spoke about her will again I suddenly thought of it and wondered if that was what it contained; the timing was right after all."

"And does it?" Philip interjected.

"It does indeed, I never realised and it's been sitting forgotten, buried at the bottom of a storage locker ever since I got the boat."

The envelope was clearly old and marked; Michael's name in ink on the front had faded almost to illegibility, but inside there was a short note and a couple of typed pages.

"Let's look," said Michael spreading the sheets of paper out on the cabin roof as they gathered round. The note, again in what Philip recognised as Abigail's clear, crisp handwriting, was brief.

Dear Mac

I know you don't want to talk right now, but put all that on one side and have a look at this. It's important. Since your Dad's death this had to be redone, it doesn't need to be complicated so I have typed it up and had it witnessed.

We should have a word about it though before I file it and regard it as final. Even if we agree to talk about nothing else let's have a word about this.

It was signed with the word "Mum" and a single X for a kiss.

The will itself seemed to meet the legal requirements as far as any of them knew them: it was on a standard form and no solicitor appeared to have been involved. Abigail had signed it and it was signed also by two witnesses and dated quite soon after her husband had died. Michael recognised one of the witnesses as a work colleague of his father.

"He was probably at the house settling work matters just when this was ready to sign," he offered.

The will consisted of a simple statement which left everything of Abigail's to her son Michael Andrew.

"Seems to be the genuine article," said Miriam. "But do you remember Philip telling you that a recent codicil was found in her house?" Michael nodded.

"Well, you should know that the additional term in that left Philip here £10, 000," she continued.

Philip immediately added, "I don't know why and in any case I didn't know anything about it until after she died." Now there was a real heir he somehow couldn't help but feel a sense of guilt about the fact.

"Well it's well deserved if you ask me" said Michael as Philip looked both embarrassed and sceptical. "You did a lot for her as I understand it," he continued, "Indeed, I guess you became a sort of surrogate son to her in my absence. Don't worry about it. I'm pleased for you. Come on now. Poy can you stow this below safely and I'll get us under way?"

He stuffed the papers back in the envelope and Poy disappeared into the cabin with them.

Despite Michael's comments, Philip still felt a little awkward about the matter and was glad to see the subject dropped. He was given the task of raising the anchor and once it was clear of the water the boat swung round, Michael and Poy soon had the sails raised and they began to make their way back towards the marina. The water crested across the bows thrown aside by their progress and the boat picked up speed. It was a great feeling Philip thought, imagining someone doing this all day and comparing it with his work in a small town library. He recognised that some of what he did

251

might be described as pedestrian and for some reason thought of Mrs Riley who always got him to read the blurbs of several books to her before she made a selection, pleading "I've left my reading glasses at home." He could see that sailing was something that someone could easily become passionate about – and Michael had certainly done that, indeed his passion had changed his whole life, but it had given him a lifestyle with which he appeared to be profoundly happy.

All too soon they were en route back to the Marina. Although Phuket was visible, they were still a good way away when they saw a powerful motor cruiser coming out towards them. Michael took no notice, knowing that motor usually gives way to sail. It progressively got closer; it's speed evident from the significant wake it left behind it.

"That's going to come close," Poy spoke up from the bow.

"It's that Jake character's gin palace," said Michael.

He altered course a little, but the cruiser remained heading resolutely straight towards them. The distance closed very rapidly.

"He's going to ram us!" Poy's shout looked to accurately reflect their situation.

"Hang on!" Michal yelled "I'm going about."

The boat slowed suddenly, the boom swung across, their direction changed and then their speed picked up again as the wind caught the sails. Just in time: the motor boat swept past only a few feet from 'Footloose's stern, the boat rocked chaotically in the wash, substantial spray drenched the cockpit, then she steadied and went on her way. The other boat did not slacken speed and was soon disappearing in the distance.

"You seem to have upset him," said Philip.

"My hope would be that's true" replied Miriam "but if he had wanted to really damage us he has the speed to have come back and he didn't, he's likely more concerned about getting to some new place to operate from."

"Well, he won't be missed back at the marina," Michael commented and then concentrated on getting the heading right for their return. He seemed to take it all in his stride.

Despite the excitement they all enjoyed the sail back, and by the time they were safely moored in the marina the day was heading for the early evening sunset which Philip and Miriam were still getting used to seeing. Soon after six the light changed and soon after, in a brief half hour or so, it was dark.

"Let's get a drink," said Michael. "I need to call into All Tours office for a moment but the rest of you go on ahead – let's go to Navigator's Bar Poy. See you all in a minute."

It seemed to be an ending. What had brought them together started a long time ago and, although there were all sorts of things to be sorted out now there was a proven heir to Abigail's estate, all that somehow seemed to be only a detail. Once Michael caught up with the others at what proved to be a smart bar in the hotel they chatted more about the way Michael and Poy lived, the trips they made and the people they had as customers.

"Some customers are funny," said Poy. "They want to sail but find the boat a bit daunting. We always make a guarantee - if the customer falls overboard they do not pay!"

She giggled at the thought.

"Does that happen often?" asked Philip, who knew so little about boats he did not know whether it was actually likely or not.

"Only once in almost 20 odd years," said Michael. "An American. And he was so drunk it was inevitable. He

253

admitted that it was all his own fault and paid up anyway. Not a bad record."

"I'm not only relieved to hear it, I do rather wish I had known that record before we went out to sea this morning," said Miriam. "It would have given me confidence."

"Go on, you loved it," said Michael, adding "Right, I discovered that the office have a job for us tomorrow so we must get set up and ready. When do you two fly back?"

"The following day," said Miriam. "We must leave the hotel about mid-morning."

"May we join you there for breakfast then?" Michael asked "It will give us a chance to say goodbye and for Philip and I to sort out any immediate tasks he might see to back in England – I've got all our contact details here for you."

He handed Philip a sheet of paper. As they went their various ways Miriam tucked her arm through Philip's.

"I bet you never dared hope it would end so well" she said.

Philip readily agreed, though he was not to know that the trip still had surprises in store.

Michael and Poy had come to their hotel to say goodbye. The four breakfasted together and arranged various details that needed to be attended to by Philip on his return. The travellers were already packed and pretty much ready to go to the airport, their flight to Bangkok departed in the middle of the day, they then had one night in Bangkok and flew on to London around midday the next day. Michael had handed over a note of all his contact details on the previous day and Philip now promised again to do anything he could to help with what needed to come next.

"Perhaps you could take this," said Michael, handing him a manila envelope.

"What is it?" Philip wanted to know.

"It's my mother's will. From what you say it needs to get into official hands as soon as possible. I won't be able to get to England for a little while and I don't want to risk sending it in the post, but I've taken a copy just to be safe. Can you send it on when you arrive?"

"Sure, no problem, I'll deliver it if that's safest. It mustn't get lost after all this!"

"Thanks again for what you've done," Michael said "I do appreciate it so much. I can't stop thinking about what happened. It's all way back, I know, but I still feel dreadful, some of the things ..."

He would obviously need time to come to terms with what he had discovered and he surely had things to regret, though both Philip and Miriam had tried to tell him that it was 'one of those things', it could certainly have been prevented but also had clearly happened all too easily as one thing had led to another. Michael shook Philip's hand and kissed Miriam on the cheek. Poy, ever smiling, hugged them both in farewell. They had settled their bill, but bade a final farewell to Noon and climbed into the taxi she had arranged for them – "Good driver, no problem." She waved and headed off towards Reception.

Michael had a parting shot. "You must come back and see us, I'm sure you'll want to visit Thailand again and it would be nice to meet up without all the drama. And one last thing: for heaven's sake, do call me Mac, everybody does."

Perhaps they would meet again. Philip hoped so, not least because he wanted to see how Michael responded to his inheritance when Abigail's affairs were sorted out. He and

Miriam both waved as the car pulled away down the hotel drive.

As the taxi drew out onto the road and set off on the first stage of the journey home, both reflected that what was an impromptu trip for both of them had turned out pretty well.

"All in all quite a trip" said Philip "we found Michael, we both loved Thailand and had a nice break and I reckon your surprise arrival topped it all, even if you did almost get us drowned by an international gangster!" We got a whole lot closer into the bargain he reflected to himself, still uncertain how much about that to put into words. The journey went smoothly and gave them more time to talk, they relived the trail that had led to their finding Michael, they wondered how all this would change Michael's life, and Poy's too for that matter, and they continued to find out more about each other.

Philip summed it up for both of them by saying, "Well, I have to say that to describe this trip as having been full of surprises is a bit of an understatement; I never dared to imagine everything would go so well ... and not just with regard to Michael."

He linked his arm with Miriam's, two flights were needed to get them home, but they had an evening in Bangkok in between.

ꝑ

Arriving back in the UK they faced the usual hassles of Heathrow airport, a fifteen minute wait for the doors to open once the plane had stopped on the stand had a fellow passenger, no doubt a regular traveller, muttering "Here we go again". Once disembarked and on a long walk past silent, unmoving walkways and finally facing a long queue in passport control Philip began to see why the airport was regularly referred to in the broadsheet newspapers as a "national embarrassment". Before they left Bangkok he had sent an email to the neighbour kindly keeping an eye on his house for him asking that he fix a taxi to meet them, he had intended to return by train, but now with Miriam with him he didn't want them to struggle with luggage on the multi-stage journey back to Maldon, besides he reckoned after what they had achieved they deserved to be spoilt.

Once they had picked up their suitcases and emerged into the terminal area outside the driver was already standing outside Boots holding up a sign saying "Marchington". They walked through to the car park with him and soon found themselves relaxing in the back of the car as it moved along the M25 ring road, for once mercifully reasonably clear of traffic and other horrors as the rush hour was effectively over.

"I know how important settling Abigail's affairs became to you. I'm so glad it all worked out - and it was not the rash young Michael we found, but a son of whom Abigail would have been proud." Miriam hooked her arm through his and smiled sidelong at him. It was dusk and car lights shone around them as she added "I love Thailand. I've had a wonderful holiday. I always really wanted to come with you you know and I'm sorry that my arrival was somewhat last minute."

"Yes, it certainly was great and I shall remember your last minute appearance in the airport for a very long time – delightful and dramatic. And everything regarding the Abigail situation did seem to work out I suppose, though there is more to do. I hope Mac will find that all this rules a line for him too. What an odd situation it turned out to be. I'm happy to help him with whatever needs to be done now here in U.K. If he does visit, and I'm not convinced he will, I doubt it will be for long; after all he has a business to run. He enjoys his way of life, he was clearly right to set up shop there, but he has obviously always regretted his alienation from Abigail and everything that followed. If only he could have avoided that. He still has some regrets now I think,

257

never has the phrase about 'the moment passing' been more apt. If only he had ... but such thoughts are just academic now."

Philip tailed off, thinking how different things might have been, if Abigail had not moved, if Mac had bitten the bullet and tried to find her rather than assuming she had turned her back on him. So many ifs; the possibilities were many, but such was life, one thing led to another and it happened the way it happened.

"You know, curiously Michael's estrangement from his mother was prompted largely by positive things you know: the opportunity to buy the boat and start a new life; and his meeting with Poy, that was something that certainly seems to have worked out well." Philip continued to reflect on events, as they both would do for a while.

"I'm sure Abigail would be pleased that finally both you and Mich ... Mac are benefitting from her inheritance. Maybe she's looking down and smiling at us all. In the end I think she would have been pleased to see what Mac made of his life, to see him happy. I would say he has both a proper job and an enviable life style." Miriam again tried to look on the good things.

"Yes. I wonder what Mac will do with the money. If he sells her house he will get a tidy sum."

"Maybe he will buy a house himself. He is getting a little bit old to be camping in a boat, though they use Poy's small apartment too. I can just imagine him and Poy living more comfortably. But I can't see him coming back to live in England, though a visit may be necessary to sort things out. Now the will has come to light, you will have a useful sum too; the codicil must be valid now."

"He said he'd contact us when he'd fixed to visit England. And yes, I guess so about the money ... I hadn't really thought." It was only just dawning on Philip that if this was the case – he really would be getting a payment in due course as the codicil could presumably now be honoured. He would need to give some consideration to that he thought, but before he could think further Miriam had a question for him:

"I have to ask, I guess it will take a while to be paid ... but what will you do with your £10,000 then?"

"Well ..."

For a few seconds Philip was silent, thinking. It was quite a thing, and quite a lot of money. Miriam was on the point of asking again; then he suddenly decided that the matter needed no more thought – none at all. He was sure, wholly sure. It might be soon, but it also felt right, even somehow long overdue. Despite the problems Michael's impromptu decision all those years ago had worked out. That success seemed to offer him an example. Although only a few seconds had passed, he was conscious of Miriam waiting for his answer.

He thought this might be one more thing of which Abigail would approve.

EPILOGUE

A few months later

The previous day had been New Year's Eve and the small hotel had hosted a special evening. About noon a white-board had been erected by the pool listing the events planned. Drinks by the pool at seven through to fireworks at midnight. It had been low key yet great fun and both Philip and Miriam had taken pleasure in being in Thailand again, somewhere they might never have visited at all but for Abigail, and in ending the evening with a toast to the future.

The following morning they walked along the beach after breakfast. The sun shone on the golden sand, small waves lapped the shore and there was hardly another soul to be seen.

"We mustn't go too far" said Philip, "Michael and Poy promised to collect us around eleven and take us for a sail."

"Can't wait" Miriam replied, "maybe we will visit the same island again, like we did when the Abigail business was settled."

They turned back towards the hotel and walked on.

"Philip, after our last visit do you remember in the taxi back from Heathrow, when I asked you what you would do with the money Abigail left you?"

Philip smiled at the recollection, and replied "Sure, I can still hardly believe I dared say it, but I said it could go towards a honeymoon ... why?"

Miriam returned his smile and gripped his hand tighter.

"Well, I'm glad you did and I'd just like you to know that it was such a good idea, really very good indeed!"

END

Author's note

I have set some of the action described here in and around Maldon in north Essex. I know it, love it and live there; this book was largely written looking out over the estuary of the River Blackwater towards which my house faces.

I have, however, taken some small liberties with the geography of the area and more important, though the official processes described as following Abigail's death are broadly authentic, there is no direct link here with the actual practices as conducted locally, which I am sure may vary. Similarly I have people populating real places in the town and all such characters are of course fictional as is anything about how such institutions operate.

Because it deserves a mention I would add that the book that Philip reads to schoolchildren at one point in the story is real - and highly recommended too should you have young children (Madrigal – the secret witch by Maldon author Elizabeth Webb).

Acknowledgements

During the gestation period of this book I was grateful for the help of a number of people.

I benefited from assistance and advice from Mary Rensten of Scriptora (linked to the Society of Women Writers & Journalists) and am grateful for her wise council and valuable suggestions I would never have thought of alone.

A variety of people, family, friends and writing colleagues made encouraging comments, ranging from "It'll be fine" to "Bloody well, get on with it". Their goading, sorry – support, was both necessary and appreciated.

I am grateful also to Lloyd Bonson at Stanhope Books for his excellent work in turning my manuscript into a finished book – and for believing in it sufficiently to take it on. Tracy Saunders, a local artist, produced a first rate cover; her contribution is much appreciated.

Last but not least, my late wife, Sue, was – as always – a great support throughout the writing and kept her cool despite the fact that anything she said fell on deaf ears when I was working at the computer. Though she read and commented on the manuscript, she sadly never saw the published book.

Thank you all

About The Author

Patrick Forsyth is the much published author of many non-fiction books. Many offer guidance to those working in organisations, for example Successful Time Management (Kogan Page) is a bestselling title on its subject. He has also written three light-hearted books of travel writing: First class at last!, Beguiling Burma and Smile because it happened. All are set in South East Asia.

Another recent title is the book Empty when half full a hilarious critique of miscommunication that misleads and amuses. He is active in the writing world, writing regularly for Writing Magazine and working with writing groups. He lives in Maldon in north Essex and this is his first novel.

Also from the author

First Class At Last!
An Antidote to Past Travel Horrors
More Than 1,200 Miles in Extreme Luxury

Fed up with the strenuous process of travel: the slow queues, the delays, the crowds and the extreme discomfort of the average economy airline seat?

Patrick Forsyth decided it was time to do something about this. He arranged a trip designed to be the antidote to the routine travel misery - and booked a trip travelling only first class.

The first challenge was to decide where to go. He decided to fly to Bangkok, stay in the world renowned Oriental Hotel, continue onto Singapore and stay at the equally famous Raffles Hotel. He then travelled in style back to Bangkok on the Eastern and Orient Express, where he spent two nights on what many people regard as the best train ride in the world, and finally concluded his travel at a luxury spa on the beach, to recover.

Along the way, the author meets a rock and roll musician; visits dubious bars and colourful markets; has an encounter with the bodyguards of the Thai Royal Family; and embarks on a boat trip along the River Kwai. This lively, amusing account of luxury travel, highlights what every traveller secretly longs to do - travel in style and grandeur.

"...witty and full of facts ..." Essex Life

"... Lively, witty and wry." Select Books

"... it reminded me of Bryson..."
Neal Asher, bestselling author of Gridlinked

Other Fiction from Stanhope Books

When Dreams Converge

Stephen Massie's first novel, charting the adventures of Luke, a keen amateur sailor, and his wife, as they set to sea to live their dream of freedom. During their voyage they are thrust into a world of crime, terrorism and murder. In a web of deceit and intrigue they are pursued by ruthless criminal organisations.

Human Rights

Ed Bush lives with his family in the coastal settlement of Chelmsford in South Britain, one of the United States of Europe. Their way of life is dictated entirely by the government known as Europarl. Every year at a four day celebration of human rights the people coming of age are assigned to their posts within the country.

Ed doesn't think there is anything he can do about it until he meets an old man on the beach who lives outside the system. Ed is recruited to join a rebel group and plans are made for him to leave, when he is distracted by the arrival of his new stepsister, Suzie.

Will Ed leave with the rebels or stay with his family and accept his fate?

The Grays Anatomy

Twelve short stories from horror author Rob Shepherd, featuring vampires, zombies and things that go bump in the night. Not for the faint hearted!

www.stanhopebooks.com
facebook.com/stanhopebooks
Twitter @stanhopebooks

Made in the USA
Charleston, SC
11 November 2014